TAKE ME

by

Lee Roberts

A HellBound Books Publishing LLC Book
Houston TX

A HellBound Books LLC
Publication

www.hellboundbookspublishing.com

Printed in the United States of America

DEDICATION:

This book is dedicated to the innocent ones who suffer in silence every day.

Take Me

Lee Roberts

TAKE ME

Take Me

CHAPTER 1

A haunting scream echoed over the deep, hypnotic waves like the dying cry of a banshee. Adriana glanced quickly toward the horizon. It couldn't be real. It was only a trick of the wind. Nothing could be happening at this hour, could it? She cocked her head and then looked down at her feet again.

Adriana was tempted, and at last she could no longer resist. Memories of the past were still too vivid in her mind. She plopped down on the wet sand and took off her shoes and socks. Clutching them in her hand, she eased closer to the rippling water and let her toes sink into the moist ground. She wiggled her toes in the sand and smiled. The feeling was heavenly. She felt like a little girl again.

The gentle waves lapped up over her feet and splashed upon her ankles. Adriana leaned over and rolled up her pants legs. She smiled and closed her eyes, relishing the intimate moment. This was the greatest benefit of working the beach patrol.

"You're crazy," her partner remarked, "you know we're not supposed to do that when we're on duty."

"I know," she replied, "you're not going to report me, are you?"

"Of course not."

"Then shut up and keep on walking, I'll catch up with you in a few minutes."

Her partner chuckled and continued on down the beach. It wasn't the first time she had done that, and it wouldn't be the last.

Adriana tilted her head back and gazed out over the Gulf of Mexico. Tiny specks of light twinkled in the clear nighttime sky. The moon was almost full now and bathed the quiet water in a soft ethereal glow. Adriana could see the lights of a few large cargo ships as they made their way through Galveston Bay. She took a long, deep breath and tasted the warm, salty breeze on her tongue.

And then Adriana heard the scream again. Her eyes popped open wide. At first, she was confused, not trusting her ears. Perhaps it was a gull or some other bird circling in the darkness. Adriana glanced toward the Kemah boardwalk, but it was closed for the night. She cocked her head to one side and listened close.

Long seconds passed. Then she heard it again, muffled and cut short this time, but she was sure it was a scream or a cry for help. It could be some late night partiers on a drunken private pleasure cruise, but it didn't sound like it. This sounded like someone who desperately needed help, and they needed it now.

Adriana began to peel off her clothes and toss them aside. She snatched up her portable radio and keyed the mike.

"Johnny, I heard something. Get back here quick. I'm going in the water."

Her partner didn't reply, but she could see him running toward her on the beach. She threw her radio down onto the sand and dashed into the surf.

The tide was still coming in. Adriana fought against the pounding waves as she sloshed out into the cool water and dove into the rushing current. The water temperature was high in the summer, but it was less than her body temperature, and there was no sun to warm it up at midnight. She ignored the sudden chill and plunged in anyway.

At the edge of the bay, the ocean floor tapered off fast. In only a few seconds, Adriana was in deep water and swimming hard. She tried to keep her head above the surface as much as possible, listening for more sounds. She swiveled her head right and left, scanning the horizon for some sign of a boat or a small craft nearby.

The noise of the water splashing around her head seemed to mask all other sound. Adriana was a strong swimmer, and in no time she found herself almost a hundred yards away from the shoreline. She glanced back and saw Johnny standing there with a radio in one hand and a flashlight in the other trying to follow her progress. By now, though, she was well beyond any contact. Adriana took a few more strokes, then she paused to rest and tread water for a moment.

There were still no running lights visible in any direction, but her eyes were becoming accustomed to the hazy darkness. Something seemed to block out the bright flickering starlight a bit farther out. There was a large, gray shape floating on top of the waves, maybe a fishing boat or a small cabin cruiser. She ducked her head down and swam in that direction.

After another fifty yards, Adriana paused and rested again. Her arms and legs were getting tired. She could see the vague outline of a boat now about twenty yards ahead and to her right. There were at least two people on board, and they appeared to be in some kind of scuffle. She heard a man's voice yelling, and then a female voice cried out in pain.

Adriana shifted to a slow breast stroke and swam up closer to the boat.

"Ahoy there!" she shouted. "I'm with the Kemah Police Department. Are you in need of any assistance?"

Everything got quiet for a few seconds.

"Um, no, we're fine here, thanks," the male voice responded, "no problem. We don't need any help."

"Help me!" the female voice yelled. "He's hurting me!"

Adriana kicked into high gear and swam for the boat.

"I'm coming on board!" she shouted. "Give me a hand up!"

A timid small hand reached over the side of the boat and was smacked away. A man's face peered over the railing.

"We really don't need you for anything," he said through gritted teeth, "you can just turn around and go back where you came from. Everything is fine here."

"No it's not," the girl squealed, "please help me!"

Adriana glared at the man.

"Help me up," she commanded, "I'm coming on board to see for myself."

The man grumbled and growled a little, but he reached over the side and pulled Adriana up onto the deck. She noticed his look of surprise when she stood there dripping wet wearing nothing but bikini panties and a sports bra.

"Do all of your police officers dress like that?" he remarked with a grin.

"Only the good ones," she replied, "my partner doesn't dress this way."

The man laughed and seemed to relax.

"Where do you keep your gun?" he asked. "I can't wait to see that."

"In a secret compartment," she said, "don't make me use it."

A small Mexican girl was cowering against the railing and glancing back and forth between them. She scooted over toward Adriana.

"Please help me," she pleaded, "this man is hurting me!"

"I'm not hurting her," the man said, "we're just on a date. And she likes it a little rough, if you know what I mean. It's all part of the game."

"That's not true," the girl pleaded. "He's lying!"

Adriana noted the bruises and lacerations on the girl's face and arms. She stared at the man. He smiled as though he were innocent.

"What's really going on here?" she demanded. "Are you holding this girl against her will, or engaging in any illegal activity? I noticed that your running lights are not on for some reason. Let me see your license and identification. I'm going to use your radio and call my partner. We can get this all sorted out."

Adriana started toward the radio console, and the man pushed her away.

"Wait a minute," he protested, "I don't even know who you are! I don't see any kind of identification on you. Maybe you should show me a little more instead."

The man reached around behind his back and came up with a long hunting knife. He grinned and held the tip high so that it gleamed in the bright moonlight.

"Watch out!" the Mexican girl screamed.

The man turned his head and backhanded the girl. In that brief second, Adriana took a quick hop forward and gave him a hard sidekick to the chest. He stumbled back and fell over the railing of the boat. There was a loud splash followed by a lot of gurgling and angry cursing.

Adriana rushed over and examined the young girl.

"Are you okay?" she asked.

The girl hung her head down and after a moment, she nodded.

"What is really going on here?" said Adriana. "I know you wouldn't go out with an asshole like that."

The girl laughed revealing a mouth full of damaged and broken teeth. Then she broke down and started to cry. Adriana held the girl in her arms and listened as she told her story. It was a sad tale she had heard many times before, a tale of people risking their lives for a chance to start over in another country. It was the familiar tale of betrayal and bondage that happens to thousands of young immigrant girls when they arrive in the United States only to be sold into sexual slavery.

"Don't worry," Adriana whispered, "I will help you."

"Are you going to send me back to them or back to Mexico?" the girl asked.

"Hopefully neither one," she replied, "let me see what I can do."

The Mexican girl smiled and hugged her tight. All of a sudden, they heard a man laugh and clap his hands. Adriana stood up and crept over to the other side of the deck. She peeked over the railing and saw a large man sitting in a small fishing boat. He was smoking a cigar and grinning.

"Bravo! Well done," he shouted, "you've given me a whole new perspective on police work! It's a definite improvement. I really like what I see."

Adriana straightened up and crossed her arms over her breasts.

"Who are you?" she demanded.

"A local fisherman," he said, "I heard all the noise and came over to see what was going on. I'm glad to see you have everything under control."

"Yeah, well, no thanks to you. How long have you been lurking out there?"

"Long enough to see you kick that guy's ass. Nice moves by the way. Did you have some training in martial arts?"

Adriana glanced around at the dark, smooth water. There was no sign of anyone splashing around or treading water nearby.

"Where did that other guy go?"

"I think a shark got him. He just suddenly disappeared."

"There aren't any sharks out here. What really happened to him?"

"I may have accidentally hit him on the head with my anchor," said the fisherman. "He went under the water and didn't come back up. I guess I'll have to take his cruiser in to the dock myself and collect the recovery fee."

This confused her for a moment, "what are you talking about?"

"Maritime salvage laws. Being a police officer, you should know all about that. Maybe I'll sell it back to the owner later, or I might claim it for myself. It looks like it would make a really nice fishing boat."

"You killed that guy so you could take his boat?"

The fisherman shrugged, "you have to admit, he wasn't a very nice guy."

Adriana shook her head in disbelief but didn't disagree.

"I wish you hadn't said that. Now I have to take you in for questioning."

The fisherman laughed at her and puffed on his cigar some more.

"I don't think that's going to happen, sweetheart. I can see a lot of interesting things right now, but I don't see any handcuffs anywhere. And judging by your nipples, you must be a bit cold. I do like those panties, though. Are those silk or satin?"

Adriana looked down at herself and tried to cover up her private parts.

"Look, mister, I'm a police officer, and I'm answering a distress call. My partner will be here any minute with more backup. You wait right there until they arrive."

The man squinted his eyes and peered toward the beach.

"Is your partner a little, thin guy with long hair? I think I see some twerp taking off his clothes back on the beach there. Oops, he just fell down. It may be awhile before your backup gets here, I'm afraid. I'm kind of busy, so I guess I'll be heading out then. I've got a lot of fish to catch tonight. Bye-bye."

"Wait! You can't leave!"

"Why not?" said the fisherman. "I didn't do anything wrong."

"You just killed a guy!"

"What guy? I have no idea what you're talking about. I don't see anybody. And, I was never anywhere near this place tonight."

"Don't leave! I'm ordering you to stay right there! I'm arresting you!"

"I don't take orders from some girl in wet underwear, bye."

"Okay, wait! I'll make a deal with you, just don't leave."

The young man floated closer in his tiny boat and puffed on his cigar.

"Okay, here is my deal," he said, "I'll come up there and help you ladies down into my fishing boat. I get to claim the asshole's boat as marine salvage because neither one of us knows what really happened to him, all right? You agree to that?"

Adriana blew out a big sigh and rolled her eyes, trying to stall for time until the Coast Guard arrived.

"Are you going to give me your name and number and wait here until some other people show up? Can I trust you?"

"Absolutely."

"Okay, then it's a deal."

Adriana smiled and helped the young fisherman climb over the railing and up into the big cabin cruiser. He paused and ogled her body for a minute.

"Yeah, I really like that outfit. Can I take your picture?"

"No," she replied, "help me get this girl down into your boat."

The man chuckled while he helped Adriana crawl over the side and down into his tiny dinghy. Then he helped the little Mexican girl do the same. As soon as he settled the ladies, he leaned over and pushed the two boats farther apart. He watched them drift for a moment, then he went over to the console and started up the cruiser.

"Wait!" yelled Adriana. "You promised to stay here!"

"I may have lied about that," he shouted in response. "I just remembered that I need to go home and let my dog out."

"You lying bastard! I bet you don't even have a dog."

"I've been meaning to get one though."

He pushed the lever forward and started to putter away.

"Wait!" she yelled. "At least give me your name and number!"

"Travis," he shouted, "and my favorite number is sixty-nine!"

His boisterous laugh rang out, and he tossed his cigar into the ocean. Adriana put her hands on her hips and watched helpless as the cruiser sailed off into the darkness. She plopped down next to the little Mexican girl.

"That didn't go too well, but don't worry, at least we still have his boat."

Adriana jumped up and tried starting the motor, but without success. She glanced around and noticed that water was trickling in along one side of the hull. After a couple more futile cranks, she found the fuel tank and unscrewed the cap. It was empty.

CHAPTER 2

Adriana paced back and forth in the interrogation room. If the room were carpeted, she would have worn a hole in it by now. It was a good thing, it wasn't.

"You're crazy," her partner remarked for the tenth time, "you wouldn't last two days undercover, and neither would I."

"I disagree," Adriana protested, "I can handle myself, believe me. I grew up with four brothers, and that wasn't easy."

"I know," said Johnny, "but that's not the same thing. You're talking about going undercover in a network of people that deal in human trafficking. They treat people like cattle. A few losses along the way is no big deal to them. If they even suspect that you're a cop, you'll wind up under a tumbleweed somewhere west of El Paso."

"Then I'll stay out of trouble. I won't let that happen."

"Of course not, like you'll have any control over that."

"There's nothing west of El Paso anyway."

"That's my point exactly. You'll just disappear, and no one will ever know."

Captain Rodriguez held up his hands and glared at both of them.

"Okay, okay, simmer down. You guys have only been partners for six weeks, and you already act like a married couple."

"I want a divorce then," said Adriana, "I don't need a coward for a partner."

"I'm not a coward," Johnny responded, "I just don't believe in suicide and doing stupid things. She's always wanting to do crazy, stupid things!"

"You're a big coward!"

"You're a reckless nut job!"

"Stop it now, both of you," said Rodriguez, "neither one of you gets to make the decision anyway, I'm leaving it up to the Feds. It's their game, so it's their call."

Dan Olivera, regional supervisor from Immigration and Customs Enforcement, stood up and leaned over the interrogation table. The others all stared at him.

"I know you both feel strongly about this situation," he said. "I discussed it briefly with my colleagues from the F.B.I., and we realize the risks associated with any kind of undercover assignment like this."

"It's suicide," said Johnny, "plain and simple. There is too much money at stake for them to let us into their network. And even if they do, there are too many chances for something to go wrong. It's just like going undercover with the Mexican drug cartels. We would become another expendable resource for both sides. One wrong word, one wrong move, even the tiniest suspicion, and we're both dead."

"Then don't do anything wrong," Adriana said in a calm tone, "we get in as far as we can without tipping our hand, and then we bail out with whatever information we have. We don't try to save the world ourselves, just try to knock a little hole in the wall."

"Exactly right," said the I.C.E. agent, "we don't expect you to make any arrests or bust up the gang. We only want information so we know who is involved and what they are doing. Right now, the biggest human trafficking ring here in Texas is a tight family business run by Big Bill Hayes and his son Billy. They don't trust outsiders and usually deal only with people they know."

"So, what makes you think that's going to change," Johnny asked, "how are we supposed to get in? If this is a family business, they aren't going to be hiring a lot of new faces that they don't know."

"Something weird has happened," Olivera explained, "Little Billy disappeared suddenly and nobody knows where he is. He was supposed to make a special delivery to a buyer in Houston last night, but something went wrong. We think that may be the deal Miss Santos accidentally interrupted."

Adriana looked around in confusion like it was the first she had heard of it.

"Is that what Norma is telling you?" she asked.

Olivera looked at her and nodded.

"Yes, the young girl you brought in last night is now in protective custody. She was treated by a doctor then taken to a safe house. She has given us a lot of information about her experience, but it is limited to only what she personally saw and heard. We would like to use this opportunity to get to the next level."

"Exactly what does that mean," asked Adriana, "get to the next level?"

The I.C.E. man shrugged.

"That's where you come in. We need to know more details and set up some kind of sting operation to get some proof. She can tell us about where she started in Mexico, but she was in the dark most of the time. We need to know who the coyotes are on both sides of the border, and how they coordinate. She was also held prisoner somewhere in south Texas and abused for a while, but we have no idea where that was. And we know nothing about how they arrange for the sales and deliveries of the girls."

"You're talking about people like they are packages," said Johnny.

"That's how they are treated," the agent replied. "That's why we need to stop it. Everyone knows about the issues with immigration and the number of illegals crossing the border, but this goes way beyond that. We're talking about slavery and murder."

The room got silent for a moment.

"Do you mean murder because of the number of people that die coming over," asked Johnny, "or are you talking about something else?"

Olivera looked down at the stocky man sitting to his right, a serious-looking guy wearing a white shirt and dark suit.

"Did I say too much, Joe? Maybe you better take it from here."

The serious guy made a face like he had just swallowed something disgusting. He shook his head a bit and then cleared his throat. The others waited.

"I'm Special Agent Joe Kelly of the F.B.I.," he said, "I'm on a task force looking for a serial killer operating somewhere in central Texas. We don't know if this person is actually part of the trafficking network or not. We've been coordinating with I.C.E. and Agent Olivera because most of the victims appear to be young Mexican girls working as prostitutes, undocumented immigrants. Needless to say, this makes it extremely difficult for us to identify them, or find out anything about them. Most of the time, we can't even find anyone who admits to knowing these girls. It gives us very little to go on."

"How do you know these murders are connected?" Adriana asked.

"We didn't for a while because they were scattered out," Kelly replied, "but we noticed a pattern and a signature on the bodies, so that's why we think it's a serial killer. We don't know if the killer is part of Big Bill's organization, or if he is only preying on the same group of victims."

"Could it be a punishment for runaways or something?" said Adriana.

"That is a possibility," Kelly admitted, "we don't know the real motive for the murders, but the profilers think they were all done by the same person."

"Maybe Adriana is right," said Johnny, "maybe it's just the way they deal with people who escape or whatever. It might even be two or three different guys who hunt down the girls and punish them to send a message to the others."

"Like I said, it's a possibility," Kelly repeated, "but it feels like something very different. Big Bill doesn't need to send a message. Who would he send it to? The others are already in transit or being held under guard. Publicity about the murders would only hurt his business and scare away customers. The profilers think it's either some sadistic son-of-a-bitch who works in the network, or it's some other psychopath who is stalking these girls because they are easy targets."

"That's why we're in this together," Olivera added, "the same group of young, naïve girls is being targeted on both sides of the border. Predators are bringing them into this country to sell them or use them, and either way their life is over before it even gets started. We want to put an end to this."

"How many girls are we talking about?" Adriana wanted to know, "is there some giant holding pen out there somewhere?"

Olivera and Kelly exchanged a glance.

"We don't really know for sure," said Kelly, "Big Bill has been operating for a while bringing in men, women, and children from Mexico, mostly for labor. His coyotes pick them up, take their money, and drop them off somewhere on this side of the border. We think the sex trade came later. They keep some young girls now and auction them off on the internet. The buyer can do whatever he wants to with them. Bill probably keeps a few for himself or rents them out as hookers. His manpower is limited, though, so our guess is we're looking for a small compound with twenty or thirty people."

"That could be almost anywhere," said Johnny, "you could fit that many people into a barn or a couple of double-wide trailers."

"Now you see why we haven't been able to shut him down," said Olivera. "Once in a while we catch a few illegals or even run down a coyote, but Hayes keeps a tight lid on things. They stay small enough for him to maintain control and secrecy. No one ever knows enough to flip on him except maybe his son, and that would never happen."

"Until now," said Kelly, "with Billy Junior gone, Big Bill has a huge hole to fill. We're hoping that one or both of you might be able to get in far enough to find out what is going on. With some good inside information, maybe we can take him down and put him away for life."

"Exactly how would we do that?" asked Adriana.

Olivera and Kelly shared another quick glance.

"We start slow," Kelly explained, "we would get you and Johnny set up on the streets as a couple of young kids looking to make a quick buck. Agent Olivera has several people on the streets already willing to work with us a little to establish a cover for you. I can also get plugged in to some of the D.E.A. and A.T.F. informants in the area."

"You're talking about using informants to establish credibility," asked Johnny, "the same people who lie and double-cross each other on a daily basis? Does anyone else think that sounds a little shaky?"

"It's not as bad as it sounds," said Olivera, "we'll be behind the scenes watching out for you. No one except the people in this room will know who you really are or where you came from. You can tell them anything you like. We can even create some false files with a criminal history and identification for you in case they check."

"Does that include some kind of fake jobs or something?" said Adriana. "We have to do something for money, but I don't want to do anything illegal."

"That may be a little tricky," said Kelly, "there is a doctor there who runs a clinic downtown. He has a bit of trouble with the I.R.S. and insurance companies right now, so we can use that as leverage to get you something, at least part-time or contract work. You both have some medical training. Adriana has a year of nursing school, and Johnny was in medical school for a while, so that should be enough to get you started."

The two of them looked at each other in total surprise. Since they had only been partners for six weeks, they didn't really know much about each other's background.

"You mean in downtown Houston?" said Johnny.

"No, Corpus Christi," Olivera replied. "Hayes owns some land northwest of there, and we think that's the center of his operation. He probably has some other places rented under different names, but we want to start with the Corpus Christi area. The clinic we're talking about is down there."

"We want you two to live there under false names and pretend to be roommates desperate for money so that you can go back to medical school," Kelly explained. "We want you to get in real tight with the streetwalkers, so we'll spread rumors that you both might have done some night work yourselves, or maybe sold some prescriptions out the back door for a little extra cash."

Adriana slapped her palm flat on the table.

"I have to sleep with him? That's not going to happen!"

"For once, we agree on something," said Johnny.

Agent Kelly looked at Johnny and smiled.

"I didn't think that would be a problem given your, um, orientation Mr. Riley."

Johnny's face suddenly turned red, and he glared at Kelly.

"What do you mean?" asked Adriana, "what are you talking about?"

"Mr. Riley seems to prefer male friends," said Kelly, "I don't think you are very likely to be sleeping in the same bed with him."

Adriana stared at Johnny in disbelief. She didn't feel nervous or disgusted by the news that he was gay, it was just another complete surprise.

"That actually makes me feel better about the whole thing," She looked over at Johnny, "I trust my partner."

Johnny smiled at her and nodded his appreciation.

"Me too," he said.

"Excellent," said Rodriguez, grinning. "We can start the preparations tomorrow, and get you both briefed and ready to go."

"One last thing," Adriana interjected, "you mentioned this serial killer that may or may not be connected, but you never told us how many girls have been murdered. Are we talking about three or four? How dangerous is this guy?"

Agent Kelly hesitated for a moment, then he answered.

"Fifteen so far."

"Fifteen?"

"That we know of."

CHAPTER 3

Adriana got the phone call early on Sunday morning. She hadn't even finished breakfast yet, but that turned out to be a good thing. It meant less food coming back up an hour later when she got her first glimpse of the body.

The Houston cop pointed and tried to wave her away as she turned the corner and eased her car down the street toward him. Adriana pulled over to the curb and climbed out of the car. She reached into her pocket and took out her badge. The nervous cop rested his palm on the holster of his gun, but relaxed when he recognized her shield.

"Good morning, officer," Adriana said in a pleasant tone as she approached. "I've been called in by Special Agent Kelly. Is this where they found the body?"

The cop glanced back over his left shoulder and nodded.

"Down at the end of the alley," he said. "Be careful where you step. This whole place is a crime scene. It's a bloody mess."

He lifted the wide strip of yellow tape, and Adriana ducked under it. She could see a cluster of people at the far end of the alley about fifty steps away. The body was not visible yet, still hidden from view by a couple of large green dumpsters.

Adriana made her way down the narrow road, not eager to see what was waiting up ahead. A C.S.I. technician watched her every step, no doubt concerned that she might step on some valuable evidence on the way. There were already several tiny plastic tents with numbers placed in various spots, and she avoided going anywhere near them. She assumed those marked the location of something they had found and thought might be important.

As she came around the dumpsters, Adriana was overwhelmed by the powerful stench of death. The smell of blood hung thick in the humid air, squeezed into the narrow confines of the alley and lingering like a malignant cloud over the mutilated corpse of the young girl. It wasn't Norma, but it was another teenage Mexican girl that could easily have been her twin.

The girl's face was frozen in a mask of terror and shock that reflected her final horrific moments of life. The agony she suffered was obvious and made the brutality of her murder even more tragic. Her eyes were still open wide, staring into the heavens as if begging for help. Below the neck, her body had been carved and cut apart, mutilated and desecrated like a slab of butchered meat.

There were three men squatting around the girl's lifeless corpse as it lay there on the pavement. They were all wearing suits, but she recognized only one.

"Good morning, Miss Santos," said Special Agent Kelly. He got up and stepped back to where she was standing a few feet away.

"Not a very good morning for her," Adriana responded, "has she been laying here very long?"

"Not too long," Kelly replied, "rigor mortis has started though, so the M.E. was guessing time of death to be sometime between midnight and four o'clock this morning. I'm sure he can tell us more after he examines her in the morgue."

"So what am I doing here?" she asked. "Do you want me to work on this serial killer case now?"

Kelly shook his head.

"No, I just thought you should see this."

Adriana blinked and cocked her head.

"You wanted me to see this? Why?"

"I'm putting all my cards on the table," said the F.B.I. man, "I want you to know what you might run into. It may have no connection at all to the trafficking ring, but we don't know yet. It will definitely be another monster roaming the streets though."

"But this is downtown Houston," said Adriana, "you said we're going undercover in Corpus Christi. That's two hundred miles from here. It can't be the same guy."

Kelly nodded toward the corpse.

"Step up and take a closer look, if you want to. You'll see what I mean."

Adriana eased forward and peered over the shoulder of the man kneeling next to the body. It was like seeing something out of a gory movie. Bloody strips of ragged flesh were peeled back, and raw pieces of disemboweled organs lay strewn on both sides of the huge cavity that had once been her abdomen. Someone had sliced the front of her body open in a deep, wide swath shaped like the letter J.

Adriana felt her breakfast burrito bubbling up into her throat. She covered her mouth and darted to the other side of the dumpsters before throwing up. The

F.B.I. man gave her a few moments to recover, then he offered her a bottle of water.

"That's okay, just take it easy, Miss Santos. You're not the first one to do that this morning. This kind of thing is hard to take, even for an old dog like me."

Adriana took a few sips of the water and felt the urge to vomit subside a bit. She wiped off her mouth with the back of her hand and blew out a deep breath.

"Whew! Sorry about that. I guess it was a little more than I expected. I've never seen anything that bad before, not even at a car accident."

"It's way beyond anything a normal human being would do," said Kelly. "We're dealing with a true psychopath here. That's how we eventually figured out that all of the killings were related. We have victims all over the state of Texas as far north as Dallas. We've found dead girls in Austin, San Antonio, and Houston that look the same. This one makes sixteen now, and we may not have found them all yet. But all of the victims were young Mexican girls working as prostitutes or living on the street. All the bodies have the same mutilation patterns, and all of them were missing their small left toe."

"Their little toe?"

The agent nodded.

"Yes, apparently the killer cuts off their toe and keeps it as a souvenir. That's one fact that is being held back from the public. If we ever find anyone that knows about it, then he is probably our killer."

Adriana stood there and tried to digest all of that information. Yesterday, she had been committed to the idea of working undercover. She had been full of confidence and ready for the new challenge. Now, she wasn't so sure. The world seemed like a much darker and more evil place than she had realized.

All at once, they heard the sounds of an argument at the other end of the alley. A thin guy in a jogging suit was arguing with the cop manning the barricade. Adriana and Agent Kelly started walking in that direction.

"It's okay," shouted Kelly, "you can let him pass!"

As they got closer, Adriana could see Johnny Riley standing on the other side of the yellow tape and yelling at the officer. Riley had a cigarette in his mouth, and he kept blowing smoke in the cop's face as he talked.

"This guy didn't have any identification," the officer explained to Kelly, "and I told him that he can't go into a crime scene smoking a cigarette."

Agent Kelly turned and looked at Johnny.

"The man is right," he said, "you have to drop that butt if you want to come on this side of the tape. Where is your badge?"

Riley rolled his eyes and sighed.

"Hello? This is Sunday morning, and it's my day off. I was out jogging when I got the call to come over here. I grabbed my keys and came right over anyway. I didn't stop to put on my uniform or anything."

"Don't you carry your badge all the time?" asked Adriana. "I do, and usually my gun, too, just in case something happens. You have to be ready for it even if you're not actually on duty."

"I was working on my physical fitness," said Johnny, "people don't carry guns when they're jogging."

"But you're not even sweating."

"That's because I'm in good condition."

"Bullshit! Do you always smoke when you jog?"

"That's enough," said Kelly holding up both hands, "I swear you two act like a couple of old married people! You should make a great team."

"I don't know about that," said Johnny, tossing his cigarette on the ground. "Let me see this body you found. I want to know what we're up against."

They all walked back to the other end of the alley and around the big dumpsters. The three of them gazed at the girl's mutilated corpse.

"So what's the big deal?" Riley asked. "It's only another dead hooker. Why do I need to see this?"

Adriana was appalled by his lack of sympathy.

"Look at her, Johnny," she said, "whoever did this is a total monster. He's not even a human being. How can you not feel something for these girls? They're lost and helpless against people like that."

"It's their own fault," Johnny replied. "They choose to sneak across the border, and do whatever it takes to get here even though they have no education or job skills to offer. They should just stay where they are instead of coming here and begging on the streets or trading sex for money. Then people like Bill Hayes would be out of business, and we wouldn't have to worry about them."

Adriana huffed and put both hands on her hips.

"Well, that's just cold Johnny Riley. I had no idea that you were so cold. Most of these girls have a terrible life in Mexico with all the poverty and the drug cartels. This is their last desperate hope to find a decent life."

"I'm not being cold, I'm only being realistic."

"So are you going with me to Corpus Christi, or are you backing out?"

Johnny rolled his eyes and paced back and forth. The C.S.I. technician kept watching him and nervously eyeing the little plastic tents.

"I probably shouldn't do it, but I'll go with you," he decided at last. "If we can shut down the trafficking ring, then at least it will get these girls off the streets.

But I'm going to warn you ahead of time that I will not spend any effort hunting this killer. Let Juan the Ripper do his thing and leave us alone."

Adriana gave him a puzzled look. "Juan the Ripper?"

"That's what they call him," said Johnny, "I guess his work reminds somebody of Jack the Ripper except with a Mexican slant."

"That's mostly right," Agent Kelly agreed, "Jack the Ripper supposedly killed a handful of prostitutes about a hundred years ago in a similar fashion. He didn't kill this many, but he cut them up and removed their organs like this maniac does."

"Why call him Juan?" asked Adriana. "Is someone trying to be funny?"

"No, not really," said Kelly, "they do have a couple of potential witnesses who say they saw a Latino man with one of the victims around the time of the murder. Since that kind of fits the profile, the investigators picked a Latino name."

"It sounds like prejudice talking to me," Riley remarked. "Just because a guy has dark features doesn't make him Latino, or the Latino guy might have been a customer."

"Exactly," Adriana agreed, "Johnny has dark hair, and he's not Latino, right?"

"I'm Irish, not an ounce of Hispanic blood anywhere in the family tree."

"Don't get too hung up on that," the F.B.I. man cautioned, "we only use that as a way to remember what type of suspect we may be looking for. Those witnesses may turn out to be completely wrong."

"It didn't help them catch Jack the Ripper either," said Johnny, "they never did catch that guy, did they?"

"No, they didn't," Kelly conceded, "I think he killed five or ten women in one particular neighborhood of

London and then disappeared. The killing suddenly stopped. Nobody knows why. Maybe he went to prison for something else, or got killed himself, or possibly went somewhere else, but the police never caught him."

"Well, I hope they catch this guy," said Adriana, "he's a sick bastard."

"Not our problem," said Johnny, "we'll just stay out of his way."

"That's great advice," said Kelly, "it's the main reason I wanted both of you to see this. We will do our best to protect you, but once you are undercover, contact with us will be minimal. We can't risk blowing your cover. Olivera will have people keeping an eye on you, but don't depend on that either. We can't watch you twenty-four hours a day. If you get inside the trafficking ring, you will be on your own. The best we can do is give you a burner cell phone and a couple of emergency numbers for messages."

"That doesn't sound very comforting," said Johnny.

"Don't worry, I'll protect you," Adriana promised.

"I'm still not too sure about this."

"Well, make up your mind quick," said Kelly, "if you're going, then meet me at the Kemah police station at one o'clock. I'll brief you on everything that we have and coordinate the details with Captain Rodriguez and Agent Olivera. We can assign you a car from the impound lot to use."

"Only one car?" said Riley.

"Yes, and I'll choose the car," Kelly replied. "You're supposed to be hard up for money. You didn't just win the lottery."

"I'm okay with that," said Adriana, "I would rather save my luck for later when we really need it."

CHAPTER 4

Adriana cruised down Agnes Street past Port Avenue. The drive from Houston had taken them a little more than four hours, but they still had plenty of daylight left. She studied one side of the street while Johnny surveyed the other.

The area was residential with small stores and businesses scattered out along the main roads. It had seen better days though. The houses were older and not in very good shape. The businesses were mostly convenience stores or supply stores. A few corner locations sold gasoline.

They drove around a few of the surrounding neighborhoods, passing taquerias, a grocery store, a local bakery, and the Salvation Army. Adriana checked her notes again and found the address. It was an old rental house they would be calling home for the next six months.

"Oh no, no, no, no," Johnny protested, "you cannot be serious! This place is a roach motel. This can't be where we are living."

"I'm afraid so," said Adriana, "this is the address they gave me. We can try the front door and see if the key fits."

"I was expecting a small condo, or at least a nice apartment."

"Suck it up, Riley. This is your new home sweet home."

Adriana cut off the engine, and they climbed out of the car stiff from the trip. Both paused to stretch a bit, then Johnny lit up a cigarette.

"This car is a piece of shit," Riley complained, "I feel like I've been riding in a hay wagon all day."

"It's a twelve-year-old Ford Taurus, not that bad really."

"I don't know why they couldn't give us one of those cars from the drug dealers. Those are some sweet rides. Those dealers aren't going to need them anymore."

"They were probably stolen to begin with," Adriana pointed out, "we don't need to attract any attention, anyway. We're supposed to be undercover here."

"I don't know about you," said Johnny, "but I'm looking at this assignment like a paid vacation. I'm going to mingle around and do almost nothing. That way we can't get into any trouble. In a few months, they'll be calling us back home."

"That may be okay for you, but not for me. I'm going to find out as much as I can about this human trafficking network. These people are ruining too many lives with all of their lies and false promises. That's just wrong, and I'm going to help them put a stop to it. There is nothing worse than stealing someone's dreams and then taking their life. That is just pure evil."

"Yeah, whatever."

Riley tossed his cigarette butt on the ground and ambled up to the front door. He slipped the key in the lock, and it opened with ease.

"Shit," said Johnny, "this must be the right place."

Adriana smiled and followed him inside. There were a few basic furnishings, but for the most part, it was bare. The two bedrooms had a worn-out bed and a small dresser. The living room had an aging sofa and a battered coffee table, but no television. A tiny breakfast table stood in one corner of the kitchen facing an ancient refrigerator and the built-in oven. That was about it.

"It looks like we won't be entertaining very much," Johnny commented, "you think there is a nice swimming pool or hot tub in the backyard?"

"I doubt it," Adriana replied. "We may want to go ahead and call Agent Kelly about springing for a few things. He might be willing to pay for a microwave and basic cable, and maybe even internet. And we probably need some sheets and towels. I don't remember seeing any when we walked around."

"How about getting a washing machine and a dryer as long as we're asking," Johnny suggested, "we could rent those."

"Good idea. You make the list, and I'll make the call."

They finished the call with permission to purchase a limited amount of stuff at reasonable prices, so they jumped in the Taurus and headed out for a quick shopping spree at Family Dollar. While they were on the road, they did an expanded tour of the city and found some other places with more to offer. It was almost dark by the time they made it back to Agnes Street.

The ladies of the evening were already out and ready to serve. Adriana cruised by slowly as they rounded the next corner onto Marguerite and then crossed over to

Mary Street. They could see the young girls lining the roadways, some half hidden next to the trees, other sauntering brazenly down the sidewalks. Every one of them smiled when they passed by.

"Can you believe this?" Johnny said in amazement. "These girls don't even look old enough to drive, and they're selling their ass on the streets! That's disgusting, I can't believe the cops aren't crawling all over this place."

"It isn't disgusting, it's sad," said Adriana, "they probably don't even know how to drive and can't afford a car anyway. Someone is just dropping them off here and then picking them up later to take their money away. This is tragic."

"You think any of these girls are from the trafficking ring?"

"I don't know. Maybe we can chat with one."

Adriana eased the car over close to the curb a few feet in front of a Mexican girl. Her face lit up, and she walked over to the car. She peeked in the open window and then smiled.

"You want a double? I will do a double," she offered in a merry tone.

"Where?" said Johnny. "You live around here?"

"I come with you," she replied.

"What's your name?" asked Adriana. She repeated the question in Spanish.

"Uhm... Mary... Maria," she stammered.

"I bet every girl on this street gives the same answer," Johnny said in his usual cynical tone, "and I bet every girl a block from here is named Marguerite or Agnes, aren't they?"

The girl began to get nervous. She stared at Johnny and backed away from the car a couple of steps.

"My name is Adriana. I'm going to start working at the clinic near here. Maybe you can come over and see me there? I'll give you a free check-up, and you can tell me some more about the area. We just moved here."

The girl was glancing back and forth between Adriana and Johnny.

"This is your boyfriend?"

Riley laughed out loud, and Adriana smacked him on the arm.

"No, this is a friend who will be working with me there. His name is John."

"Have you ever heard of Juan the Ripper?" Johnny shouted.

The young girl screamed and ran away as fast as she could on stiletto heels. Riley slapped his thigh and cackled. Adriana glared at him.

"Wow, that was real subtle partner. Why didn't you just whip out a long butcher knife and wave it around? Maybe she would have peed in her panties for you."

"Ha, ha," Johnny responded, "very funny but I don't think she was even wearing panties. I only wanted to scare her a little. Maybe she will go home and get her skanky ass off the street."

"Maybe she doesn't have a home," said Adriana, "maybe all she has is this shitty job working for some shitty pimp who lives in a crack house. Maybe her only alternative is to go back there and get knocked around while he keeps her high on drugs all day. Did you ever think of that?"

Riley stared out the window and didn't say anything.

"You need to quit being so self-centered," she added, "not everyone gets to grow up in the suburbs with a nice house and a family that cares about them."

Johnny turned and glared at her.

"I didn't either," he snapped, "I grew up on a patch of barren land that my father called a goat farm. If I wanted meat for dinner, I had to kill it and cook it myself because he was always too drunk to do it. Believe me, eating goat meat every day is no picnic. I was the youngest, so my mother and my older brothers all left before I did. How is that for your happy family?"

Adriana stared at him and saw the rage and humiliation on his face. She had no idea that he had escaped from a life like that.

"I'm... I'm sorry, Johnny. I didn't know. I shouldn't have said that."

"Don't apologize, and don't feel sorry for me," he whispered, "it made me what I am today. I'm not going to look back, but I'm not going to feel sorry for anyone else."

Adriana nodded.

"I understand. And we don't ever have to talk about it again."

Riley went back to staring out the window. Adriana put the car in drive and eased away from the curb. She drove the short distance to their rental house and pulled into the driveway. They unloaded the things they had purchased and carried them into the house. There was no more conversation that evening.

CHAPTER 5

driana reported for her first day of work at the clinic early on Monday morning. Though reluctant, Johnny came along, eager to get out of the house. The customers were already lining up at the door when it opened. An older woman wearing a cheap smock and a frown pushed the door back and waved them all inside.

Adriana and Johnny stood off to one side and waited for the customers to sign the register first. Then they walked up to the reception desk. The woman ignored them for a moment, but then she glanced up.

"Good morning," Adriana said, "my friend and I are supposed to start work here today. We're your new temp help. I'm Adriana Santos, and this is John Riley. This is the medical clinic for Dr. Richards, right?"

The woman at the desk seemed perplexed for a second and then brightened up.

"Okay. No one tells me anything around here, so I didn't expect you, but that's not a problem. We can always use more help. As you can see, there is no shortage of patients that need our attention, and it's like this every single day."

She waved her hand at the waiting room behind them. The chairs were already half full, and there were more people coming in the front door.

"Kathy," the woman yelled over her shoulder, "temp help is here!"

A middle-aged woman wearing a nurse's uniform came out of the back offices and stood behind the receptionist. She glanced back and forth from Adriana to Johnny and smiled. Adriana returned the smile. Johnny didn't.

"So you'll be working with us now," she asked, "it's very nice to have you. We can certainly use the help. Come on through that door, and I'll show you around."

John and Adriana walked through the door separating the back offices from the waiting room. Kathy was waiting on the other side. She gave them a quick tour of the place. Behind the reception desk was a large office area used for file storage and some computers for scheduling, billing, and dealing with insurance. There were two wings of treatment rooms branching off each side of that. In between the wings were larger rooms set up with simple lab and x-ray equipment. In the back part of the building, there was a second smaller waiting room, a nurses' lounge area, and the doctor's office.

"This place is a lot bigger than it looks from the outside," Adriana observed.

Kathy smiled and nodded.

"Yes, it is. I think it used to be some kind of real estate office when it was first built, but that was probably over fifty years ago. Dr. Richards bought the building and parking lot about ten years ago when he started the clinic. He had another partner back then, another doctor, but he left, so now it's just us.

Sometimes we get young interns or physician assistants, but they come and go. Mostly the nurses have to carry the load."

"When does the doctor come in," Adriana asked, "is he here now?"

Kathy glanced at her watch.

"No, it's only a little after eight. Dr. Richards usually comes in around nine or nine-thirty and stays until six or seven o'clock depending on the last patient. We try to close the doors at five, but people always come later."

"What kind of treatments are you doing here?" said Johnny.

"General medical care," Kathy replied, "but not urgent care or anything that will require a specialist. We do physicals, some basic testing and blood work, simple x-rays, some vaccinations and injections. No emergency room stuff, a few referrals."

"That sounds good," said Adriana, "are most of your patients local people and walk-ins then?"

Kathy nodded.

"Yeah, mostly, but we also have a few contracts with some local companies to do things like a pre-employment physicals, drug testing, back-to-work certifications, things like that. It's pretty routine stuff really."

"Works for me," said Johnny.

"Who deals with all the documentation for patient treatments and insurance?" asked Adriana. "What do we do if patients don't have any identification or coverage, do you treat them anyway?"

Kathy rolled her eyes and blew out a long sigh of exasperation.

"That's the real sore spot around here. A lot of them don't have anything. They might show you a fake license or something, but most of our people don't have any sort of insurance coverage at all. A lot are illegal immigrants and not U.S. citizens, but we don't turn anybody away. Dr. Richards always takes the time to see every patient who comes in here. Sometimes he has to do some creative stuff with the paperwork though. Brenda Castro works up front in the business office and deals with all of that."

Adriana looked at Johnny and smiled. He shook his head no, but she ignored it.

"John is actually a lot better with the paperwork side than I am," said Adriana. "He might want to spend some extra time with Brenda to learn more about that."

"That would be wonderful," Kathy exclaimed, "Brenda is always so behind on her filings! She has to answer questions all day from the patients so she never gets caught up. Are you an outgoing person with good people skills?"

Johnny shook his head no again, but Adriana pushed on.

"He is fantastic," she gushed, "you just would not believe how well John deals with people and high-pressure situations. I'm sure he would love to jump right in and help Brenda with that."

Johnny glared at her and mumbled, but he managed a weak smile.

"I would be delighted, Kathy. I can't tell you how much I would appreciate the chance to learn and pitch in."

"Wonderful," said Kathy, "let me take you both up front right now and introduce you to Brenda. She will be so thrilled."

They walked back to the front office, and all squeezed in around the ladies sitting there. Kathy made the introductions, and everyone pretended to be happy about it. Brenda found an extra chair and rolled it up next to her work station. Johnny parked himself there and prepared for a long day of training. Adriana fell in behind Kathy and started helping with the patient backlog.

Patients came and went throughout the morning, but the waiting room seemed to always be nearly full. Most of the complaints were trivial things requiring only cursory examinations and minor treatments. The more serious cases were referred to specialists or sent to the hospital for follow-up care.

Adriana was appalled by the general condition of the customers. Many of them had little or no medical history at all, no record of basic immunizations or previous care for childhood illness and injuries. Some even presented classic symptoms of the problems that resulted from a chronic lack of proper medical care and treatment. Even worse, most seemed to have almost no knowledge of how to take care of themselves now.

Lunchtime rolled around with no break in the workload. Adriana peered out at the waiting room and saw that almost every seat was still occupied. People were stopping by on their lunch hour and joining those already waiting. Customers were waiting more than an hour now to get called back for treatment.

She blew out a sigh of weariness.

"Don't let it get to you," Kathy whispered, "pace yourself and take it one step at a time. Don't feel pressured to do things any faster."

"Is it like this all the time?" Adriana asked.

"More or less. Some days are worse than others. This is the Monday right after a holiday weekend, so it's a little heavier than usual. Tomorrow and Wednesday will be a lot easier."

"Is the clinic open tomorrow? Tomorrow is the fourth of July."

"We're open every day, dear. People don't schedule when to be sick or get hurt based on their calendars. Once you get the hang of everything, we can come up with a more reasonable work schedule for you. We expect you to be flexible, but we certainly don't expect you to work every day."

"I'll have to coordinate with Johnny too," she pointed out, "we are roommates, and we share a car."

"I'm sure we can work something out," Kathy responded, "why don't you go to the lounge and take a short break?"

"Thanks, that would be great."

Adriana went to the back of the building and found the lounge area. She grabbed a soft drink and settled into one of the soft, padded chairs to rest for a few minutes.

She had just closed her eyes and relaxed when the door burst open and Johnny came rushing in.

"Hey! How is it going?" he asked in a cheerful voice.

She opened one eye and squinted at him.

"I thought you were lost in paperwork hell," Adriana remarked. "Why are you so happy now?"

"This is going to be great," he answered, "I get to see all the details for every one of the patients! Even if they don't have any insurance or identification, we have to make up something for their medical records. I'm sure most of the names are probably fake, but it doesn't really matter. It gives me a good reason to press them for more information. I can usually tell when people are lying, so I know what part is true and what isn't. It will give me something to go on."

"What do you mean something to go on?"

"It helps me pick out the most likely targets."

"What kind of targets?"

"The girls that are probably hookers. I'm going to make a list of those girls and find out whatever I can. Then I can stalk them later and get more details."

Adriana sat up straight in her chair and stared at him in surprise.

"Wait a minute, I thought you told me this was going to be a vacation for you, and you didn't want to get involved. Now, you're talking about stalking people. Why are you going to stalk them?"

"Those will be the most likely people to know something about this trafficking network or be potential targets for the serial killer, right?"

Adriana nodded.

"Yeah, that's a good point."

"So, I figure we can take turns stalking a few of them and see where it leads."

She thought about that for a minute.

"You don't really mean stalking them, you mean hanging out with them."

Johnny shrugged and frowned a little.

"Whatever you want to call it. You do it your way, and I can do it mine. If you want to go make friends and share a salad together that's fine. But, I would prefer to just watch them and see where they go and who they talk to."

"Are you looking for a reason to get out of the house at night?"

He laughed and tried to look innocent.

"Of course not! How could I possibly not enjoy spending a relaxing evening in our beautiful rental home with you? But, since we only have one car, I figure we can do this thing separately. Besides, it will be a lot easier to blend in alone than as a couple, especially if we are hanging around with hookers."

She had to admit, it did sound like a pretty good approach.

"Okay, it makes some sense, but don't tell Agent Kelly that we're going to stalk some targets. That makes it sound like we're the serial killers. Let's tell him we are going to establish some connections on the street and do some surveillance."

"I'll let you tell him whatever you want to."

Johnny poured himself a cup of coffee. He stirred in a generous helping of cream and sugar, then he sat down in the chair next to Adriana. He leaned back with a smug grin on his face.

"See? I told you this would be a great assignment."

"Bullshit! You've done nothing but complain up until now."

"Sometimes it takes a while for my good-natured personality to come through. But you know I've always got your back. We're partners, after all. Don't forget that."

She gave him a skeptical look.

"Yep, we're partners. You just better be there whenever I need you."

"Oh absolutely, pumpkin. Now let's get back to work. We've got a lot to do."

Johnny jumped up and dashed out the door spilling coffee as he went. Adriana leaned back with a sigh and closed her eyes again.

CHAPTER 6

Traffic was light on Tuesday because it was a holiday. Johnny and Adriana got to the clinic in less than twenty minutes. They still had to wait outside for a few minutes since neither of them had a key to the door. The receptionist from yesterday was on duty once again, and she recognized them. This time she smiled.

"Good morning, Alma," said Adriana, "how are you today?"

"Oh, I can't complain," she responded, pulling the door aside. It sounded like something she said every day more out of habit than sincerity.

With most of the insurance companies closed for the day, Brenda didn't come into the office. Johnny was free to spend more time digging around in the medical records and making notes for himself. The other ladies commented on how much they admired his dedication and work ethic.

Adriana followed Kathy around again and helped with patient treatments. Now that she was more familiar with the procedure, Kathy let her handle some routine things like taking the patient medical histories and basic information. The more experienced nurses would come into the room to deal with the case. Dr. Richards also insisted on seeing every patient, even if only for a few minutes.

The morning passed with a continuous stream of walk-ins. The holiday seemed to be a good opportunity for many people to make time for a quick visit to the clinic. By lunchtime, Adriana was already tired and ready for a break.

She had brought food from home this time, so after checking with Kathy, she ducked into the nurses' lounge for a bite to eat. A twenty minute rest was enough to recharge her batteries again.

Adriana came out of the break room and started toward the front of the building. As she walked up the short hallway, Kathy caught her eye and then pointed to a treatment room. She grabbed the clipboard on the door and stepped inside ready to meet the patient.

A young Mexican girl sat on the cushioned exam table. Judging from appearance, the girl was only sixteen or seventeen years old. She was covered in bruises, her left eye was swollen shut. Her clothes were worn and tattered.

Pushing the door closed, Adriana smiled a reassuring smile and said hello to the girl in both English and Spanish. The girl tried to return the smile, but it was obvious that her face was hurting. She sent a nervous glance toward a young man sitting on the chair in the corner of the room.

"What is your name, sweetheart?" Adriana asked, doing a quick visual exam of the bruises on the girl's arms. The patient didn't respond. "Can you slip off your clothes and let me examine the rest of your body?"

"I was about to ask you the same thing," said the guy in the corner.

The voice sounded familiar. Adriana spun around and stared at the man. It was the same one she had seen in the fishing boat last Friday night.

"What are you doing here?" she demanded.

He chuckled and moved over to block the door.

"You must be reading my mind," he said, "that's two times in a row. Is it just my imagination, or did you change jobs? I thought you were a cop up in Galveston."

"Well, uh... I used to be. I got fired because of the incident on the boat, so now I work here at the clinic. I only started yesterday."

The man eyed her suspiciously.

"Now, I wonder why I don't believe you," he said, "let's go back to that first question again. Can you take off your clothes and let me see your underwear? Then I could be sure it was really you."

"No, I'm not taking off my clothes!"

"Yeah, it's you. I recognize your stubborn attitude. So they fired you because of what happened on the boat? I wouldn't have expected that. Weren't they happy because you rescued the girl from that asshole?"

Adriana shrugged.

"Well, yeah, but they weren't happy that I didn't arrest anybody. It made me look kind of incompetent. Why did you leave anyway? You should have stuck around so you could verify my story. You promised to do that, but then you left and took that big boat. We were floating around in that little fishing dinghy with no fuel or anything. It made me look kind of stupid."

"I thought you looked pretty good myself. Are you wearing the same underwear today? I wouldn't mind seeing that again."

"Forget it, Jack! I'm not showing you my underwear."

"The name is Travis, not Jack. Did you forget me so soon?"

"No, Travis, I didn't forget. What was your last name again?"

"I think it will be Jones today, I was Smith yesterday."

"Well, Travis Jones, I'm about to step out of this examination room and go call the police. You can explain your side of the story to them while I take care of this poor girl. Who is she anyway? Is this another one that you guys were going to sell?"

Travis reached into his pocket and pulled out a small handgun.

"I wouldn't do that if I were you," he said, "my version of the story is probably a little bit different from yours. I like my version a lot better, so I would prefer to stick with that one, if you don't mind."

"And what's your version?"

"In my version, we were suddenly surrounded by the harbor patrol and little Billy went overboard in a scuffle with the police. I was lucky to escape with my life when they killed him and then tried to confiscate the boat. Fortunately, I managed to get away in the darkness and not leave any incriminating evidence behind. My boss was very grateful."

"You left that poor Mexican girl!"

"She doesn't know anything, and I knew you would take good care of her. See? I even brought you another one to fix up."

Adriana glanced back at the young girl on the exam table.

"What happened to her anyway? Did you beat her?"

Travis held up the hand not holding a gun.

"Not me," he said, "one of the other guys did that. Sometimes the girls get a little upset when they finally realize that their situation is not exactly what they signed up for. When that happens, we have to explain to them the new rules and then train them."

"This is not a job, this is slavery," Adriana protested, "do you promise these girls a job? Is that how you talk them into coming here?"

"It's a job, and it's really an easy one if they cooperate. They already have all the right equipment; they just have to learn how to use it."

"Oh, come on! This is sexual slavery. You people are using these girls or selling them, right? Do they ever get a choice about it?"

"Why do you care?" he asked. "You're not a cop anymore, or at least that's what you're telling me. Or am I wrong about that?"

Travis narrowed his eyes and pointed the gun at her chest. Adriana backed up a step and hesitated. She put both hands in front of her as if she would block any bullets that came flying in her direction.

"Okay, you're right. I'm not a cop anymore," she lied, "I shouldn't care. But, I do really care about these young girls getting hurt like this. This isn't right. You should take better care of them. Aren't they worth more to you if they are healthy and good-looking? That should be worth something."

Travis shrugged.

"It doesn't matter to me. I'm not making any money out of this. It's only a job for me, like herding cattle or something."

"Yeah, but it matters to your boss, right? You need to take care of these girls just like you watch out for the cattle and make sure they don't get sick or hurt. That way they are worth more. Doesn't that make sense?"

The man stared at her and thought about it for a minute.

"Okay, you've got a point," he nodded, "taking them to the clinic or taking them... someplace else is a pain. I really hate that part."

Adriana had a brilliant idea.

"What if you never had to do that again?"

Curious, Travis cocked his head and eyed her.

"What do you mean?"

"What if you had someone there to take care of these girls all the time?"

"Oh, don't worry; we take good care of them."

Adriana looked at him and rolled her eyes.

"That's total bullshit and you know it, otherwise you wouldn't be here. I don't mean feeding them or clothing them. I'm talking about real medical care, making sure they are healthy and attractive. What if you had a full-time nurse like me? I know what girls need and want. I can take care of them when they are hurt or sick. I can even help them with clothes and make-up so they look their best. Isn't that a good idea?"

He stared at her and thought about that for a minute.

"Yeah, I guess so. It would sure save me a lot of headaches. But that's not my decision. Something like that has to come from the big boss."

"But you can ask him, right?" Adriana pressed. "Just ask him. You can say that it's your idea, if you want to get the credit for it. I don't care. I only want these girls to have a better life. I can't stand to see anyone treated like this."

She stepped back and showed Travis the ugly cuts and bruises on the girl's arms and face. Then she began to remove the girl's clothes and examine the rest of her body. The young girl stared at the wall and hung her head in shame.

Adriana motioned for her to lie flat on the table. She made sure her movements were gentle as she took off the girl's skirt and blouse. As expected, her thighs and ribs were covered in scrapes and bruises. Her wrists and ankles were swollen and chafed.

"Do you keep these girls tied up or chained?"

"That's none of your business," he replied.

She studied the girl's body for a few more minutes, then Adriana turned and headed for the door. Travis reached out and stopped her.

"Where do you think you're going?"

"I'm going to get some antibacterial ointment and medication for my patient. Please get out of the way so I can do my job."

"You're going to call the police, aren't you?" he smirked.

She shook her head.

"No, I promise I won't do that. I only want to get the medicine to help this girl. After I get her bandaged up, then you can both leave. I won't say anything, and I won't charge you anything. All I ask is that you make sure this doesn't happen again. I don't want to see her back next week for the same thing. Is that a deal?"

Travis hesitated for a moment.

"I'm going outside to wait," he said at last, "you fix her up and send her out in less than fifteen minutes. I better not see any police show up or things could get messy. Fifteen minutes, is that clear?"

Adriana nodded.

He shoved the gun back in his pocket and slipped out the door. She glanced back at the girl on the table once more and said a few reassuring words in Spanish. Then she went down the hall to the supply cabinet to get some ointment and pain killers. By the time Adriana got back to the room, the girl was gone.

CHAPTER 7

It preyed on her mind all day, thinking about the young girl, wondering about all the others out there somewhere. The girl's wounds had not been fatal, but they were serious. Adriana felt sure they had killed what little hope the girl had of finding a decent life. She had no illusions about the kind of people who had brought her into this country with vague lies and false promises they never intended to keep.

She moped through the rest of the day and wondered what had happened. Did the girl escape and run away? Was Travis waiting outside to catch the girl again as soon as she came out the door? Adriana didn't know, and it bothered her a lot. She searched the waiting room and the parking lot, but there was no sign of Travis or the girl.

Johnny stopped her as they passed in the hallway.

"Are you alright?" he asked.

"I guess so," Adriana replied, "something strange happened this morning, and it kind of got to me."

He glanced at his watch.

"It's almost six o'clock now. Let's get out of here, you can tell me about it on the way to the house."

They checked out and exited through the back door of the building. The majority of the parking lot was empty. Johnny paused and lit up a cigarette while Adriana fumbled in her purse for the car keys. She unlocked the car, and they both climbed in.

Adriana pulled out of the parking lot and guided them through the light traffic on the way home. There weren't many cars on the road. She glanced over at Johnny and saw him studying the little notebook he had been carrying around all day.

"What are you writing down in there?" she asked. "Are those notes about how to do the job or about the patients?"

"A little of both. The insurance forms are complicated, so I write down a lot of the tips Brenda shows me. Most of the stuff is computerized now, but it still takes a lot of this special coding and shit. I'm trying to learn the special codes they use most of the time. It makes a huge difference. For example, if the nurse writes down 'removed ear wax' and I put that on the insurance form, then the charge is twenty-five dollars to the insurance. But if the doctor writes down 'extraction of infectious materials' and I use a different special code, then I can charge the insurance company two hundred dollars."

"Wow, that is a huge difference."

"Yeah, even if they are doing exactly the same thing. I can see why Dr. Richards gets into trouble doing shit like that."

"Yeah, me too. So what do you write down about the patients?"

"I'm trying to identify girls who might be from the trafficking ring or potential targets of the serial killer. I was thinking we could check out a few of them late at night and see where they live or where they go. It might give us a lead on something."

"Don't you think that's illegal? Medical records are supposed to be confidential. Most of the information they give is probably made up anyway, right?"

Johnny shrugged his shoulders and blew smoke out the window.

"It doesn't really matter if the information is true or not. False information tells us something, too. If we check out a girl's address, and it turns out to be a vacant lot or some abandoned building, then we know she is hiding something. Even the fake names tell us that. You have no idea how many girls are named Isabella Garcia around here."

"Or Rodriguez," she added, "even our captain is named Rodriguez. I know that's a pretty common name, too."

"Exactly. So if a girl uses one of those real common names and combines it with a bogus address, then that tells you something. It might be an illegal, or a prostitute using a street name. Those go on my list to check out. Maybe they are legit, but most of them are probably not. Either way, it gives me something interesting to do at night besides sitting around in that shitty house."

Adriana laughed.

"You don't look forward to spending time with me in our love nest?"

Johnny looked at her like she had three ears.

"Are you serious? I would rather have a root canal."

"Maybe that will change when we get the internet hooked up."

They rode the rest of the way home in silence. Johnny spent the time playing with his smartphone. Adriana stayed lost in her thoughts about Travis and the young girl. A few minutes later, they were pulling in the driveway.

"Leave it running," said Johnny, "I'm going out for a while to get some dinner and drive around. You want to come?"

Adriana shook her head.

"No, I'm going inside and relax for a while, maybe take a long bath or something. I'm not really hungry right now."

"Can I bring you back something?"

"Don't worry about it. If you want to get a pizza or a hamburger, you can bring me something for later, but I'll be okay with a sandwich."

"Okay then, I'll see you in a little while. I'm going to check out one of these girls on my list. The address she gave is a taco stand."

Adriana slid out of the car and Johnny got behind the wheel. She waved goodbye, and he backed out of the driveway.

She unlocked the front door and walked into the rental house. Without Johnny's constant chatter, it felt cold and lonely to be there by herself. She peeled off her uniform and ran a hot bath. The cable television wasn't working yet, so she settled for some music through her phone. At least, it was some kind of noise to fill the empty vacuum.

The warm water felt good on her skin as Adriana eased herself down into the tub. She didn't have any bubble bath, but there was nothing to stop her from imagining it was there just the same. All she had to do was close her eyes and lean back.

She heard a loud knock on the front door, and her eyes snapped open. Adriana shivered, the water was ice cold. Had she fallen asleep? How long had she been in there? She heard the knock again and got out of the tub.

Adriana grabbed a towel and wrapped it around herself. Then she edged up next to the living room window and peeked through the blinds. It was still light outside, but the sunshine was fading fast. She could see the back and shoulders of someone standing on the front porch close to the door. It was a big man holding a gun.

Moving silent, Adriana crept back into the bedroom and found her own pistol. She started toward the living room, and then she heard a loud crash coming from behind her in the kitchen. She ran that way instead. A man staggered through the back door and stood there with a long knife in his hand. The blade was dripping blood all over the floor. Adriana leveled her gun at the intruder and then stared at him in shock.

"Johnny! What happened? Where did you get that knife?"

He looked down at the knife in his hand as if it belonged to someone else. Then he glanced at his chest and Adriana saw the blood soaking through his shirt.

"I think I killed someone," he stammered, "I didn't mean to, but they surprised me. Don't worry, I'll protect you."

Johnny's eyes rolled back, and he collapsed face down onto the linoleum floor. Adriana dropped her gun and ran over to check on him.

"Johnny, tell me what happened! Who did this to you? Who did you kill?"

A few seconds later, the front door of the house flew open and slammed into the wall. She heard the noise and glanced back over her shoulder. Travis sauntered into the kitchen and pointed a gun at her head.

"Congratulations," he said, "my boss really liked your idea, and I'm here to offer you the job. I think your boyfriend has just created another opening in our organization, so there should be plenty of opportunity for advancement."

Adriana jumped up and flew at him in a rage, her fists landing harmlessly on his arms and shoulders. She cursed and screamed in frustration. Travis laughed at her.

"You do realize that I'm holding a gun, don't you? I could blow your pretty little brains out with this. You're lucky that I like you so much, especially since your towel fell on the floor."

She stopped and looked down at her wet, naked body.

"I don't care!" she shouted. "Why did you kill him?"

"I didn't do anything," Travis responded calmly, "apparently your boyfriend had a little disagreement with one of my associates. I had nothing to do with it."

"You liar," she yelled, "don't you ever tell the truth about anything?"

"If you don't believe me, just look out your back door. You'll probably see some other guy lying there and bleeding to death. Not my problem. If your boyfriend had come to the front door, I would have shot him instead. You didn't hear any gunshots, did you? I'm completely innocent."

"You are not innocent! You're part of this mess! Why are you even here?"

Travis laughed again.

"I told you, I'm here to pick you up and take you to your new job. You're going to be in charge of taking care of all those girls now. That's what you wanted, isn't it? Come on, let's go."

He motioned toward the front door with his gun. Adriana stared down at Johnny and balled up her fists again.

"Can I at least call an ambulance for him? He may still be alive."

Travis walked over and kicked Johnny hard in the ribs.

"I'm fairly certain he's dead, but I can make sure of it, if you like."

He pointed his gun at Johnny's head.

"No wait! Don't do that. Come on, let's go."

She grabbed Travis by the hand and began pulling him toward the front door. He gave her a puzzled expression, and then shrugged his shoulders.

"Okay, that's a much better attitude. I think we're going to get along just fine. My boss is going to love having you around."

Adriana paused in the living room and stared down at her bare chest.

"Can I please put on some clothes? This is very embarrassing."

"Honey believe me, you've got nothing to be embarrassed about. From where I'm standing, you're looking as good as butter on a hot biscuit."

"Thanks for the compliment, I guess, but I would still like to put on some clothes. Can I at least get some underwear?"

Travis peeled off his t-shirt and tossed it to her.

"Try this," he said, "it should cover most of the top part anyway."

She slid the shirt over her head and let it fall down over her shoulders. Travis was a little bigger and more muscular than she had noticed before. The shirt was stretched out and the soft cotton felt good against her skin. Adriana glanced up and saw him staring at her with a strange expression on his face.

"What? Why are you staring at me?"

He shook his head as if to clear the cobwebs.

"Nothing," he mumbled, "come on, let's get out of here."

She hesitated, and he pushed her through the open front door. They walked the short distance to the driveway where a dark panel van was waiting. There was no sign of her car. Travis slid the side door open and shoved her inside. She fell on top of the thin air mattress covering the open space in the back.

"Lie down and put both hands over your head," he ordered.

Adriana flopped onto her back and complied. She stretched her arms up, and he grabbed her by the wrist. Then he snapped a thick metal bracelet around it and secured the other end to an iron loop welded onto the floor.

"This isn't very comfortable," she complained, "I thought you said I was going to be an employee. Why can't I ride up front in the passenger seat?"

"I didn't say you were an employee. I said you had a new job. You're going to be responsible for taking care of the other girls."

"Everything out of your mouth is always a lie, isn't it?"

But Travis didn't respond. He was busy staring at Adriana. The shirt had ridden up higher as she fell back onto the mattress. Now the bottom hem of the shirt just covered her hips. Both of her legs were spread open wide giving him a clear view of her most private area.

She watched as Travis tilted his head. Then he put down the gun and began to stroke the inside of her thighs with his hand, going up one leg, across the crevice in between, and then down the other side. Back and forth he went again, this time pausing longer as he passed over the middle of her body. He pressed his fingers against her and nudged her lips apart.

Adriana held her breath, trembling with fear and... what? Excitement? She was terrified of what he might do, but at the same time she liked it. Every muscle and nerve below her waist was tingling. She felt herself getting wet and sweating as her heart beat faster. She closed her eyes and groaned.

"Oh, you like that?" he whispered.

"No... stop touching me! Get away from me!"

He raised his hand as if he was going to slap her, and she cringed.

"Don't hit me! Just... don't hurt me... please."

Travis stared at her for a moment. He licked his first two fingers, and then he slid them deep inside her. With his other hand, he pushed the shirt up higher and grabbed her breast, pinching her nipple. She gasped at the sudden pain.

His fingers moved in and out of her, back and forth, going deeper and harder now. Adriana felt the heat building up inside. Her leg muscles tensed.

All of a sudden, she cried out as the unexpected orgasm flooded over her body.

Curious, he looked at her for a moment and then stepped back. Travis licked his fingers and smiled. He handed her a plastic bottle with a straw attached.

"Have some water," he offered, "it's going to be a long ride."

Adriana's eyes were still closed, but she heard Travis slam the door shut and walk around to the driver's side. He opened his door and climbed into the van. She heard the engine crank up and felt the motion as they backed out of the driveway.

Her heartbeat was beginning to slow down again, so she took a long swig of water from the bottle. After a quick pause to catch her breath, Adriana took one more drink, and then lay back. In a matter of seconds, she realized that something was wrong. Her head began spinning, and her vision became blurry. Travis must have mixed something into the water.

"You devious bastard!" she yelled, and then she passed out.

CHAPTER 8

Adriana woke up the next morning on a metal cot with a stained, wafer-thin mattress. It felt a little more comfortable than the air mattress in the van, but not much. Her body was sore and hurting all over, her head hurt the most. Whatever drug Travis had put into the water must have been strong. She couldn't remember any details of the long journey to wherever she was now.

Her eyes itched, so she reached up with both hands and tried to rub the sleep away. Adriana's eyelids still felt heavy, but she opened them wider to get a better look at her new surroundings. What she saw surprised her.

The room was a boring rectangle of beige and gray, maybe twenty feet across and about three times as long. There were two rows of identical cots, one along each wall. In the middle of the room sat an island of plastic storage bins. It reminded her of a military barracks, or maybe a cheap dormitory at a summer camp. Everything was organized, but the atmosphere was dismal and impersonal, as if it didn't matter to anyone.

She sat up and surveyed the room. Most of the other cots were occupied by young girls that looked somewhere between fifteen and twenty-five years old. None of them appeared to be older than her. There were a couple of empty places that made her wonder about things. What had happened to those girls?

The door rattled, and all the girls turned to stare in that direction. The door swung open and a short Latino man pushed a wedge of wood under it. The man disappeared back through the doorway without saying a word. The girls climbed out of their bunks and walked hesitantly toward it. Adriana could smell the scent of cooked food drifting through the air.

They all filed through the door and into the big room adjacent. Adriana found herself in another large open area, but this one was arranged like a crude dining room with buffet tables and folding furniture. Like obedient zombies, the girls all shuffled along beside the food table and filled paper plates with what they wanted. Then they each grabbed a paper cup full of water and took a seat.

There was no smiling or chatting. Every person in the room wore the same sad, haggard expression on their face. An older Mexican woman presided over the buffet and she tried to make conversation with the girls. A few of them smiled, but most ignored her. All of them glanced often at the short Latino man standing in the corner with a long bullwhip in his hand.

Adriana selected some food and walked toward one of the tables. She started to sit in the next available chair, but the girls all reacted. They all started shaking their head and waving her away.

"No! No! You cannot sit there!"

She stopped and stared at them in confusion.

"Why not? Is this seat taken? Do you have assigned places?"

The girls all continued to shake their head and pointed toward the man with the whip. He frowned and sauntered toward them. He stopped about three feet away and glared at Adriana.

"What is your problem?" he demanded.

The room went quiet, and she shrugged.

"I don't know where to sit," Adriana replied, "is there some special order to this? I only arrived last night, so I don't know the rules yet."

The Latino man unfurled his long whip and let it drop to the floor. The other girls all gasped and watched the drama with wide-eyed fascination. Adriana took a quick step forward and got right in the man's face. She smiled at him.

"Would you be kind enough to explain the rules for me, please?"

The Latino man cocked his head and stared at her. The room was so quiet she could almost hear the steam coming off the tortillas.

"We sit in order by name," he said, pointing at the chairs one by one. "Amanda, Bianca, Claudia, Diana–do you understand?"

She shrugged and nodded.

"What is your name?"

"Adriana."

He glanced at the chair on the far end of the table and then back at her.

"No, it cannot be. We have Amanda now. What is your given name?"

"My name is Adriana Santos, from Corpus Christi." She held out her hand. "What is your name?"

The short man wrinkled his brow and frowned a lot. She could see the color rising on his face and knew he was getting upset, but she didn't know why.

At that moment, a familiar figure walked in, and every head turned to stare at him. He swaggered through the middle of the room smiling and nodding.

"Good morning, everyone," Travis called out in a cheerful tone, "I trust you all had a lot of sweet dreams about me last night! I know I did. Has everyone met the new girl?"

The Latino man backed off a little and glanced at Travis.

"This girl does not know the rules," he grumbled. "She says that her name is Adriana, but it cannot be. We already have Amanda."

Travis chuckled.

"Ah, I see the problem. No worries, Chaco, I will explain."

He walked over to where they were standing and draped his long arm around Adriana's shoulders; then he smiled and scanned the room.

"Everyone, this is Adriana. She is a nurse, and she is here to take care of you. So whatever problems you have, you will go to her first. Then she will talk to me or Chaco, and we will provide what you need. Adriana can keep her name, but she will always sit in the last chair. Okay?"

"But we already have Amanda!" Chaco whispered.

"It's okay," said Travis, "just pretend that her name is Zadriana or something so she is always the last one. It's really not a big deal."

Adriana glanced back and forth between the two men.

"I don't understand, why is my name a problem?"

Travis laughed.

"It's the system they use here to keep track of all the girls. Each girl is given her new name when they arrive, and there can be only one for each letter of the alphabet. It's kind of weird, but it works. Instead of trying to memorize a number or whatever, we can learn a name for each face and keep them organized that way. If someone is missing, we know which letter is not here and instantly we know which girl that is. We never have more than twenty-six girls at a time. If one leaves, then we replace that letter. Chaco is upset because we still have Amanda here, so Adriana doesn't work for him."

"That's crazy," she responded, "why not let them keep their real names?"

"It's too complicated, and we have to get new identification for them anyway."

"Do they at least get to choose their new name?"

"No, we do this so we can keep them organized the way we want."

"Why not let them choose?" she argued.

"Let it go," said Travis, "this is a battle you're not going to win."

Adriana crossed her arms and sighed with exasperation. After a brief moment of sulking, she looked at the short man and smiled.

"Nice to meet you, Chaco," she said, "my name is Zadriana."

He grinned and nodded with satisfaction.

"I want to give you a quick tour of the place," Travis said, "I'm sure you already have some ideas, but I need to explain some things to you before we talk to the boss. As I said, he likes the idea of someone taking care of the girls, but he also has a lot of doubts about it. You need to say things that he wants to hear, especially the first time you talk to him. If you make him mad, then he will tell me to get rid of you."

"You mean take me back to Corpus Christi?"

"Um, not exactly. I mean get rid of you... permanently."

"Oh."

"Go eat some breakfast, and then we'll go for a walk."

She took her food and sat down at the last empty chair on the end of the table. The other girls ate in silence with only a few whispered words here and there. Adriana sat by herself and watched them all, trying to get some feel for each girl's personality. Many were upset by their situation, but most were glum and resigned to their fate, whatever that might be. Travis and Chaco stayed in the room and carried on their own private conversation in the far corner.

They had plenty of time to eat, but the food wasn't that good. Adriana noticed that most of the girls just picked at their breakfast for a few minutes and then pushed the food around for a while. In less than thirty minutes, everyone was finished. A younger Latino man entered the room carrying trash bags and set up a garbage drop. The girls all picked up their paper plates and plastic utensils and deposited them in the trash bags.

Adriana got in line and followed the other girls back into the dormitory. There was another door in the back of the room she hadn't noticed before. She followed some girls in there and found a crude bathroom with concrete walls and floors. It was laid out similar to a roadway rest area with a short row of sinks along one wall, primitive toilets opposite, and an open area for showers at the far end. There was no paper or hot water.

Without toiletries, the morning rituals went fast. She had only the t-shirt from last night, so she asked the other girls where to find some clothes. They all shared the clothes in the big storage bins, so Adriana searched through them until she found something that would fit her. It wasn't flattering, but it would have to do.

About an hour after breakfast, Travis and Chaco came back into the dormitory. All the girls were ready by then, and they herded them out like cattle. There was another door in the dining room, and this one led outside.

Two more men were waiting there for them. Both were rough-looking older guys. They reminded Adriana of aging cowboys who had spent their best years staring at the backsides of cattle. Neither of them carried whips, but they were armed with handguns in small holsters on their wide, leather belts.

Travis grabbed her arm and pulled her away from the others.

"You come with me," he ordered.

The other girls glanced at her and then continued walking with the older guys. The crowd drifted on toward some wooden tables that sat beside a small lake.

"Where are they going?" Adriana asked Travis.

"Those other guys have the morning watch. That's Raul and Jimmy Ray. You'll meet them later. They usually take the girls over there until lunchtime. Two other men have afternoons, and then they rotate again. Basically, they're working six-hour shifts babysitting the girls."

"What do the girls do?"

Travis shrugged.

"Nothing really. They usually just sit around and talk to each other unless they get assigned to a work detail."

"What kind of work?"

"Mostly cleaning or washing clothes. Some help with the meals."

Adriana stared toward the girls and shook her head.

"That is so boring. It's like being in prison."

"That's more or less what this is," said Travis. "It's not our job to provide any entertainment. Come on, walk with me."

He led her off in the opposite direction around the corner of the building. Other than a few trees and a small patch of green, there was nothing but open fields on every side. In the distance, Adriana could see a sprawling ranch house with a barn and some smaller buildings clustered nearby. Travis pointed toward it.

"That's where the boss lives. The guys have a place there, and that's where we keep our vehicles and horses."

"You have horses?"

Travis nodded.

"Yep, although most of the time we use four-wheelers now. The boss owns about a thousand acres of land, and he likes to ride, so we have to take care of them. Sometimes he buys cattle or sheep. This whole place is fenced in by miles of posts and wire, and it is electrified. A few people have found that out the hard way."

Adriana cringed. She noticed sunlight gleaming off a pair of metal railings about fifty yards away from where they were standing. She pointed.

"What's that out there? Is that an oil well or something?"

Travis chuckled.

"Not hardly. That's the stairs leading down into the bunker. It was actually built for a tornado shelter, but we use it for other things."

"What other things?"

He looked at her and smiled a wicked smile.

"You'll find out tomorrow."

A moment of pregnant silence begged the question, but Adriana let it go for now. They shuffled on around to the back of the building.

"So what's the boss's name?" she asked.

"We aren't allowed to use his name," said Travis, "we just call him boss."

"Tell me a little about him. If I'm going to be here a while, I have to know how to deal with him and what he expects."

They walked on as Travis thought about it for a minute.

"He's an older guy, like a retired cowboy. He's a hard man, doesn't talk much."

"Do you like working for him?"

Travis shrugged.

"I like the money he pays me. I don't always like what I have to do, but I've been trying to change that little by little."

"You seem to be a pretty important guy around here."

"Not really. His son was really the one who ran everything. With him gone now, the boss doesn't know exactly what to do, so he's relying a lot on me to handle things. I don't know if that's going to change or not. We're all just waiting to see what happens next. He might decide to shut down the whole place, but I'm hoping that he will let me step up and take over things instead."

"Exactly what is it that you people do here? I'm not really clear on that. Are you helping these girls to get across the border and then renting them out as migrant workers or prostitutes or what?"

Travis stopped walking and glared at her.

"Like I said, everything is changing. Don't ask a lot of questions right now. The boss started out just bringing people back and forth from Mexico for money, simple and easy. Junior got the bright idea to hand-pick some girls and sell them, so we started doing a little of that. The ones that didn't get sold, he turned out on the streets to bring in some extra money and sort of advertise the business. Without Junior to manage things, it could either fold up or go a completely different direction."

"What other direction? You mean back to the immigration thing?"

"No, I mean a darker direction. The old man is tough, and he's really angry right now. A couple of the other guys suggested making some films, and he seemed to like the idea. They weren't talking about the kind of movies that earn awards though."

"You mean porno movies? Is that why the girls are treated so rough?"

Travis laughed.

"You really don't have a clue, do you? Let's just say that a porno movie would be a walk in the park compared to what Junior and the other guys had in mind. The little bit of rough stuff that you saw is nothing compared to this. I'm talking about the kind of film where the star doesn't get to make a sequel. There is no point in taking them to the clinic when they don't survive the last scene. Now do you understand?"

A cold shiver went down her spine despite the summer heat. Adriana shook her head and tried to block the horrible images from her mind.

"Maybe I should go spend some time with the other girls," she suggested.

"Yeah, that's probably a good idea. And think about what I said. I know you think that prostitution and porno is a terrible life, but you have to keep in mind what these girls are coming from. There are other alternatives that are much worse. You need to convince them to go along with my plan. At least, they will have some kind of future. Even a hard life is better than none at all."

CHAPTER 9

Visions of dead girls and gory nightmares haunted her dreams, and she woke up the next day feeling exhausted and filled with dread. Adriana had never imagined coming face to face with true evil like this before. But in less than a week, she had seen the carved-up remains of a Ripper victim, and was now inside an organization planning to make snuff films as a form of entertainment. She was seeing the real dark side of humanity, the part most people never knew existed. It was something beyond her comprehension.

Adriana crawled out of bed and muddled through the same morning ritual as the day before. She shared a bland breakfast with all the other girls, and then they cleaned themselves up again. Chaco seemed pleased that she remembered to be last in line this time and didn't mess up his naming system.

Travis was waiting outside when the girls filed through the doorway. He grabbed Adriana by the arm and pulled her to one side. One of the other cowboys had also taken a young Mexican girl from the group.

"Today your dreams come true," said Travis, "you two ladies get to see the inside of our pleasure palace and enjoy some special treatment. Are you looking forward to this as much as I am Jimmy Ray?"

"You know it," the other cowboy responded, "how about you, Claudia?"

The young girl began to cry and plead.

"No! No! Not me! I do not do this! Please!"

Jimmy Ray laughed and jerked her toward the path leading around the building. Adriana glanced at Travis, and she saw that he wasn't smiling. He nodded in the same direction, so she followed a few steps behind the others.

They wove a path toward the gleaming metal railings with Claudia bucking and fighting all the way. Jimmy Ray had a firm grip with one hand and used his other to slap her whenever he got the chance. All the struggling only resulted in more bruises and a bloody face by the time they reached the railings.

Between the two metal railings was a steep concrete staircase leading down into the ground. Travis went down first, and then Jimmy Ray dragged Claudia down behind him. Adriana hesitated for a moment, then summoned her courage and descended after them.

There was a thick steel door at the bottom. Unlike most shelter doors though, this one could be bolted and locked from the outside. Travis unlocked it, and they all stepped inside. He switched on the lights.

It was a simple block space, but a little bigger than the average storm shelter. The walls were made of thick concrete like the steps. The only furniture was a long, flat table in the middle and some wooden shelves in the back cluttered with various things. Adriana had no idea what those things were, but she could guess how they were used.

What set the mood was the row of heavy hooks, straps, and chains along one wall. There was also a thick hook in the ceiling with chains dangling down over the center of the table. Blood stains lingered on the floor, and the odor of bodily fluids hung in the air like a sick perfume.

Claudia took one look and began screaming at the top of her lungs. Jimmy Ray hit her in the face a couple of times to shut her up. Adriana cringed, but Travis showed no emotion at all. They both stood by as Jimmy Ray stuffed a dirty bandanna into Claudia's mouth and threw her onto the table.

The young girl tried to curl up into a fetal position, whimpering and crying like a baby. Jimmy Ray grabbed some rope off the shelves in the back of the room. He pushed Claudia over onto her back, and then he wrapped the rope around her wrists. She tried to work free, but he jerked the knot tighter, pulled her hands up over her head, and tied the other end of the rope to a big metal hook in the wall.

He walked back around to the other end of the table. Claudia kicked her legs when Jimmy Ray tried to unfasten her jeans, so he snatched up a small leather whip. After three or four hard lashes across her thighs, the girl stopped moving her legs. She did not resist the next time when he unzipped her jeans and slid them off.

Adriana and Travis stood against the wall and watched in silence as Jimmy Ray went back to the shelves and got more rope. This time he looped one end of it over Claudia's ankle, passed it under the table, and then back up and tied to the other ankle. The girl was now laying on top of the table with her legs spread wide, her body in an inverted Y position.

Claudia closed her eyes tight and sobbed, preparing herself for whatever came next. The big cowboy continued to work with no concern for the girl. He picked up a short rubber post that looked like a sawed-off broomstick. Placing his left-hand firm on the girl's stomach, Jimmy Ray spit on the rounded end of the post and shoved it into her ass.

The young girl screamed in pain and blood began to trickle from her anus. The big man ignored it, focused on his task. He grabbed a large vibrating dildo and pushed it into her vagina, working it in and out with a hard, rhythmic action. Claudia continued to cry and groan in pain.

Adriana glanced at Travis, her eyes pleading with him to intervene, but Travis didn't move a muscle. He only watched with morbid fascination.

"Make him stop," she whispered, "he's hurting her."

But Travis did nothing. Jimmy Ray continued to thrust the dildo in and out of the girl for several minutes. At last, he seemed to get tired of it. Leaving the vibrator inside her vagina, the man turned back around to the shelves. He found a small, square electrical box and some short wires with sticky pads. After studying them for a moment, he placed the device on the table.

Claudia lay flat on her back and stared at him, her eyes filled with fear and pain. Jimmy Ray pushed the flimsy t-shirt up to her neck, exposing the soft flesh around her breasts. He put one of the electrical wires on her nipple and pressed down the pad. Then he started to place another one on Claudia's other breast.

"Stop," Adriana shouted, "you can't do that!"

Jimmy Ray swiveled his head around and glared at her. Adriana starting moving in that direction, but Travis grabbed her by the arm and held her back.

"Don't interfere," he warned, "Jimmy Ray has his own way of doing things. This is how we train the young girls. They need to build up some endurance and toughness for... for what they are going to be doing."

"I know that," Adriana argued, "they don't have much sexual experience, maybe none at all, but there are other ways to learn it. You don't have to abuse them and torture them like animals."

"This isn't torture," said Jimmy Ray, "this is sex. She just doesn't know it yet. This is my way of breaking them in."

"It doesn't have to hurt like that. You can train them with pleasure."

"These girls aren't going to a high school prom," said Travis, "they're going straight to the professional level, and they need to be ready for that."

Adriana blew out a huge sigh of exasperation.

"I know that, but you're not thinking about it right. If you wanted to train a guy for professional baseball, would you just stand him up at the plate and throw fastballs at him for hours? Of course not! You start at a lower level and build the basic skills until he gets better and better. Sex is no different. You can teach these girls the basic skills and let them practice until they get better at it. But in order to do that, you have to make it more fun and less painful."

"Just shut up and let me do it my way," said Jimmy Ray.

"You're going to kill her! If you hook up that thing and run electricity from one side of her chest to the other, the current will pass right through her heart. That can cause her to have a heart attack. Did you even think about that?"

Jimmy Ray looked down at Claudia's breasts, and then he glanced at Travis.

"Is that true?"

"Hell if I know," Travis replied, "but it kind of makes sense."

"Why don't you let me show you how to do it?" Adriana offered, "I know how a woman feels and what she wants. I can show you how to teach them the skills and make them want to learn more. They won't fight you at all. And not only will they cooperate, they will beg you for it."

Travis and Jimmy Ray looked at each other and grinned.

"That would be great," said Travis, "show us how to do it then."

"Do you ever fuck them," Adriana asked, "do you make love to them?"

The two men glanced at each other again and shook their heads.

"Boss says we're not supposed to do that," said Travis, "we can use anything except our own dick. Don't know why, but that's the rule."

Adriana nodded and moved toward the table. The men stepped back. She leaned over and smiled at Claudia. Then she whispered into her ear, touching and caressing to calm her down.

Claudia watched her with curiosity, not sure what was coming. Adriana moved slow and carefully, removing the electrodes from the girl's breasts. She put her hands between Claudia's legs and placed the pads on each side of her ass so the current arced through her genital area instead.

Using both hands, she slid the rubber pole out of Claudia's butt and tossed it on the floor. An expression of profound relief spread over the girl's face.

"Do you have some massage oil or some lotion?"

Travis and Jimmy Ray searched the shelves.

"I found some hand soap," said Travis, "that's the only thing we've got."

"Okay, give me some of that, but you really need to get some better lubrication, especially something that smells nice. It goes a long way toward enhancing the feeling. That kind of thing makes a huge difference to a woman."

Adriana leaned over and kissed Claudia's nipples, gently sucking on them until they both stood firm and erect. Claudia closed her eyes and relaxed. Using a generous handful of liquid soap, Adriana massaged the girl's breasts with smooth swirling motions, pausing to pinch and tease her sensitive areas.

Both men were mesmerized and watched it all in stony silence. Adriana shifted her movements lower on Claudia's abdomen, massaging her flat stomach and then the soft flesh below her waist. The girl kept her eyes closed and stayed motionless on the table, relishing the sensations.

Claudia relaxed even more and allowed her legs to rest spread open on the table top. Adriana took the vibrator out of her vagina and began to rub it across the girl's pubic mound. She increased the pressure and direction then to slide up and down on her clitoris. Using her other hand, she spread more soap to lubricate the area and then inserted the tips of her fingers into the two moist openings. The young girl tensed her thigh muscles and moaned with pleasure.

The vibrator moved up and down as Adriana pressed it harder. The men gazed in awe as Claudia began to moan louder, and her crotch became pink and wet as her heart rate climbed. Inserting her delicate fingers faster and deeper, Adriana massaged the interior canals of the girl's body, touching all the nerves and triggering more intense sensations. A few moments later, Claudia's entire body went rigid as the powerful orgasm rippled through her. She rode the waves for several seconds before finally collapsing back on the table.

Adriana glanced at the two men. Their eyes were wide with excitement and both were drooling a bit. Their eyes were locked onto the girl's limp body.

She turned off the vibrator and the electric stimulation so that Claudia could rest for a few minutes. The girl opened her eyes and stared at Adriana. She reached up and removed the bandanna from Claudia's mouth.

"Do it again," she whispered, "please."

Travis cocked his head to one side as if he couldn't believe his ears.

"Can I try it?" asked Jimmy Ray. "I want to try it your way this time."

"Let me check first," Adriana replied.

She reached up and put one hand on Claudia's breast. Then she leaned over and kissed her on the mouth. The girl hesitated, but then she responded, eager and passionate. Adriana whispered some reassuring words into her ear. Claudia thought for a minute and then nodded.

"Yes, she says you can do it this time, but please be careful. Do what I did."

"All right!" Jimmy Ray shouted.

Travis chuckled.

"That was amazing," he said, "I had no idea you could do that."

"That's only the tip of the iceberg. There are a lot of other things I can show you, but you really need some supplies. To start with, you need some antibacterial ointments and salves. Paper towels and sticky bandages aren't enough. To do training right, you're going to need some oils, lotions, and better, uh... toys. And lots of batteries."

Both of the men laughed. Jimmy Ray stared at Claudia's wet crotch.

"Wouldn't you like to lick that right now?" said Adriana. "I know she would like that, too, but a little strawberry and vanilla flavor would taste a lot better than hand soap, wouldn't it?"

Jimmy Ray tore off a paper towel and picked up a bottle of water. He poured the water on Claudia's genital area and rubbed off some soap. She closed her eyes and lay back. He inserted his fingers the same way Adriana had. Then he started licking her, and the moisture returned in a more natural way.

"What about the rope?" asked Travis.

"You can leave it at first," Adriana answered, "but you might consider replacing it with something softer that doesn't rub the skin so raw. Some of the girls will probably like being tied up, but some of them may not. You might want to leave them free to use their hands more or change positions. The possibilities are endless, and everybody likes something different."

Travis moved closer and looked into her eyes.

"And what about you," he said, "what do you like?"

Adriana flashed a coy smile.

"Just be patient and behave yourself. Maybe you'll find out someday."

He laughed.

"Can I make some other suggestions?" she asked.

Travis shrugged.

"Why not? No promises though."

"Okay, just something to think about. Imagine what this would be like if the girls all had nice underwear. You know, some sexy lingerie? And wouldn't everyone be in a much better mood if we had music to listen to all day?"

He thought about it and nodded.

"I can see that. I don't know if I can sell it to the boss, but I like it. I'll suggest it and see what he says. I think bringing you here might turn out to be the best idea I ever had."

CHAPTER 10

Claudia had persuaded only one other girl to volunteer for the training on Thursday, but three girls volunteered for it on Friday morning. Travis and the other guys were ecstatic. They insisted that Adriana do the "break-in" part every time, but then all of them wanted to try it for themselves afterwards. The girls seemed to respond well to the new approach and were chatting among themselves about it.

Adriana sat silent and listened to their gossip. Most of them were skeptical and still didn't trust the men, but that was to be expected. Life had thrown these girls a lot of hard knocks. They had worked to escape from one bad thing after another for years, and now they found themselves in a difficult situation once again.

The girls gathered in small groups, sitting around beside the lake waiting for dinner time. Claudia and the other volunteers were still rehashing their experiences in hushed conversations with the others. No one was crying, so Adriana took that as a good sign of progress.

"Hey there Z," Travis said as he walked up and sat down, "or maybe I should call you X instead, given your area of expertise."

"Hey, I never said that I was an expert. I just know how a woman feels and what they usually like, but everybody is different."

"Well, that may be true, but you've made a big impact already. All of my guys are swaggering around here like high-school jocks, and the girls seem happier. At least, they are complaining a lot less."

"It doesn't take much to make a big difference when you're starting from nothing. Did you talk to your boss about the underwear and the music?"

Travis nodded.

"He's thinking about it. The biggest problem with the underwear is the cost. You know how expensive that stuff is. I think he will be okay with the music though."

"That's good. Music means a lot to Latina girls. That's probably more important to them anyway."

He hesitated for a moment, and then he changed the subject.

"I need a favor from you."

Adriana shrugged, "Okay."

"We have some business scheduled for later tonight. I have to take one of the girls up to Galveston and collect some cash. One of the guys is going with me, but I want you to come with us and keep the girl calm during the whole thing."

She leaned back and glared at him.

"What sort of thing?"

Travis blew out a sigh and looked away.

"It's a sale. We have a buyer coming, and we need to complete the transaction."

The blood pumped faster, and Adriana could feel the anger surging in her body. She was furious but trying hard to contain it.

"You're selling one of the girls? I thought we weren't going to do that anymore. You told me that things were changing."

"I told you that I was trying to change some things, but I'm not the boss around here. This deal was set up months ago, so it's too late to back out anyway. We have to take Elena up to Galveston on the boat tonight and finish it. You can either go with us and try to keep her calm, or stay here and get mad about it–your choice."

"Is there anything we can do to stop it?"

"No, it's a done deal. All we can do is make it a little easier."

Adriana fumed about it for a minute, but she knew it would do no good.

"Okay, I would rather go with you and keep her company. Maybe, the buyer won't show up, or he will back out of it."

"Hey, you never know. I get paid the same either way."

Travis shouted something to one of the other guys and made some hand motions. The Latino man nodded and walked over to one of the younger girls. He grabbed her arm and whispered something in her ear. She got up and followed him around toward the back of the long dormitory building.

"She can't be more than sixteen years old!" Adriana protested.

"Let it go," Travis warned, "there's nothing you can do about it."

He started walking away and Adriana followed along behind him. When they got to the other side of the building, she saw that the Latino guy already had Elena gagged and was tying her hands together with a zip tie. The van was parked there and waiting. The man opened the rear door and shoved Elena inside.

The young girl was scared and struggling to escape, so Adriana ran up and tried to calm her down. She climbed inside the van and put her arms around her. Elena cried and laid her head on Adriana's chest. She leaned back against the side wall and tried to make them more comfortable for the long ride ahead.

"Okay Omar, let's roll," said Travis.

The Latino man closed the back doors and checked them, and then he stepped up into the passenger seat in front. Travis cranked up the engine and pulled out.

This time Adriana could see where they were going. She peeked out the windows and through the windshield to catch glimpses of the countryside. It was still light outside, and on occasion a road sign was visible. She tried to make a mental note of each one as they passed. Nothing looked familiar.

She expected to see Corpus Christi, but three hours later they were still driving. Darkness came, Elena lay motionless snuggled up against her in the back of the van. It was well past sunset when Adriana spotted the small sign for Freeport and knew where they were headed.

Travis drove them through the town and all the way to the coast. They went along the shore for a while and at last arrived at a secluded dock. The van eased to a stop next to one of the boat slips. The men transferred them onto a large cabin cruiser, and then the group continued the journey by sea.

Omar navigated to some pre-arranged location by GPS while the others sat on the deck in back and stared up at the stars. It was past midnight now, and everyone was tired and irritable.

"Can't you take these things off her hands now?" Adriana asked. She had pulled the gag out of Elena's mouth hours ago.

Travis looked at her and frowned.

"You remember what happened the last time, don't you? Things didn't go so well, especially for Junior. I don't want a repeat performance."

"Want me to tell Omar not to hit you with the anchor?"

"You don't need to mention that part. No one else knows about that, and I would strongly suggest that you forget it. That never happened."

"What if I tell your boss?"

"That would not be a good move. He wouldn't believe you anyway, but just to be certain, he would probably kill us both."

"That doesn't sound good. Is he really that tough?"

Travis nodded.

"Yeah, and more so every day. He's getting to be a bitter and angry old man with less patience for anything now. You need to tread lightly around him."

They both fell silent and thought about that. Elena laid her head in Adriana's lap and cried herself to sleep. A little while later, she overheard Omar talking with somebody on the radio. Travis went over to take command and coordinate the meeting.

Both of the boats had their running lights off, but Adriana heard the other vessel arrive and come up beside them in the water. They lashed them together with two heavy ropes, fore and aft. Adriana could see two men on the deck of the other boat, and both were armed. One of them approached the railing.

"Ahoy there! Permission to come aboard?"

"Yes sir," Travis responded, "come ahead."

She sat on the deck and watched as a middle-aged man climbed over and stood in front of Travis. He glanced down at the two girls.

"Is this my merchandise?" the man asked.

Travis nodded and pulled Elena up to her feet.

"This is the one you wanted, right? Do you have the money?"

The other man grunted and turned back to his companion.

"Toss me the bag!"

A black duffel bag flew through the air and landed on the deck at his feet.

"Fifty thousand is what we agreed on, right?"

"Fifty thousand?" Adriana exclaimed. She jumped up and stood next to Elena. "You aren't going to pay fifty thousand for her, are you?"

The men stared at her in surprise, annoyed by the interruption.

"What do you mean?"

"Just look at her," Adriana answered, "she's only a kid. She has small boobs and not much of an ass. She has no sexual experience at all. Look at her armpits and her legs. They are covered with hair. This girl isn't even very good-looking. Why would you pay fifty thousand for her?"

Travis made a face and glared at Adriana. He did a silent slashing motion across his throat. The other guy looked at Elena with a curious expression on his face.

"This is the same girl, right?" the man asked.

"Oh, yes sir, this is the one you wanted," Travis replied.

Adriana grimaced and shook her head.

"No, you really don't want her. She's way too skinny and ugly. I think you can do much better, mister."

"He didn't ask for your opinion," Travis interjected, "this is the one he wants."

The man seemed confused for a moment. He stared at Adriana.

"What are you suggesting? Are you wanting to take her place?"

Adriana shook her head.

"No, I'm not for sale. I'm their nurse and their trainer. I'm just thinking we could offer you a better deal."

The other man smiled.

"Okay, I like the sound of that. How about forty thousand?"

"No," Travis protested, "fifty thousand is what we agreed on!"

"How about a rental agreement instead," said Adriana, "if you take her home, then you will have to feed her and give her a place to stay and take care of her. And for what? A good fuck once a week? You'll probably get tired of fucking the same girl over and over, won't you?"

Travis rolled his eyes and sighed.

"Doesn't sound so bad to me," the man said, "you got a better idea?"

Adriana smiled and spread her arms.

"You could have a different girl every week. Think about it–fifty different girls during the year. And instead of paying fifty thousand to buy something you're going to get tired of, you pay only one thousand a week to rent something fresh and new. You can choose the same one or a different one, whatever you want."

The man thought about it and started grinning.

"I like the way you think, sweetie. Let's do that instead."

"Wait a minute," yelled Travis, "she can't make deals! We already have a deal! You agreed to take that one for fifty thousand. You can't back out now!"

"It's my money," the man shouted back, "I can do whatever I damn well please, and I want what this girl offered instead. You take that other one back."

"I can't do that! My boss will kill me!"

"That's your problem. You tell him I want the new deal starting next week."

"Where should we bring her?" asked Adriana.

"What do you suggest? You seem to be full of ideas tonight."

"Well, we have basically two choices. If you want to maintain control over that, then you will need to rent a small apartment or something where we can meet you. But that will cost you some money and leave a paper trail."

"What's the other option?"

"The other option is for us to rent a place. Less convenient for you, but nothing is traceable that way. All you have to do is show up, have fun for a few hours, and then go home. We'll take care of the rest."

"I like that," he picked up the duffel bag and tossed it back onto his boat, "tell your boss to send me the address. Nice doing business with you, lady!"

The man turned around and climbed back over the railing. The other guy with him untied the ropes, and the boat drifted away. Elena ran over and gave Adriana a giant hug. Travis watched in stunned silence with his mouth hanging open.

"You've just killed us all," he mumbled, "my life is over now."

"You want to jump in the water and swim for it," said Adriana, "or do you want to go back and explain to the boss how we're going to make him two million dollars?"

He cocked his head and stared at her.

"Run that by me again?"

"I'll explain on the way back. Tell Omar to get us out of here first before the Coast Guard shows up."

CHAPTER 11

The sun was already up by the time they arrived back at the ranch. Travis dropped them off at the dormitory, and then he and Omar disappeared to get some sleep. Elena was far too excited about the whole experience and insisted on retelling the story for all the girls to hear. In that instant, Adriana was launched into sainthood and cemented her status as their new hero and protector.

She snuck away after lunch for a quick nap herself. The afternoon passed, and Adriana was still groggy when she crawled off the cot and rejoined the girls outside. She sat and listened to their small talk again, but the mood was different now. Everything seemed a little more upbeat and normal. A slender ray of hope had crept in to replace the dismal gloominess that existed before.

They had just finished dinner when Travis reappeared again. She watched him saunter through the dining room observing things as usual, but something seemed to be weighing heavy on his mind. The sparkle and self-confidence that normally lit up his face was gone.

He walked over and sat down beside Adriana. The girls sitting nearby got up and left the table. Travis stared at her for a moment.

"I still can't believe what you did last night, blowing a sale like that. The boss is going to be furious. He's probably going to kill us both."

"Don't panic yet, Travis. I explained it all to you on the way back. He can make a lot more money running an escort service, and the girls would be a lot more cooperative. It's a much better way to go."

Travis rolled his eyes and looked at the ceiling.

"I'm not sure he's going to agree with that. He spent years building up this kind of business. Junior had everything set up the way he wanted it."

"Yeah, but Junior isn't here anymore thanks to you. And they were starting to go down a darker path that would have been worse for everybody. This is the time to make a change. We can make it work, and everyone will be better off in the long run."

"You really think the girls would go for that?"

Adriana thought about it for a minute, and then she nodded.

"I think so, but we need to start recruiting some different girls. Instead of getting these young kids, we should look for some that are a little older and more mature about this sort of thing. We need young women that have some sexual experience and might be willing to use that."

"I'll let you explain that to him tomorrow when he gets back. In the meantime, we need to make some money to cover what we lost. Are you up for a trip to Corpus Christi? Maybe we can take some girls into town and drop them off for a while."

"Sure, let's go. Tell Chaco to put his whip out of sight, and I'll try to round up a few volunteers. Maybe we can shop for some supplies while we're there?"

Travis sighed.

"Okay, but don't spend too much until we have something to show for it."

"You can't catch fish without good bait. I'll meet you around back."

Adriana threw away her trash and hurried outside to talk to the other girls. Most were still reluctant and suspicious. Even the ones with an open mind weren't convinced yet that prostitution was a big improvement. It took some persistence, but Adriana persuaded six of the girls to go.

The girls all made a final pass through the bathroom to freshen up, then they went around to the back of the building. Adriana gathered them up and waved them into the rear of the van. Travis kept the gags and restraints out of sight, but he had them close by just in case. Raul was driving this time.

The van pulled out a little before sunset and arrived in Corpus Christi an hour and a half later. Adriana spent the time encouraging the girls and preparing them mentally for what lay ahead. They were curious about the city and kept peeking out through the front windshield to get a better look. Four of them had been there before, but they hadn't seen much except the block where they worked.

"Please clear your head and stay focused," she said, "remember to smile, and try to keep a positive attitude. You want to attract nice men who will spend money to be with you. If you look cheap and angry, you will attract people who are cheap and angry. Try to show some class and be sexy with self-confidence. Make the men think you are choosing them, and you won't go with just anybody. Choose the best and expect them to treat you that way. You are sexy young ladies, and you deserve only the best."

The girls all smiled and giggled. Sofia looked at her.

"Do we have a hotel this time, or do we have to go wherever they want?"

Adriana glanced up at Travis.

"I don't know the rules yet," she admitted, "I would rather rent a place for all of us to hang out. It's much safer that way. What do you say, Travis?"

He shook his head.

"That's not usually the way we do things. It's too easy for the cops to find us and shut us down. Nobody wants to spend the night in jail and get deported, do they?"

The girls all shook their head and stared at their shoes.

Adriana didn't agree, but she didn't want to argue the point.

"Okay then, maybe we can think about that for the next time. Since none of you has a cell phone why don't you pick a partner? You can walk around together and keep an eye on each other. You can even work together, if you want, just remember to jack up the price for that. You are not cheap whores, you are professional escorts. When you look at a man, you should not see his face. You will only see the faces of Benjamin Franklin and his little green friends. Got it?"

They all nodded.

"Can we have cell phones?" one of them asked.

"I'm working on it," Adriana responded, "Travis and I are going shopping right after we drop you off. We're going to get some make-up and other stuff for you. Maybe we can get some of those disposable cell phones so that we can all stay in touch. Don't trust anybody and don't take any chances. If something doesn't feel right, turn around and walk away. Your safety is the most important thing to me."

"But your cute little ass is the most important thing to me," said Travis, "so get out there and show your stuff. Don't be shy. You're not here on vacation, you're here to work. I expect to get at least a thousand dollars from you when we come back to pick you up later. It's Saturday night, so there are a bunch of horny guys roaming the streets with a pocket full of money tonight. Find a way to take it from them, any way you can. We will come by and check on you every hour, so stay close to the drop zone or get back there as soon as possible. Now everybody get out there and have some fun!"

The girls were all quiet, still staring at their shoes.

Raul eased the van over to the curb and two of the girls got out. They were only two blocks from the house where Adriana had been living a week ago. A mental image of Johnny lying face down in a puddle of blood floated through her mind. Then, she thought about the disemboweled body of the Ripper victim in the Houston alley.

"Be careful ladies!" she shouted as they drove away.

They made two more stops, and the other girls got out in pairs. Adriana repeated her warning each time. She waved to them as Raul pulled away.

"We need to change this, Travis. The girls aren't safe out there like this."

He blew out a big sigh and leaned back in the seat.

"They'll be fine. There are people all over the place on Saturday night. All they have to do is watch out for each other."

"I don't like it," Adriana argued, "we should rent one place and keep them all in sight. That way we don't have any problems or any risk. We can have a couple of men right there to handle any troublemakers, and we will always know where the girls are. I think we should rent an old house. That will give us some privacy, too."

"The boss will never go for that. Not only would it be expensive, it would be too easy for someone to report us or call the cops."

"Not if we do it right. I'm not talking about setting up a crack house; I'm talking about a quiet, classy place that caters to a different kind of customer. We can target guys like the one on the boat last night. They know how to keep a secret, and they have lots of money to spend if you make them happy. And the girls will be safer because they know how to treat a lady. Those guys don't want a twenty dollar blowjob; they want a young, sexy mistress who can blow their mind with sexual fantasies."

Travis snorted.

"I think you might be surprised by what those guys want. Talk to the girls on the way back and ask them how many times they sat in the back seat of a luxury car tonight and sucked on some rich old man's dick."

"We just need to upgrade our talent. We need show horses, not baby colts. We can attract a different kind of client if we have something to catch their eye. Come on, give it a chance. Take me shopping, and I'll show you how to turn these young kids into dream girls."

"I think it's a waste of time and money."

"Give it a chance. You'll see."

Adriana sat back and sulked, but Travis gave Raul directions to a few stores and they picked up some things for the girls. Most of it was cosmetics and medical supplies, but they did stop at a specialty shop and buy a few lubricants and sex toys. At least that part of the list got his attention.

They rode around in the van for a while and gave the girls plenty of time to work the streets. Every hour or so, Raul would swing back around to the drop-off points, and Travis would check on them. It was half past midnight when they made a final turn near the taco stand and saw one girl standing by herself on the curb. She flagged them down and dashed up to the van.

"I think Keyla is in trouble," she shouted. "You need to go check on her!"

Raul stopped the vehicle, and Travis opened the door.

"Where is she?"

The girl pointed toward a dark alley that ran between two old buildings.

"We went back there with some creepy guy, but he yelled at me and told me to go away and leave them alone. She's still back there with him."

Adriana climbed around the seat and got out on the curb beside her.

"Why do you say he is creepy? Did he say something weird?"

The girl shook her head and moved closer to Travis.

"It's just the way he acted. He kept staring at our boobs and making these strange grunting noises. He made us both stand against the wall, and then he just lit up a cigarette and stared at our ass."

Adriana looked for signs of cuts or bruises.

"Did he attack you or try to take off your clothes?"

"No, and that was even more weird. He's wearing a jacket, and it's the middle of July. He never even unzipped his jacket."

Travis put his arm around the girl, but Adriana took off down the narrow alley. Images of the Ripper's last victim flashed through her head. She had almost reached the far corner of the building when she saw them. Keyla was lying motionless on the ground. A small, wiry man was hunched over her.

"Stop!" she shouted. "Leave her alone!"

Adriana ran full speed and dove right into the man, knocking him over onto his back. The momentum caused her to fall too, and she wound up face down on the rough pavement. The man was lightning fast. He jumped up and grabbed her by the throat, yanking Adriana to her feet. He held her in front of him and spun them both around as Travis came running up the alley seconds later. She felt hot breath on the back of her neck. A long, curved blade was pressed tightly underneath her chin.

"Let her go," Travis yelled, "drop the knife and let her go!"

She saw Raul lumbering down the alley to help. The tip of the blade nicked her skin, and Adriana felt the warm trickle of blood running down her neck. She heard the man's ragged breathing. Time seemed to stand still for a moment.

"I would never hurt you," he whispered into her ear.

The man shoved her hard in the back, and Adriana stumbled forward and fell into Travis's open arms. He wrapped his arms around her and hugged her tight. Raul pointed his pistol over her shoulder and aimed, but the man had already disappeared into the inky darkness.

"Are you alright?" asked Travis.

"I'm fine," Adriana wiped the blood off her neck, "check on Keyla."

They both kneeled down and looked at the girl. Her eyes were closed, but she was still breathing. There was a wide, shallow gash across her throat with blood pouring out of it. Her clothes were ripped down the middle of her body and spread open. There were more vertical slashes down her torso. Keyla wasn't moving at all, possibly unconscious or in shock.

Adriana yanked a piece of clothing off and wrapped it around her neck.

"We've got to get her to a hospital. She needs a doctor."

Travis shook his head.

"I can't do it. They ask too many questions. You have to fix her."

"I don't have the supplies for this. She needs stitches and antibiotics. We have to take her to the hospital right now!"

"Let's get her to the van."

Travis picked up the injured girl and carried her back up the alley. Raul opened the back door of the van, and they loaded her inside. Adriana looked all around, but the other girl was gone. She climbed in and sat beside Keyla. The men got in front and Raul stomped on the accelerator.

"Where to?" he asked.

"The hospital!" Adriana shouted.

Raul glanced over at Travis, but neither of them said a word. They made it to the emergency room in less than five minutes. The van skidded to a stop outside the big glass door. Raul kept the engine running. Travis ran to the back of the van, and Adriana helped him lift Keyla into his arms. She started to climb out.

"Stay," he ordered, "if I'm not back in one minute, you guys take off!"

He cradled the girl against his chest and ran through the door. Ten seconds later, he came running back out with a nurse chasing him. He jumped into the front seat and slammed the van door shut. Raul peeled away.

Travis leaned back in the seat and stared at the roof of the van. He blew out a big sigh and mumbled a string of angry curse words. Adriana reached forward and laid her hand on his shoulder.

"Thank you," she said.

"I don't know why I keep listening to you."

"You did the right thing, Travis. You probably saved that girl's life."

"Yeah, but it will probably get us both killed. We lost two girls tonight, and that's assuming the others will still be there waiting for us."

"Everything will be fine, you'll see."

Travis just shook his head in disbelief and kept mumbling to himself. Raul drove to the other drop-off points, and they picked up the other four girls. They handed over the money that they had earned and settled into the back of the van. When everyone was on board, Raul headed back toward the ranch.

There were some curious expressions when the others realized that two of their group were missing, so Adriana huddled them together and explained what had happened in a hushed tone. The news about the assault terrified the girls, but they accepted it. A couple of them gave Travis a curious, sidelong glance.

There was no more conversation as they drove back to the compound. Everyone was lost in their own thoughts, their mind filled with questions that no one could answer. No one slept.

CHAPTER 12

Travis pulled up in a pickup truck and parked outside the dormitory. Adriana saw him arrive and walk toward where she was sitting. She noticed that the image of tough self-confidence had vanished. He didn't smile or speak to anyone.

She turned away and pretended to be watching and listening to the other girls. She heard his footsteps coming closer and glanced over her shoulder.

"Good morning!" Adriana said in a cheerful tone.

"I don't think so," he replied, "we have been summoned to the big house. I guess the boss is back and wants to discuss some things. You might want to say goodbye to all the girls before we go. It may be the last time they see you."

"Don't be so glum. We can explain everything. I'm sure he will understand."

Travis shook his head.

"You don't know this guy. He's hard, and he's not going to be happy with what has been happening while he was out of town. We cost him a lot of money. I'm thinking real serious about making a run for it instead."

"Don't worry so much. Running away isn't going to solve anything."

"But the odds of survival might be a lot better."

Adriana stood up and put her hand on his arm.

"Come on, let's go face the music. We can do this together."

She took him by the hand, and they walked back to the pickup. He started up the truck and drove them to the big ranch house where Hayes lived. A couple of men she didn't know were milling around outside. They parked the truck near a side door. Travis nodded to the other guys as they walked inside.

The interior of the house looked like the set of an old western movie. The heavy furniture was made of thick, polished wood. The walls were wood paneled and decorated with bullhorns and gun racks. The only artwork was Remington pictures and sculptures. There was no sign of a feminine touch in anything.

She followed Travis down a hallway to a room that looked like a business office. An old man sat behind a huge oak desk studying a stack of papers and puffing on a cigar. He glanced up and frowned when they stepped through the door.

"Come in, Miller. I see you brought the new girl."

Adriana grinned at hearing Travis's real surname for the first time.

"Yes sir. We came as soon as we heard you were back. We wanted to give you an update on everything."

"You have the money?"

Travis leaned forward and handed him a small stack of bills. The old man took it and stared at his hand in surprise.

"Where's the rest of it?"

"Well, that's a long story." He glanced at Adriana for help.

"We ran into some changes, sir," she said, "so we had to improvise."

She could see the color rising quick in the old man's cheeks.

"What kind of changes? Explain it to me."

"Well, the buyer on Friday night didn't seem very happy when he saw Elena in person, so we offered him a different deal. Instead of buying a girl, we talked him into renting a lady every week for a thousand dollars. That gets you fifty thousand dollars a year of steady income, plus you still have the girl."

The old man stewed on that for a minute. Adriana could see him doing the math in his head, but he didn't seem too happy about the result.

"How is fifty thousand over the year better than fifty thousand today? Plus I still have to take care of the girl?"

Adriana smiled and tried to personalize the situation a bit more.

"You will still have Elena and the rest of your girls working for you. We can rent a house or some place in town to meet with the customers so everyone is safe and things stay quiet. All the business takes place away from here, so there is no risk for you. And you have about twenty ladies, so if every girl brings in fifty thousand, then that makes a million dollars a year for you. And some of them could be busy more than once a week. You might make ten times that much."

The boss sat back in his chair and stared at the ceiling. His face was beet red, but she could tell that he was trying to keep an open mind. He glared at Travis.

"What do you think, Miller?"

"Um, well, I think it's a good idea, sir. The exchanges are always a big risk as you know. At least this way the girls and the customers are all anxious to cooperate, and that makes things a lot easier to control."

"It's going to require a lot more communication, though, right? No more one and done deals. So how are you going to keep them all booked up?"

"We'll have to use the computer more, sir," Adriana explained, "but we can still rely mostly on word-of-mouth. In order to do that, we need our ladies to be better than the competition and worth the money. We need to give them an upgrade, provide them with better clothes and make-up, and get some mature girls with better skills."

The old man stared at the computer on his desk as if it was an alien monster.

"I hate computers," he said, "I like doing business face-to-face. It's too easy to lie and deceive people with computers."

"We can use that to our advantage," said Travis, "we can make some fancy web sites and take a bunch of sexy pictures to draw out the customers. We'll make sure that none of it can be traced back to you. We could even make extra money from porno web sites and phone sex lines."

"Especially, if we can set up a place away from here," Adriana added, "we could rent a place near Corpus Christi or San Antonio and run the computers from there. It will also be safer for the girls and the customers. We can set up our own security and cameras to monitor everything that goes on there."

The boss got out of his chair and stomped around the room, puffing on his cigar. She couldn't tell if that was a good sign or a bad sign.

"I don't know," he grumbled, "that sounds expensive. I wish Junior was here to handle this."

"I can handle it, sir," Travis offered, "and Adriana can help. She is great with the girls. They will do whatever she tells them. We can hire some contractors to do all the computer stuff, maybe some college kids. They work cheap and won't ask any questions. I'm sure this will work."

The old man's face was still bright red, his anger subdued by his love for money. The stark contrast with his silver hair made it appear even more dramatic. He paced back and forth behind the big desk for several minutes, cigar smoke billowing into swirling gray clouds.

"What's it going to take to make it happen?" he asked at last.

Travis looked at Adriana and blew out a big sigh.

"I don't know, sir. I've never done anything like this before."

"Maybe ten grand," Adriana guessed, "we need to rent a place and set everything up. And we'll need some clothes and stuff for the girls."

"Ten grand? Are you out of your fucking mind?"

"We want to be first class, sir. We're not talking about some fly-by-night sort of operation. We want to be the best, like one of those places in Nevada."

"This isn't Nevada, missy. Prostitution is legal there, it's not in Texas."

"But we know it goes on. Anywhere you have men and money, you're going to find ladies willing to please them for a price."

"The girls we have don't seem too willing. That's why we have the guards and the fences. How are you going to change that?"

Adriana shrugged.

"Maybe we need some new girls, some that are a little more experienced. We can start with those first. Once the other girls see that, then they will come around. They can learn how to do it. It's not rocket science, just basic biology."

The boss plopped down in his chair and stared hard at them both.

"This better work. I mean it, your ass is on the line. I'm going to warn you both ahead of time, if I don't see some results immediately, neither one of you is going to live to enjoy your next birthday. Do I make myself clear?"

Travis and Adriana nodded. The old man reached into his desk drawer and took out a stack of bills. He tossed it onto the desk.

"There's your seed money, and that's all you're getting. I suggest you spend it wisely. I want all of that back and then some within a month. Do we understand each other?"

"Yes sir!" said Travis, snatching up the cash.

"So what's your first move?"

"We need some experienced girls," said Adriana, "we need to kick this off with models the same way they do in clubs and restaurants. That will establish our reputation right off the bat."

"When can you start?"

"We'll leave tomorrow," said Travis, "at first light. I'll go with Adriana and Omar to Laredo and find some working ladies. Three or four maybe. We'll be back in a couple of days and try to get things set up this weekend."

The old man ground his cigar out in a big metal ashtray.

"Don't let me down," he warned, "this is your last chance. Now, get out of my sight before I change my mind and feed both of you to the coyotes."

Adriana and Travis scrambled out of the office and up the hallway. They didn't slow down until they were back in the truck again. The doors slammed closed and Travis cranked up the engine. Adriana glanced at him and smiled.

"You see? That wasn't so bad. You owe me big time."

"What? You're the reason we're in this mess. Everything was going fine until you decided to interfere. I think you owe me big time. You're lucky we're not dead."

"I'm the lucky one? You kidnapped me, remember?"

"You wanted it. You're the one that asked for it in the first place."

"I asked for a job. I didn't ask to be kidnapped and held prisoner by a bunch of psycho cowboys. You people are all crazy."

"It's not crazy. This is just like the cattle business. We buy, and we sell. It was really simple until you started screwing it up."

"Buying and selling people is not a normal business. You can't look at it that way. These girls are human beings with their own hopes and dreams. They aren't a bundle of meat on four hooves. This is totally different."

"It's all the same to me."

Adriana reached over and put her hand on his arm.

"You don't really mean that, Travis. I saw the way you looked at Keyla when she was lying on the ground. You carried her to the van and took her to the hospital. You care about these girls."

He paused for a moment and stared at the floorboard.

"Yeah, well, now you've got us on the hook for this whole new thing. We're on thin ice with the boss, and I'm not sure we can deliver."

"Would you rather go back inside and explain to him why Junior isn't around to handle things?"

Travis looked at her, and she could see the fire in his eyes.

"I'm putting my life on the line for you," he said, "don't make me regret it."

CHAPTER 13

Omar was driving when they left the ranch on Monday morning. They were all sitting in the cab of a big flatbed diesel truck. On the back of the truck was a late-model German luxury car that was dirty and a little banged up on the outside.

Adriana was wedged in between Travis and Omar on the bench seat. She rested her hand on Travis's thigh as they pulled out. He didn't say anything about it, but she saw the corners of his mouth twitch up a tiny bit.

"Where did you get the car?" she asked, "does that belong to the boss?"

"I don't think so," he replied, "we don't usually ask questions like that."

"Oh. It looks like a nice car. Was it in an accident?"

"I'm pretty sure all of that damage happened in the barn last night. We're taking it to a place in Laredo to get it fixed."

"There isn't any place closer that can work on it?"

Travis turned his head and stared at her.

"We're taking it to Laredo to be repaired. End of story. That's all you need to know, so quit asking questions about it, okay?"

"Okay."

They rode in silence for a while. Omar turned onto Highway 59 and they headed in a southwesterly direction toward the Mexican border. The big truck was loud and very uncomfortable with three people jammed into the front seat. It was still July and hot, but the truck had no air conditioning. Her clothes were already sticky with sweat even with the windows rolled down.

Adriana glanced over her shoulder at the car again.

"Are we going to trade that for a different vehicle? I don't see how we can bring four new girls home with us in this truck. Do they ride in the back?"

"Yeah, something like that. You'll see. Why don't you shut up and take a nap or something? We're still a long way from Laredo."

It sounded like a good idea, so Adriana turned toward Travis and tried to snuggle up against his shoulder. He sighed with exasperation and with some reluctance, put his arm around her. She slid her left hand onto the inside of his thigh and saw the corners of his mouth twitch upward some more.

When she opened her eyes again, they were cruising around the outskirts of the city. Laredo appeared to be a little smaller than Corpus Christi and a lot more compact. The atmosphere was different. Laredo was dirty, crowded, and industrial, a big change from the laid-back resort feel of Corpus Christi. Lots of people were packed closer together in neighborhoods that resembled slums more than suburbs.

The people were different, too. Adriana felt like she was in Mexico. Everywhere she looked, the grim, brown faces of Latinos stared back at her. Conversations in Spanish floated through the open windows of the truck.

"So where are we going," she asked, "are we going to look for some girls here, or do we go into Nuevo Laredo on the Mexican side of the border?"

"First, we drop off the truck and talk to a guy. Then, we go have some lunch and place the order."

"I don't get it. Are we going to get the car fixed?"

"Don't worry about it. Just stick with me and forget everything else you're going to see. You're only job is to help us pick the right girls."

Omar navigated the truck through the side streets of Laredo until they came to a large block building with three wide bay doors on the front. A small sign over one door said "Cesar's Body Shop". They eased to a stop outside the open door and sat in the truck with the engine idling.

After a minute, a young Latino man with a dirty red bandanna on his head came sauntering out and waved them inside. Omar maneuvered the big truck with care through the open bay door and put it in park. A handful of guys seemed to appear out of nowhere and stood around the truck. Travis got out and had a brief conversation with one of the guys. He turned his head and nodded, and Omar cut off the engine.

Adriana crawled out of the cab and stood next to Travis. The young men in the garage all stared at her like they had never seen a woman before. They started mumbling to each other.

"What's wrong with these people?" she whispered to Travis.

He grinned at her.

"These guys aren't used to seeing a girl involved in this kind of thing. As you can probably imagine, the sex business is usually a male thing. They can't figure out who you are or why you are here. It's making them real nervous, so play it cool."

She glanced around the garage as if appraising the quality of the equipment or the service and tried not to act feminine. Some young men leered at her, their eyes roaming up and down her body. They appeared to be appraising her equipment and service as well, but in a very different context.

One man crawled up onto the flatbed to examine the car while another man handed Travis a yellow baseball cap. He slipped it on.

"Okay, let's go."

Adriana followed Travis and Omar out of the garage. They walked down to the end of the block and around the corner. They ambled around the side of the garage and turned the corner again. Five minutes later, they were in the gravel parking lot of a large Chinese restaurant that sat in back of the body shop.

"What was that all about?" she asked in confusion. "Are they going to fix the car? Why are we here?"

"We're here to have lunch," said Travis. He held the front door of the restaurant open, and they all walked in. "Welcome to the Rice Palace."

The hostess looked somewhat Oriental, but the rest of the staff looked Mexican.

"Lunch buffet for three," said Travis.

She glanced at his yellow hat and led them to a small table near the door to the kitchen. Travis placed his hat down on the table in front of one chair, and the three of them took the other places. They were the only customers in the restaurant.

"This is creepy," Adriana whispered.

"Don't freak out," said Travis. "Enjoy the buffet, lunch is on me. You can eat as much as you like."

She surveyed the long buffet tables for a while, then decided to try a bowl of soup first. It was hot and steaming, and the aroma was fantastic. She carried it back to the table and took a sip. Despite what the sign said, it tasted like tortilla soup.

After the mediocre cooking at the ranch, the restaurant food tasted delicious. A giant plate of chicken and broccoli went perfect with the fried rice. There was plenty more to choose from, but Adriana felt full after the first helping.

Omar and Travis both made multiple trips to the buffet table. Everything looked great, and it must have been delicious judging by the satisfied smiles of their faces. They all seemed to get finished after a while. She saw the hostess come by one last time and snatch the yellow cap from the table. In its place, she left a small brown bag.

Travis picked up the bag and looked inside.

"We got four," he said with a smile. He dumped the fortune cookies on the table and broke them open. Little pieces of paper tumbled out. Omar grinned.

"What does that mean?" Adriana asked.

"It means that we get to pick four girls when we go recruiting later tonight. We have to go to the Mexican side of the border for that."

"Are we taking the car? Will it be fixed by then?"

"Forget the car. The car was to buy our line of credit. It's long gone by now."

"We're trading the car for four girls?"

"Yeah, more or less."

This confused Adriana.

"So how do we get to the other side of the border? And how do we get home?"

"You ask too many questions," said Travis, "come on, let's go."

He threw some money on the table, and they walked outside. They retraced their steps, walking all the way back around to the body shop again. All the bay doors were pulled down and closed this time. Their flatbed truck was parked near the curb with the keys dangling from the ignition.

"What happened to the car?" she asked.

"Forget the car," Travis replied with a sigh.

They all climbed back into the cab of the big truck and Omar drove away. It was still very early on a Monday afternoon, and traffic was light. They cruised along, and the neighborhoods took on a different flavor. Adriana saw a few small hotels and a few other shops aimed more at tourists. On one corner, she spotted an adult novelty store.

"Oh! Stop there! Stop there!"

Omar looked surprised, but Travis told him to pull into the lot. He waited in the car while Travis and Adriana walked around inside the shop.

"What are you looking for?" said Travis.

"Tools of the trade," she answered, "we're not here to get some young kids who are barely past puberty. This time, we're here for some working girls that know how to handle things. We want girls in their prime who have the right skills."

Adriana went through the store picking out toys and love-making accessories. She selected sensual lubricants, vibrators, whips, and blindfolds. Travis seemed to get excited just holding the stuff as they went. She chose a few more things, and then lots of batteries to go with it. They paid for it all and went back outside.

Omar laughed when they climbed in with their bags of merchandise. He leaned over and stirred around in one of the bags.

"Training equipment," Adriana explained. "I'll show you how everything works when we get to a hotel, but only a quick demonstration. I want both of you guys to be full of, uh, energy when we do the recruiting later."

"The recruiting?" said Travis. "Usually we just point to the girls, and that's all there is to it. That was always good enough before."

"It's different this time. We're not choosing these girls based on their looks. We want girls based on their attitude and skills. We need some kind of testing before we commit to take them back with us."

Travis and Omar looked at each other and grinned.

"That sounds great! We need to get a hotel room on the other side of the border though. Omar, head for the bridge."

"Wait," said Adriana, "I don't have my passport!"

"No problem. I've got one for all of us."

He pulled some documents out of his back pocket and held them up. Adriana took the passports out of his hand and studied them for a minute.

"Wow, this looks better than my real passport. How did you do this?"

Travis shrugged.

"We've got connections. You can get anything you want if you have the money."

"I guess so."

Adriana glanced over at Omar. He was holding up a double-pronged vibrator and looking at it with curiosity. She chuckled.

"Don't worry, that's not for you, but I'll show you what to do with it. You could do things that will make a woman beg you to make love to her."

Omar nodded his head and grinned.

"Show me how to use that one," said Travis, "I want to try that out on you. I want you to beg me for it."

"Maybe that's not what you need with me."

She gave him a mischievous smile. Travis cocked his head and stared at her.

They slowed to a halt on the U.S. side of the long bridge over the Rio Grande River and waited in line. Lines were short and most were commercial vehicles, so things moved quick and smooth. Travis had all the paperwork that they needed to get through customs and immigration.

A couple hours later, they were past the bottlenecks and cruising through the narrow streets of Nuevo Laredo on the Mexican side. Adriana saw a different city as they got farther away from the border. She studied the faces of the people as they passed and saw only the hardship of lives filled with danger and desperation. She could not imagine growing up in a place like this where life was cheap and hope was a fairy tale that no one could afford. People would kill you for the food it would take to survive until tomorrow.

Welcome to Mexico.

CHAPTER 14

Omar seemed to know the city well. They stayed on the quieter side streets until they found a respectable motel at the edge of the commercial district. It was old but spacious, with a small kitchenette and two separate beds.

They checked in and grabbed the small bundle of overnight supplies that each of them had brought. Omar volunteered to carry in their purchases from the novelty store. He seemed anxious to give them all a closer look, but Adriana made them wait.

"Okay, what now?" she asked.

"Now it's nap time," said Travis, "we'll go out again after dark and probably be out late, so we need to get some rest first."

Travis and Omar both kicked off their boots and flopped down on a bed. Adriana lay down near the edge of Travis's bed and then scooted back against his side. It was no luxury mattress, but compared to the cots at the ranch, it felt like floating on air. Within moments, the three of them fell asleep and slept through the rest of the afternoon.

When Adriana opened her eyes again, it was already twilight. The men were still sleeping, so she took advantage of the opportunity to enjoy a nice, private shower. The water coming out of the faucet was a sterile beige color, but it washed off well. She felt cleaner than she had in days.

The boys began to stir, so she threw on some clothes and muddled around in the kitchen area while they got ready. Half an hour later, they were filing out the door.

"What's the plan for tonight?" she asked.

"We're going to a strip club," Travis replied, "we look over the girls, talk to them if we want, and choose four to meet us back here tomorrow."

"Is that the same way you always do it?"

"No, this is different. Usually we choose the girls based on photos and that's it. I asked them for a little more flexibility this time since we're looking for a different kind of girl, a different kind of personality anyway."

Adriana chuckled.

"You see? You guys are already getting used to a new way of doing business."

"Don't count your chickens yet," Travis warned, "this is a trial run. If we can't find the right people, or they don't work out for some reason, then the result will be the same. The boss will still want to sell them."

"Don't worry, we'll find the right girls, but you need to be honest with them right up front. Sometimes you have a tendency to lie a little."

Travis laughed.

"Hey, lying is a basic survival skill. The more people know about you, the easier it is for them to take advantage of you. You need to learn that too, or you won't last very long in this kind of business. Only show people what you want them to see and tell them what you want them to believe. Perception is reality. Anything else can get you killed."

They bypassed the truck and left it in the parking lot of the motel. It was a good night for a stroll, so they sauntered down the street pretending to be interested in the various shops along the way. Five minutes later, a cab came along and Omar flagged it down. He gave the driver some directions, and the car sped off.

The Black Cat Bar was a nondescript block building tucked away behind a small stone fence with palm trees in the yard. Parking was in back, but the cab driver dropped them off right at the front door. Omar paid him, and they all went inside.

Adriana had been to a strip club before, but nothing like this one. Just inside the door were three large men wearing clothes that were a size too small. Any of them might have succeeded as a professional wrestler. They were all big, muscular men with no sense of humor.

Behind them on the wall was a large metal cage for holding the weapons that they confiscated from the patrons as they entered. It was not a voluntary procedure. The three men were quick and thorough as they searched every single person that walked through the front door, both men and women. Judging by the number of weapons in the cage, it was a good precaution to take with their clientele.

Omar and Travis each surrendered a knife, and the men were happy. It seemed to be the minimum cover charge required to show you were a serious customer. Adriana had nothing to offer. The men stared at her curious, but they let her pass anyway.

Travis led them over to a table near the wall, and they took a seat. There weren't a lot of people inside, but the arrangement of the tables and small stage platforms gave the place a cramped and cluttered feeling. Like most clubs, the music was too loud, and the patrons cranked up the volume of their voices to compensate.

A half-dressed server came by and took their drink order. Adriana surveyed the smoke-filled room. As expected, the crowd was primarily male. There were a few girls scattered around, but it was difficult to tell whether they were customers or performers. Some might have been working girls trolling for their own private business.

They sat there and sipped on their drinks for a while. More customers poured in as the time passed. Sometimes, Travis or Omar would crook their finger at one of the girls and they would come over for a lap dance.

The boys looked happy, but Adriana was very bored by the whole process. The music was so loud that it was almost possible to even have a conversation. Any exchange of words had to be done by shouting into each other's ear. Unless she wanted to have a lap dance of her own, there was no way she could interview the girls.

Fed up with the noise, Adriana decided to find a bathroom and relieve her aching bladder. She yelled at Travis and made some hand motions to tell him where she was going. He was preoccupied admiring the assets of a busty dancer and may or may not have gotten the message. Omar had a different girl on his lap pouring beer down her bare chest and letting him lick it off her nipples.

She eased her way through the room, stepping around chairs and tables to avoid any accidents. One of the waitresses came by, and Adriana tried to follow in her wake. She managed to make it all the way to the bar and ask where the bathroom was. A quick nod toward a side corridor was the only answer.

Adriana slipped out of the main room and ducked into a dark hallway. A narrow passage led past two doors to a bigger door that appeared to be an emergency exit. She walked past the first door and paused to look for signs. Since the doors were identical, it was impossible to tell which might be for the women's bathroom.

The dilemma was resolved a few seconds later when the first door opened up and five men came pouring out. The men were laughing and joking, but they went quiet when they noticed her standing there. One man stared at her and smiled.

"Are you looking for someone?" the man asked her in Spanish.

She shook her head and tried to remain calm.

"Are you waiting for someone?" another man asked.

Adriana shook her head again and started toward the second door. The five men moved to block her path and surround her in the hallway. She felt the cold breath of fear on the back of her neck. The first man stepped up close and got right in her face. She could smell the strong scent of beer and cigar smoke.

"What's the matter, we are not good enough for you?"

The man put his hand around her arm and showed her a smile of crooked, rotten teeth. The others all crowded in as well, feeding off his aggressive lead. She was trapped in the hallway with no way out. Her eyes darted all around looking for a way to escape. The man misinterpreted her intentions.

"Ah, okay," he said, still in Spanish, "then we will take our business outside. We will have more privacy there anyway."

The man grabbed her and shoved her hard toward the emergency exit. The others followed them out through the door and into a small, dimly-lit yard. One of the men held her from behind in a loose bear hug and dragged her away from the doorway to a darker spot underneath one of the trees. The leader of the group edged up to her again.

"So what is your price, little girl," he turned to the others, "what do you think, boys? Is she worth a thousand pesos?"

Everyone laughed.

"I am worth a lot more than fifty bucks!" Adriana responded. She made a face as if she was offended, "my boss will not accept that. Nine thousand pesos for all of you, and that is my final offer!"

The men were surprised by her bravado, but then they all looked at one another and laughed.

"You talk tough," the leader said, "but let's see how tough you really are. We will all have you, and then I will pay you. And if you are good enough, we might come back later and do it again. But only if we are satisfied."

He showed her the disgusting smile again. Adriana squirmed around a bit, still in the grasp of the other man.

"Let me use my hands," she said with a sly grin, "and I guarantee that I will make all of you very satisfied."

"Does that include me?" Travis asked as he strolled through the side door. "Sorry to interrupt, but I was getting a little tired of waiting for you, babe."

Omar came through the door right behind him. They both stood to one side of the gathering. The five Mexican men glared at them.

"This is none of your business," said their leader, "we are entertaining ourselves with this girl. If you want some ass, then you go back inside and find your own girl!"

Travis stared at him and spoke in Spanish.

"I think I've seen all the assholes that I want to see for a while," he said, "you give her to me, and I will let you go with no broken bones."

The Mexican men all laughed.

"You think that you can handle five of us?" said the leader of the group. "You may be in for a big surprise."

"That's funny, I was about to say the same thing," Travis responded, puffing out his chest, "ask yourself why I speak Spanish with a Colombian accent. Omar and I have tangled with much tougher men than you bunch of street fairies."

Adriana saw the emotion boiling up in the faces of the Mexican guys.

"I've got these two," she said, "you guys take care of the others."

She jerked her arms free of the loose bear hug and pulled up the front of her shirt.

"Hey asshole, look at this!"

All the men froze and stared at her breasts.

The leader's head swiveled in her direction. In one swift motion, Adriana lunged forward and smacked both of her open palms on top of the man's ears. He cried out and bent over in pain just in time to feel her foot coming up hard into his groin. He collapsed and starting bawling like a baby.

Using the same leg, Adriana spun around low and kicked the other man's feet out from under him. As soon as he hit the ground, she pounced on top of him and slammed an open palm square into his nose as hard as she could. Blood and mucus flew all over the place, and the man cried in agony.

Adriana looked up at the other men who were still staring at her. She cocked her head to one side and winked at Travis.

"Okay, big guy, it's your turn."

Omar was already on the move. He leaped forward and gave one of the thugs a hard punch to the gut and then a back-fist to the jaw. Travis was one second slower, but he started with a powerful sidekick that knocked both of the other guys off their feet. They scrambled up and ran away.

"I think we're done here," Travis said, glaring at the Mexican guys, "we need to get out of here before the others come back with help."

"Shouldn't we wait for the police or something?"

Travis and Omar both laughed.

"That would be even worse," he explained, "down here, the cops are just as bad as the bad guys. Most people are on the payroll of the drug cartels, or some organization that's a lot bigger than us. You don't know who you can trust, and any of them might kill you just for the hell of it. Let's go."

He grabbed Adriana by the hand, and they started jogging down the street behind the strip club. A block away, they found a cab parked near a busy intersection. The three of them crawled inside, and the car pulled out into traffic.

"What about the girls?" Adriana whispered.

"We found some possibilities," Travis replied, "they're coming by to see us at the hotel tomorrow."

"Get plenty of rest then," she said, "you're going to need it."

CHAPTER 15

They all slept late the next day. Travis gave Omar some money and sent him out to get food for everyone. He got back as the first of the new girls arrived.

Her name was Yasmine, which was a perfect fit with their odd system for choosing new names for the girls. Adriana sat with her and made small talk while they waited for the others. As expected, Yasmine's personal life was a tale of tragedy and desperation at the hands of the Mexican cartels. Her family was all dead or scattered, and she was just looking for some way out of the madness.

Travis wolfed down the last bite of his lunch.

"Should we go ahead and start?" he asked. "I'm not exactly sure what you've got in mind for this. Are we supposed to interview them or test their, um... skills?"

"I want to do something like our training sessions," said Adriana, "I think asking more questions will be a waste of time. These girls will probably all have the same kind of background, and it will either come out as a bunch of lies or questions about the future that we can't really answer for them. We're still hoping the boss will change things, but we can't make any promises yet."

Travis nodded. There was a tentative knock on the door. Two more of the girls had arrived, and Omar let them in.

"By the way, what was all that bullshit about your Colombian accent last night," she asked, "is that really where you learned Spanish, Travis?"

The guys glanced at each other and chuckled.

"Omar and I were both in Special Forces," he replied, "we spent some time in Cali and a few other places."

"Ah, okay, that explains why you trust each other so much. What about the other guys at the ranch? Are they former military, too?"

Travis shrugged.

"Raul and Jimmy Ray are alright. I haven't known them long, but I think they were both in the military, and they seem like good guys. I can't vouch for any of the other guys. Dusty is a suck-up who kisses ass all the time and tries to dress like the boss. And Chaco, well you've met him. I wouldn't trust him as far as I could throw him."

Adriana nodded. That was pretty consistent with her impressions. She heard a soft knock on the door, and the fourth girl was ushered in. They all finished lunch and looked at her.

"Okay," she began, "this will seem a little strange at first, but what I want to do is try some bondage techniques."

"Are you serious?" Travis sputtered.

"Yeah, I know what you are thinking, but it's because you don't really understand how it works."

"Enlighten me then, oh wizard of the whip."

She took a deep breath. The girls all giggled.

"The whole dominant/submissive thing is really a fantasy foreplay designed to get everyone excited about what comes after. It gets the adrenaline jacked up, and the sexual hormones flowing, and the blood rushing to the right places. I can tell by looking at your jeans that you are excited just thinking about it."

Travis cleared his throat and crossed his legs.

"It's a natural response. Men get excited faster than women anyway."

"Exactly," Adriana agreed, "men have separate responses: one is mental, the other is physical. Men can fuck a wet sock and get physical pleasure. They don't have to feel love or emotional commitment. Women are different. A woman can have an orgasm five times for every one time a man reaches a climax. Women's bodies are made for sex. We have more hormones, more blood vessels, more nerve endings, and more muscles in that area designed for strength and stamina. We are made to reproduce, and that's where all of it comes together."

She paused, explaining it all slow again in both English and Spanish. Everyone listened in wide-eyed fascination.

"The bondage game kicks everything into motion for a woman. It spikes the fear factor which engages the hormones and the physical stimulation. The emotional strength of that reaction bypasses the need to feel love or some other strong desire. And contrary to popular belief, it is the submissive one who has the power and control in bondage."

"Ha," Travis laughed. "How do you figure that?"

"Think about it," said Adriana, "rape is merely a power game. It isn't really sex. It's a desire to control somebody and hurt them. Rape is an act of violence."

"Yeah, so how is bondage any different then?"

"It's different because bondage has rules. The goal is physical pleasure. There may be some pain involved, but only what the submissive one wants and allows. It is done to heighten the excitement for her. She is the one who is really in control of the situation. She decides what happens and how far it goes. She decides when it is over. When the submissive person is exhausted and stops, then there is no more pleasure for either one of them. The game is over."

She repeated it again in Spanish. They all stared at her in awe. Travis nodded.

"I get it. If you have someone tied up or whatever, then it's exciting for both of you even if neither one of you is feeling real love. It becomes purely physical, and you can both enjoy it for what it is. As long as you follow the rules, then no one really gets hurt, and no one takes it too far."

Adriana shrugged and nodded.

"That's a little simplistic, but that's basically it. If our girls are good at playing the game, then they can actually control the situation and still please the customer. Everyone will go away satisfied and happy, and we all live to love another day."

The room was quiet as they all thought about that.

"Where is the stuff we bought at the store?" she asked.

Omar scrambled to find the toys and handed her the bags.

"Let's all go into the bedroom now and practice with each other," said Adriana. "We need to get comfortable with the techniques and the boundaries. Not everyone will have the same boundaries, but that's okay. We don't all like the same things, and that is okay, too. The important thing is to relax and enjoy it."

"What about the dick thing?" asked Travis. "The boss always told us that we can use anything except our own dick. Is that still the rule?"

"What do you think? Why would he make that rule?"

Travis thought about it and shrugged.

"He doesn't want you to feel an emotional connection to the girls," said Adriana, "he doesn't want you guys to fall in love with them. That's why you could never make love to them. He wants you to control them, not protect them or please them."

"So what about now," he asked, "what are your rules?"

Adriana smiled and began taking off his clothes.

"I want you to love them, all of them. I want you to protect them and please them and make them all happy. I want the girls to feel happy and content and stay because they are loved, not because they are prisoners."

She peeled off his shirt and then her own.

"I don't know," said Travis, "I don't think the boss is going to like this at all. He's not going to let us do things like this."

She pulled down his jeans and got on her knees in front of him.

"Then maybe it's time for a new boss. Think about it."

Reaching into his boxers, Adriana took his penis in both of her hands and began to massage it. She leaned forward and licked the tip with her tongue two or three times. Then she slid it into her mouth. Her delicate hands continued to massage his genitals as she moved her head forward and back, sliding his penis in and out of her wet mouth until it was firm and erect.

Travis stood there with his eyes closed, every muscle in his body tensed with excitement. Adriana could sense that he was nearing a climax, so she stopped and backed away.

"Are you in love with me yet?" she asked in a playful tone.

"Yes! Yes! Please finish what you're doing! That feels so good!"

She chuckled and stood up.

"That's not real love. It's pleasure for you, but not for me. Even if you forced me to do something more now, there would still be no emotional connection between us."

She could see the anger and frustration in his face.

"What you feel now is purely physical. It is fueled by adrenaline and aggression. You are furious with me. But truthfully, you could finish this yourself without me. All you need is some lubrication and your own fingers."

Adriana took Yasmine by the hand and led her over to the bed. She motioned for the girl to take off her clothes and lay flat on her back with her legs open wide.

"Now let's play the game," she said, "spread her arms out and handcuff both of her wrists to the head of the bed. Then tie her ankles down in this open position, but keep everything very loose and relaxed."

The other girls found the handcuffs and some soft nylon rope in the bags from the novelty store. Omar helped them tie Yasmine to the bed.

"Now blindfold her."

Omar took a blindfold and fastened it over her eyes. Adriana rummaged through the bags and came up with vibrators, batteries, and some flavored lubricant. She handed them to the other girls and got them started.

"Okay ladies, you know what a girl likes. Let's make Yasmine feel good."

The other girls got busy as Travis and Omar watched and grinned. The girls were gentle and started slow.

They spread oil over Yasmine's body, caressing and rubbing it in. A generous amount was applied between her legs and inside her crevices.

Adriana sat on the bed next to Yasmine and squeezed her breasts with her fingers. Every few seconds, she would give the nipples a quick pinch, and then massage them again. The other three girls focused on the lower areas, rubbing the vibrators back and forth over her clitoris, deep inside her vagina, in and out of her anus.

Yasmine began to squirm around and moan with pleasure. The girls were in no hurry. The excitement was contagious, and they all seemed to feel it. The feelings grew stronger until Yasmine finally arched her back as the powerful orgasm rippled throughout her body. Moisture gushed out between her legs. The girls paused for a moment, and then they continued. A minute later, Yasmine climaxed again.

Adriana glanced at Travis and Omar.

"You see guys? A woman can also experience the pleasure without any emotional involvement, but it has to be done a different way. At this point, Yasmine no longer cares who is making her feel like this. She is only focused on making it last. Omar, put yourself inside of her, but leave the blindfold in place."

Omar took off his jeans and moved over to the foot of the bed. The other girls looked at him and continued to caress Yasmine's body. He slid his penis inside of her. Yasmine moaned and smiled.

"Now they are both thinking about nothing but pleasure. Everything is just a fantasy," Adriana explained, "they are not really in love with each other, and no one gets hurt. When she is finished, the game is over for both of them."

Travis was sitting on the other bed wearing nothing but his boxers.

"When do I get to play?" he asked with a sly grin.

Adriana took off the rest of her clothes and moved over to stand in front of him.

"We're going to play a different game. You need to get naked."

He pushed his boxers to the floor and sat back up.

"Now lie back on the bed and pretend that you are the one tied up."

He smiled and then complied.

"In this game, there are no blindfolds. I want you to see the difference."

Adriana crawled over and sat on top of Travis, straddling his hips. She leaned forward and let her legs slide down. She kissed him on the lips and then opened herself to let him deep inside. He began to throb as she moved her hips in a slow, circular motion. Adriana squinted her eyes and saw Travis looking at her.

"Can you feel the difference?" she whispered.

"Um-hm," he groaned. "I definitely feel something."

"This is not pleasure; this is making love. You are falling in love with me."

She started to move her body faster, and she felt him thrusting deeper inside. In less than a minute, Travis's body went rigid as he erupted deep within her. Adriana felt herself come at the same time, their bodies in sync together.

Travis had his eyes closed, but he was relaxed and smiling. She gave him a quick kiss and lay down on his chest.

"Now, tell me which one you like better."

"Love," he whispered, too soft for her to hear, "definitely making love."

CHAPTER 16

All four of the girls demonstrated that they were willing and able to do what was asked, so Adriana recommended they keep them. There was no argument from Omar or Travis. No one was eager to leave, but this was not a vacation. They played around and had fun for a couple more hours, then Travis began to get nervous.

"We need to head north," he said to the group, "those guys from the strip club might come looking for us. We don't know who they were. If they work for one of the cartels, we could be in big trouble. They don't tolerate anybody stepping on their toes, especially in their own back-yard."

"What's the next step," Adriana asked, "how do we get back across the border with these girls?"

"We have a plan, but we need everyone to cooperate, and we need to move fast. I want to leave tonight. Omar, make the call."

Omar got busy on the phone. Travis and Adriana rushed to pack up everything they didn't want to leave behind. Omar ended his conversation and hung up.

"They'll be ready by the time we get there," he said.

Travis nodded.

"Okay, everybody, let's go."

They all grabbed a bag or a bundle and carried it out to the truck. The men took a few minutes to walk around it and make sure no mischief was done. They didn't want the police to have any reason to pull them over. Travis pointed to the back, so Adriana and the girls climbed up on the flatbed and huddled together next to the cab. Everyone was hoping for a short and uneventful ride to wherever they were going next.

Omar cranked up the engine, and they rolled away. The truck bounced along a few city streets and then into the countryside. It was a bone-jarring experience, but the girls hung on to each other and tried not to scream too much.

About an hour later, Adriana felt the truck slowing down, and they pulled into a long dirt driveway. A few more minutes of bouncing through ruts and potholes, and they arrived. Omar eased the truck to a stop in between two huge barns and honked the horn. A couple of men walked out and waved.

One of them ambled up to the cab and spoke to Omar and Travis. They turned off the engine, and both got out. Travis walked around to the back of the truck.

"Okay, ladies, this is your last chance to take care of any personal business. After we get loaded, we won't be stopping until we get to the ranch. That's going to be several hours from now."

He pointed toward a wooden outhouse nearby, and the girls headed that way. The farm hand started up the truck and backed it into one of the barns. Omar walked inside, but Travis stayed outside and stretched his legs. Adriana strolled around next to him and did the same.

"What happens next," she asked, "do we change trucks or something?"

Travis shook his head.

"No, this one is fine. They are going to load some compartments on the back of the truck, and the girls will get inside. Then they will stack a bunch of those hay bales all around them to cover them up."

"You mean those things?"

She pointed to the hundreds of giant rolled bundles of dry grass.

"Yeah. We have some with a black plastic compartment in the middle. They load those first. Each girl will get in one of them, and we'll close it up. The compartment is all wrapped with real hay, so you can't tell that it's hollow inside. Then they will stack some more bales around and on top of those."

"No one ever looks at those?"

"Hell no, those bales weigh about eight or nine hundred pounds each, so they can't ask us to move them around. And hay is a real common thing to haul in Texas with all the horses and cattle ranches there. Nobody ever gives it a second glance."

Adriana was still concerned.

"Won't the girls get hot in there? Do they have to sit inside them all the way back to the compound?"

"That's why I wanted to leave now, so we can travel at night when it's cooler. I know it's rough, but it's a lot better than some other ways I've seen. At least, they have a good chance of surviving. We did cut some air holes in the plastic, but it will be hot. Tell them to relax and try to stay calm, and everything will be fine."

"How long will it be until we can get them out again?"

Travis looked north and shrugged.

"I would say at least four hours and probably closer to six. We have to go back to the Rio Grande bridge, get across to Laredo, drive all the way back to the ranch, and then get all the bales unloaded at the other end. It's going to be a long night."

It seemed like a horrible plan that would be torture for the girls, but she couldn't think of a better way to do it. What they were doing was not legal, but the girls would be desperate enough to try anything for a chance to escape their horrible life in Mexico.

The girls returned from the outhouse, and they all went inside the barn together. Adriana explained the plan, and they all nodded somewhat hesitantly in agreement. The hollowed bales had already been loaded on the flatbed. Each of the girls crawled inside of one and tried to make themselves as comfortable as possible. Travis closed them up, and Omar got the farm hands to stack a few real bales around and on top.

Adriana stood back and watched the whole thing. Once they finished, there was no obvious way to tell that anything was other than what it appeared to be. She gave it one last look, and then she climbed up into the cab next to Travis.

Some money changed hands, and Omar drove away. They left the farm and went back through Nuevo Laredo. Traffic was light until they got closer to the border. At one point, Omar stopped the truck and turned off the engine. Travis leaned his head out the window.

"What is it?" Adriana asked.

"Listen," Travis replied, "you hear that sound like popcorn?"

She concentrated, but heard nothing.

"Gunfire," he explained, "there is something going on west of here. We'll go down to the other bridge.

Usually, it's something involving the drug cartels. We don't want to get in the middle of that."

Omar turned the wheel in the opposite direction, and they took a different route through the city. Since it was the middle of the night, the line to cross the border wasn't long, but the guards were moving like they were half asleep. One of them checked their paperwork while a second man took a cursory glance in the back. They were cleared and moved on without any problems.

On the U.S. side, the people of Laredo were quiet, and they passed through the city unnoticed. When the streetlights were behind them, everyone began to relax. Adriana was feeling sleepy and exhausted but couldn't stop thinking about the girls.

"Can we stop soon?" she asked.

Travis glanced at Omar and then shrugged.

"We don't usually do that. We don't want to attract any attention. It's better if we push on and get to the ranch as soon as possible."

"I only want to check on the girls for a minute and make sure they're okay."

"We can't unload anything or open the compartments yet."

"I know, but I still want to talk to them and tell them where we are."

He glanced at Omar again and nodded.

"Okay, pull over anywhere you can, Omar. We'll stop for one minute, no more."

They were on an open stretch of two-lane highway now. Omar found a deserted spot to pull off the road and onto some level ground. The truck hissed to a halt. Travis swung the cab door open and got out. Adriana climbed out right behind him and dashed to the back of the truck.

"Help me up!"

Travis lifted her up, and she crawled onto the flatbed. She scrambled over and through the large, round bales of hay looking for some way to get between them. At last, she found a tiny open space and slid down into it.

"Hey girls," she yelled in Spanish, "we're in Texas now! Is everyone okay?"

There was nothing but silence at first, and Adriana began to get worried. Then she heard a muffled voice from inside one of the bundles.

"Yes! I am okay!" shouted Yasmine.

"Me too!" said the others.

Adriana laughed, overcome with relief.

"Okay, hang in there a little longer. Not much further now!"

She fought her way back out of the hay and jumped down into Travis's arms.

"They are okay," she repeated.

"I told you they would be," Travis replied.

She kissed him hard on the lips, and he acted surprised.

"What was that for?"

"Thank you," she said with a smile, "thanks for taking care of us and getting us safely back home again."

Travis shrugged.

"I was only doing my job."

"Well, thanks for doing a great job."

She ran up and climbed back into the cab of the truck. Travis got in right behind her and slammed the door. Adriana leaned over and kissed Omar on the cheek. He stared at them both for a moment.

"Don't ask," said Travis, "just take us home."

CHAPTER 17

It was a long night, but they made it back to the ranch safe and sound. Adriana and the four new girls slept late and missed breakfast. They came into the dining room for lunch, and Travis showed up to make the introductions. After a brief conversation with Chaco, he assigned them new names. They all got some food and took a seat at the last table next to Adriana. Travis strolled to the center of the room.

"Everyone, please welcome our new ladies," he said, "they just arrived last night. This is Ursula, Vera, Wanda, and Yasmine from Laredo. They will be working with us."

The others studied the newcomers. There was a flicker of a smile here and there, but Adriana detected a lot of suspicion still evident on their faces.

"As long as we are all here together, can we talk about some things," Adriana asked, "maybe some of our ideas for changes?"

Travis hesitated a moment, and they heard approaching footsteps. Omar walked into the room and leaned against the wall.

"I don't think so," he replied, "it's too soon to talk about that."

"Aw, come on," she persisted, "I think our girls need to hear about what we have in mind for the future. I think they will be very excited about it."

He rolled his eyes then glanced around the room.

"Maybe I'll let you do the talking about that. Why don't we all finish up our food and then go out and sit by the lake? It's a nice day, and we can relax out there."

Adriana wrinkled up her brow but nodded in agreement. She wondered if Travis was having second thoughts or trying to back out. Or maybe he was paranoid about some kind of electronic listening devices inside the buildings?

They all finished lunch and filed outside. It was a typical July afternoon in south Texas, hot and dry. The girls gathered around the wooden tables in small clumps. The four new girls stood together under a mesquite tree.

Travis and Omar walked out a few minutes later, and he gave her the nod.

"Okay ladies," she began, "I wanted to share with you some thoughts and ideas. I think most of you know me by now. My real name is Adriana, but Chaco probably calls me something different."

There were a few smiles and chuckles since Chaco was still inside.

"Anyway, Travis brought me here about a week ago to help take care of you. We want everyone to stay safe and healthy, at least as much as possible. I am a trained nurse, so I can help with some basic things."

"Do you know how to cook?" asked one of the girls. "The old woman is a terrible cook. Can we get some better food?"

Several of the other girls nodded and mumbled. Adriana glanced at Travis, but he shrugged.

"I don't know about that," she responded, "but we can make a list of things to ask about and maybe discuss it later with the boss."

Adriana pretended to search her pockets for a pen and paper, but she had neither so she moved on.

"We have purchased some basic medical supplies like bandages and ointments. I know it isn't much, but it's a start. I'm hoping we can go into town and get some stronger things like antibiotics, but it will take some time. We can always use the clinics, or even the emergency room if necessary."

"What about things for women," Sofia asked, "can we have birth control pills? Can we get some tampons and panty liners?"

"I want some nice panties," said Bianca, "it would mean a lot to me if we had some real underwear. I feel like I'm wearing my brother's clothes."

Everyone looked down at themselves and frowned. Travis threw up his hands.

"We will work on that," Adriana promised, "I don't know what you were told or what you expected when you came here, but obviously things are different. I want to be honest with you, and hopefully you can accept things for what they are. Then we can all work together to improve them."

The group went quiet then, anticipating some kind of revelation. Adriana looked around at all the sad faces and hopeful eyes staring in her direction.

"You all came here looking for a better life, or maybe just to escape a life that was already very bad. I respect you for that. It took a lot of courage and strength. I know that many of you are disappointed. This is not what you expected or what you wanted. But do not give up hope. We can make this better. And it is this same courage and strength that will enable you to achieve it."

Adriana looked at Claudia and saw that she was crying.

"No matter what you thought, you see now that this is a business. And we are not the employees, we are the merchandise. We are what they are selling. The man who runs this business is only interested in making money. He does not really care about us. If we can make money for him, then he will keep us. If not, then he will sell us. That might be hard to understand, but it is the truth. That is just the way things are. Spending money to make us happy is not important to him at all."

Travis stared at the ground and nodded.

"Then why are we even talking about this," asked Jenny, "why are you raising our hopes if there is nothing more for us in the future?"

"Because, that is what I want to change," Adriana replied, "I think if we are smart and use our heads, we can change our future. The key to this will be to show this old man that we have more value. If he treats us well, then we can make more money for him than he will get by treating us badly. That is what I want to show him."

"But that is obvious," Jenny argued, "everyone knows this. Latina women want to be beautiful and enjoy life. If we are happy, then everyone around us will be happy. How can he not see that?"

Adriana shrugged and sighed.

"I cannot explain it," she admitted, "he is an old and bitter man who is angry at life and doesn't know how to be happy. He seems to have given up for some reason.

Now, he wants only to accumulate money by selling happiness to others. That's why he sells or rents you to other men for their pleasure. The sad thing is that many of the other men are exactly the same as him, so they treat us badly, too."

"So what can we do then?" Sofia asked. "If all men are the same, they will all treat us like animals."

"I didn't say that all men are the same," Adriana replied, "many men will be the same, but some are different."

She glanced over and pointed to Travis and Omar.

"Those two men work here, but they are not like the others. They want to be nice to us. They want to make us happy."

"Will you let us go then?" Elena shouted.

Travis shook his head.

"No, I can't let you go. It's my job to keep you safe and secure. In order for me to do that, you have to be here where I can watch over you."

"Then you still treat us like animals," said Elena, "we are your pets."

"We are your pussy cats!" Claudia added.

The girls all laughed and murmured to each other.

"There are worse things to be," Adriana reminded them. "Keyla was attacked last week by the Ripper. You have all heard about that? And our new girls can tell you about what the men are like in Nuevo Laredo. What do you say, ladies?"

Yasmine giggled and pointed at Omar.

"I like that one," she said, "I will be his pet any day. He certainly knows how to make a woman happy."

Omar smiled, and his face turned crimson. Vera and Wanda nodded, and Ursula blew him a kiss.

"You see," said Adriana, "that is what I am talking about."

"So you want us all to be happy by having sex with Omar?" asked Sofia. "I may be wrong, but I don't see that as a good solution."

Travis laughed, and Omar's disappointment seemed genuine.

"That's not what I mean," Adriana clarified, "my point is there are good men, and there are bad men. If we let things continue as they are, the man who owns us will always keep selling us or renting us to the same kind of people. Those will be men just like him. Those will not be the good ones like Travis and Omar."

Ursula blew them both another kiss.

"What I'm suggesting is that we show him how to find the good ones. We could make ourselves into better women, and we will attract better men."

"But we are still just selling ourselves for money," Sofia argued, "that is not my idea of happiness. That is not the kind of life I wanted."

"Maybe not," said Adriana, "but it is better than what we have now. Would you rather go suck a dirty *picha* in the alley for twenty dollars or make love to a gentleman on soft, satin sheets for a thousand dollars?"

The girls got quiet and looked at each other.

"How do we find these gentlemen if we are prisoners here?" asked Elena.

"That will be our new goal," Adriana explained, "we will go to the city looking for men like that. We will dress better. We will fix our hair and our makeup to impress them. We will show the world that we are beautiful ladies who deserve something more from them. Travis and Omar will help us, but we are the only ones who can change this business into something different. We must do whatever it takes to satisfy the customers that we want. If we can do this, we will make a lot of money for the old man, and then we will have more money to make our lives better. Our future will be in our own hands. We can continue as we are, or we can become the best at what we do and enjoy the rewards that come with it."

"You're still talking about selling our bodies," said Jenny, "it doesn't matter how you say it, this is still prostitution."

"Everything is selling yourself in some way," she replied, "working in an office is selling your time and your mind. Working in a restaurant is selling your kitchen skills. Even marriage is trading sex to another person in order to gain a partner. Marriage is a partnership, but the commitment is for more than just money. It also demands a serious emotional commitment. I am not asking for you to love this business or the customers. Use this as an opportunity to make your life better. It may not be where you want to go, but maybe it can get you one step closer to it."

The girls all stared at the ground for a moment then at each other.

"Okay," said Adriana, "today is the first day of the rest of your life. I say that we take control of our future, and we choose to make it better. Who is with me?"

Adriana raised her hand high. The four new girls hesitated for a second, then raised theirs. Elena raised her hand, then Sofia, then Jenny. In less than a minute, all the girls had their hands raised high.

She looked over the crowd, and then she glanced at Travis and smiled. It wasn't much, but it was a start. It was time to make some changes.

CHAPTER 18

Adriana didn't sleep much at all, but she woke up on Thursday eager to start the day. She had so many ideas about a new way to do business. Hayes was still locked into the old way of doing things and didn't see the potential. But she would keep working on the other guys, and she knew they would all come around sooner or later.

She was certain that Travis would support her. He had his faults, but Adriana was convinced that underneath all of his macho bullshit and cocky, self-centered attitude there was a decent man. It would take a little work to peel off the dirty layers and polish him up, but she could handle it. She was finishing her eggs when Travis came sauntering into the dining room with his usual bravado.

"Good morning, ladies," he said, "I trust you all slept well and dreamed about me. We have a fairly light day today. Jimmy Ray would like to have a couple of volunteers for training sessions, and I think Chaco needs a crew for some cleaning at the big house. Finish up your breakfast, then come see me outside."

Travis nodded at the other men, then he came over and sat down at the table next to Adriana and Yasmine.

"What's up, girls?"

"My, aren't we the happy little minion today," Adriana replied. "Did the boss give you a big raise when he heard about the trip to Laredo?"

He laughed and shook his head.

"No, I actually have a meeting with him set up for tomorrow, so he doesn't know anything about that yet. I guess I'm just in a good mood today. Everything seems to be okay for a change. Everybody seems pretty content."

"I don't know if content is the right word. It's a little too early to say that. I think everybody is still waiting to see how things shake out. We've made some promises to the boss and to the girls, but we haven't really delivered on anything yet."

Travis shrugged.

"Okay, you're right. So what do you think we should do?"

"I think we need to start making some changes," said Adriana, "we need to show people that we are serious, and it isn't just talk."

"For example?"

"Let's go into the city today. We can talk about it on the way, but I would like to look for a place to rent and buy some more things for the girls."

"We can't keep spending money," he argued, "we're not generating any cash yet, and the money is almost gone."

"Then let's take some the girls and drop them off. We'll take Yasmine and the new girls. They need to learn the city anyway, so they can do that while we drive around. We can take some the others, too, and let them work in pairs again."

"But it's Thursday and business will be slow, especially in the day time."

"So what," said Adriana, "it doesn't cost any more to take ten people than two in the van, and it will be safer. Anything we make is better than nothing."

"Good point. Okay, we'll go right after lunch."

They all went through the usual morning routine. A couple of the girls went off with Jimmy Ray to practice their skills in the underground shelter. Four more left with Chaco to do some cleaning at the big ranch house. The other girls settled outside next to the lake to chat and gossip with each other.

The girls were still curious about the trip to Laredo and fascinated by the details. It was very different from the experience that most of them had coming across the border. Adriana and the new girls spent the morning telling and retelling their story over and over.

Time passed, and soon they were through with lunch and getting ready for the trip to Corpus Christi. Travis came by the dormitory with the van, and they loaded up eight of the girls. Nobody had to be tied up or blindfolded. They jumped in and made themselves comfortable in the back. Raul was driving again this time.

A little more than an hour later, they were riding around the outskirts of the city. Raul maneuvered through the familiar streets to the same part of town where they had been the previous week. He dropped the girls off in pairs again, one new girl and one of the others working together.

After the last two had stepped off, they swung by a couple of stores and did some shopping. Adriana picked up a few supplies and some new underwear for the ladies. The streets were empty and traffic was light. They found an interesting adult boutique nearby and picked up a couple of new toys. It was still early in the evening, but they had run out of things to do.

"Let's look for a place to rent," Adriana suggested.

"I hope you're not thinking about calling a real estate agent," said Travis.

"No, I was actually thinking about the place where I was living before. It was paid up for a while, and I'm sure they haven't rented it out to anybody else. We may be able to use that place for free."

"It's a crime scene, remember? I doubt if we can just move right in."

"Why not? The lease is probably still good. Nobody knows what really happened there. I could just show up again and take it back."

Travis shook his head.

"That wouldn't work. The cops would have too many questions, and they would be hanging around all the time looking for answers. And those are things that we do not want to talk about, right? I thought you were on my side now."

"Of course, I'm on your side, but we want to do what is best for the girls. I don't like the idea of them walking the streets all the time, especially with Juan the Ripper out there killing people. Let's go by and take a quick look, okay?"

"Okay, but just a quick look. If I see any cops or reporters or even a curious dog snooping around, we're getting out of there."

"Alright."

She gave Raul directions, and he drove by the old house. There were still a few strips of yellow crime scene tape on the front door, but there were no police cars in sight. Raul pulled into the driveway.

"Can we go inside for a minute?" Adriana asked.

Travis sighed and nodded. The two of them crawled out of the van. Raul stayed in the vehicle. They approached the front door and studied it for a minute.

"You think it's locked?" she wondered.

He raised his right foot and gave the door a hard kick right below the knob. It flew open and banged against the wall.

"Not now," he said.

"You are such a gentleman. I love it when men open doors for me."

Adriana peeled the crime scene tape off and walked in. The memories came flooding back. Everything was a total mess. It was difficult to tell what chaos had been left by her abduction and what had been done by investigators afterwards.

It was obvious that someone had spent a lot of time in the house looking for some clue about what had happened. She wondered if that was the local cops or someone from the F.B.I. team. In the end, it didn't matter. Everyone would know by now that she was gone, and they would have no doubts about who had been responsible for taking her. They may have assumed she was already dead, then she thought of Johnny.

She dashed into the kitchen and stopped at the entrance. The back door was closed and taped. There was a huge blood stain on the dirty linoleum floor, but there was no outline where Johnny's body had been. Could he still be alive? It seemed almost impossible that he would have survived. No, it wasn't possible. She had seen him lying there covered in blood.

And then she smelled the noxious odor of cigarette ash. On the counter by the sink was a paper cup. She tiptoed over and peered inside. It was half full of old cigarette butts. Sitting on the counter next to the cup was an empty pack of cigarettes, the same brand that Johnny smoked. But that didn't mean anything. Maybe one of the cops smoked. Maybe they had left it there.

Adriana felt her skin crawl and gave a quick glance back over her shoulder. Travis was standing in the doorway staring at her.

"Have you seen enough?"

"Do you think he survived? Could he still be alive?"

"Who, your boyfriend? No way. We both saw what he looked like."

"I know, but it's possible, right?"

Travis shook his head.

"No. He killed my guy, and my guy killed him—end of story. Why do you care anyway? Was he your lover or something?"

Adriana smiled.

"No, he was gay, but he was a good friend. I miss him sometimes."

She glanced around the room and sighed.

"You're right," she said, "this wasn't a good idea. Let's get out of here."

They left everything as it was and walked back outside. They climbed into the van, and Raul started it up again. Adriana stared out the window, lost in thought.

Following the usual routine, Raul drove back around to the drop points to check on the girls again. Amanda and Wanda were fine, so they left them there and moved on. A block further on, they slowed down to look for the next pair. Adriana spotted Ursula and Jenny sitting under a big tree talking to another girl. Raul eased the van over to the curb close by.

"Who is that with them?" Travis wondered. "It can't be a customer. Are they out here making new friends or what?"

"It's Laura," Adriana shouted, "they found Laura!"

She yanked open the door of the van and scrambled across the sidewalk. Travis got out and followed her over to the cluster of girls. Jenny glanced up.

"Look who we found walking around," she said, "Laura said she's been living in the streets ever since you left her here last week."

"We didn't leave her," Travis replied, "she ran away."

"Laura was with Keyla last week when that guy attacked her," Adriana explained. "We chased the guy off, and Travis carried Keyla back to the van so we could take her to the hospital. Laura disappeared somewhere in all the confusion."

"She told us that she was hiding because she got scared," said Jenny, "she thinks that you guys abandoned her."

Adriana leaned over and studied the girl close. Her clothes were covered in filth and torn, it was apparent that she hadn't bathed in a week. One of Laura's shoes was missing. Her face was severely bruised and had a blank expression. Both of her eyes were bloodshot and dilated.

"I think she's high on something," said Adriana, "somebody gave her something and put her back out on the street."

"This girl is definitely on something," Ursula agreed, "everything that she says is crazy. She doesn't even know where she is right now."

"Relax, baby, we're going to take care of you."

Laura glared at Adriana as she reached out to pat her arm.

"Don't touch me," she screamed, "you're a cop! Leave me alone!"

The girl jerked her arm away from Adriana and scooted back on the grass. The others all turned and stared at her.

"I was a cop, but I'm not anymore," said Adriana.

"Then why did she say that?" asked Jenny.

"The girl is high as a kite," said Ursula, "she's talking crazy."

"But where did she even get that idea?" Travis wondered. "I never said anything about that. Did you talk to them?"

Adriana shook her head.

"No, I don't know where she heard that. It must be a rumor on the streets."

"That's a very dangerous rumor," said Travis, "if the boss hears that, he will kill us both in a heartbeat."

"So it's true," asked Jenny, "you are a cop?"

"I was a cop in Galveston," she replied, "that's where I first met Travis. But then I screwed up trying to arrest him, and they let me go."

Jenny narrowed her eyes and stared at Adriana.

"I'm not sure that I believe that," she said, "you could be undercover trying to win your old job back. I may not be educated, but I'm not stupid. If you're smart, you'll leave that bitch here, Travis."

The other girls helped Laura get to the van, and they all climbed inside. Travis stood on the sidewalk looking at her.

"What," said Adriana, "you don't believe me now either?"

He shrugged.

"I don't know what to believe. I'm just looking out for myself. If I take you back to the ranch and word gets around, we'll be taking a long walk in the desert with a shovel. That doesn't seem appealing to me. It might be safer for both of us if I left you here."

Adriana moved close to Travis and kissed him on the lips.

"Do what your heart tells you," she whispered.

He looked into her eyes and thought about it for a minute, and then he sighed.

"Get in the fucking van. Let's pick up the others and go home."

CHAPTER 19

After a long and sleepless night, Adriana sulked through breakfast with her head hanging low. She could feel the eyes of the other girls upon her. They were all watching, waiting, judging her words and her actions. Whatever trust she had earned up to now seemed to have vanished overnight. It was back to square one again.

She wondered if maybe Jenny had been right. Maybe she should have stayed in Corpus Christi. If her cover was blown, coming back here was suicide. And if Big Bill decided that she was a risk, Travis would be guilty by association. Hayes would have nothing to lose by killing them both.

Yasmine sat next to her this morning, but she wasn't smiling. Instead, she turned and whispered with the other Laredo girls. Adriana glanced around the room and caught some others staring in her direction. They looked away to avoid catching her eye. The dining room was quiet.

Travis seemed to be thinking similar thoughts when he showed up a few minutes later. He didn't laugh or greet the girls with his normal banter. After exchanging some brief conversation with Chaco, he pointed at Adriana and left the room. Chaco looked at her with a wicked grin on his face. She didn't take that as a good sign.

Adriana pushed her scrambled eggs around on the plate for a while and then got up and went outside. Travis was standing by himself near the corner of the building. He pointed at her and nodded toward the back. She followed him around the corner and saw the pickup truck waiting there.

"We have a meeting with the boss today?" Adriana asked as she climbed in.

Travis nodded and started the engine.

"Yes, but please don't say a word. Let me do all the talking."

"What if he asks me something?"

"Keep the answer short and sweet. We're on thin ice right now."

He drove the short distance to the big ranch house, and they got out of the truck. A couple of men she didn't know were standing around. Travis ignored them, and she followed him into the house.

They walked past the same bronze statues and cowboy art again. This time, she was even more nervous and apprehensive. The self-confidence that she felt before had shriveled to nothing.

Hayes was sitting behind his big desk again when they walked into the office. A thin stream of smoke was curling up from the long, brown cigar sitting in the ashtray. The piles of paperwork on his desk appeared to have grown.

He glanced up and frowned as they took a seat.

"I hope you two have some good news for me this time," he grumbled, "I haven't heard much lately, and it's putting me in a very bad mood."

Travis let out a nervous chuckle.

"Sure, boss, we've got some good news. The trip down to Laredo went well. We came back with four new girls that are super-hot. I think they're going to make us a lot of money on the streets."

"Oh, really," said Hayes, "You have some money for me?"

"Uh, no, not at the moment. We had to buy more supplies. But we did take them down to Corpus Christi yesterday and got them all started learning the routine. I think they're going to be great on the street."

"If they are so great, then where is my money?"

Travis shifted around in his chair and cleared his throat.

"Well, like I said, we needed some more supplies, clothes and stuff. The new girls didn't bring anything from Mexico. And we're trying to get some new stuff for the other girls, too. We want to upgrade them a little in order to attract some better customers that will pay a little more."

Hayes snatched up his cigar and took a few big puffs. Smoke clouds hovered over the desk. He glared at them through the thick haze.

"I heard you had some trouble on the trip to Laredo," he said, "my friends there told me that you and Omar had a disagreement with some of the local boys. Should I be concerned about that? Is that going to come back and bite us?"

"Nah, it was nothing," Travis responded, "a couple of guys were drunk, and they were giving Adriana a hard time. Omar and I just ran them off. It was really no big deal at all, nothing to be concerned about."

The old man stared at Travis for a moment, then he looked at Adriana.

"I'm beginning to think that we don't need you around here anymore, little lady. So far, I've heard a lot of promises, but we've had nothing but trouble since you showed up. Give me one good reason why I shouldn't throw your ass in the lake right now."

"Because I'm a good swimmer," Adriana replied with a smile.

The room went quiet for a second, and then Hayes burst out laughing.

"You've got spunk, little girl, I'll give you that much. I can see why that dopey bastard there is so struck on you," he grinned at Travis. "So tell me again how you plan to make me a millionaire."

"We're going to change the business," Adriana explained. "Instead of bringing girls across the border and selling them, we want to use them as an escort service for the high-end market. You have twenty girls in their sexual prime with no criminal records or birth certificates to worry about. Rich men will pay a lot to spend time with them. All we need is a place to set up the business somewhere in the city, a place that is safe for them and convenient for the men. You can make a fortune with that."

Hayes grinned.

"You're basically talking about setting up a brothel? A whorehouse?"

Adriana shrugged.

"Well, we don't really think of it that way, but that's one way to look at it."

"What do you think, Miller?"

Travis sat back in his chair and crossed his legs.

"I think it might work. That's why we needed some new girls with better skills and a different attitude. They need to buy into the idea that it's a better future for them."

The old man puffed on his cigar some more and thought about it.

"Then I think we need to sell a couple of the others, cull the herd a little. We don't have any cash coming in, and you two screwed up that other deal for me. Get me some photos of the new girls and let me make some phone calls. Then we can use the cash that we get for those to finance this new business."

"No! We can't do that!" Adriana protested.

Hayes cocked his head and stared at her.

"I thought this was what you wanted to do. If you want to start a new business, then you're going to need money. Nothing happens for free, little girl."

"No, we can't sell the new girls. We recruited them because they have the right attitude and the right skills to make this work."

"Then sell a couple of the others. I really don't care which ones you get rid of, but a couple of them have to go. We need the money."

"You can't do that! It's not right!"

Travis covered his face with his hands and sighed. Hayes glared at Adriana and his cheeks began to get red. He puffed harder on the cigar.

"I think you're forgetting who is in charge around here," the old man said, "I've been hearing some disturbing rumors about you and Travis lately, and I don't like what I'm hearing. I'm not sure that I can trust you two anymore. Maybe it's not the girls that I need to replace, maybe it's you."

"You can trust me, boss," said Travis, "you've known me for years. I always do what you want and what's best for the business."

He stared at Miller for a minute.

"That's what I thought until a couple of weeks ago. Junior trusted you more than I do and look what happened to him. I'm thinking your leash was just a bit too long. And now you've gone and brought in this uppity filly that don't know her place yet. Maybe I should get rid of you both right now."

Travis jumped to his feet and pleaded with the old man.

"Please, boss, give me another chance! You can trust me!"

Adriana sat there and glared at them both. She could think of nothing useful to say that wouldn't be an outright lie.

"Chaco," the old man bellowed, "get in here!"

Chaco strolled into the room carrying his beloved bullwhip. Dusty was lingering in the hallway right behind him. Hayes glanced at Travis. Then he looked at Adriana and smiled a wicked smile.

"Take these kids and put them in the shed. We'll leave them there for a couple of days to think about things. They need to get their stories straight and adjust their attitude a bit. Then we can try having this conversation again."

"I would be happy to do that, boss. Anything else you need?"

Hayes stood up and puffed on his cigar some more.

"Yeah, find Omar and Jimmy Ray, and tell them to come up here. We have some business to take care of this weekend."

"No," Adriana screamed, "you can't sell any of the girls!"

"Get them both out of my sight!" Hayes ordered.

Chaco tried to grab Travis, but he jerked his arm away. Dusty stepped up closer. After a few tense moments, Miller relented and walked out of the room without a word. Adriana glared once more at the old man, and then she followed Travis.

They exited the ranch house and turned to the right, heading toward a wooden shed about fifty yards away. It looked like an old place that had been used as a storage building of some kind. It was small and square with one door and no windows.

Adriana had taken about ten steps when she heard the soft rustle of leather right behind her. A few seconds later, the end of the long whip popped across the middle of Travis's back. He yelped in pain, but he kept on walking. Five seconds later, it snapped again, ripping a gash in his shirt and drawing blood, but Travis staggered on. Halfway there, the whip cracked across his shoulders a third time, knocking him to the ground.

Adriana dashed over and knelt beside him.

"Leave him alone!" she shouted, but Chaco only laughed. All of a sudden, the big whip snapped again, and she felt the fire leap across her back like hot lightning.

"Move!" Chaco commanded.

She helped Travis get up on his feet, and they both stumbled on toward the shed. Another ten yards, and the whip popped again two more times, hitting them both square in the back. Adriana screamed in pain. Travis only groaned and hobbled on.

The last twenty steps seemed to take forever, but they made it to the shed. Dusty yanked the door open and shoved them both inside. They collapsed onto the hard plank floor and heard the click of a lock on the door latch. Two sets of footsteps faded into the distance.

"Thanks for letting me do the talking," Travis gasped.

Adriana smiled at his sarcasm.

"Sorry, but sometimes I have to say what I'm thinking. It just comes out."

Travis swiveled his body around and sat up, careful as possible.

"It's going to get pretty hot in here this afternoon. Try to stay calm and save your energy. I don't know if they're going to bring us any food or water."

"Okay," she replied, "well, at least look at the bright side."

"Yeah? What's that?"

"We get the rest of the day off."

CHAPTER 20

A day in the shed felt like a year in a furnace. It was still mid-July, and the temperature outside hovered over a hundred degrees for most of the day. Inside, it was at least twenty degrees hotter. With the door bolted and no windows, the only hint of a breeze came through the narrow slits between the boards in the wall. It felt like hell.

Adriana and Travis sat on opposite sides of the shed and tried not to crowd each other. Shared body warmth would only make the situation worse. The small building was just twenty feet square, so it didn't make much difference anyway. The only other things inside were a pair of wooden benches, some stacks of animal feed in large bags, a few rusty gardening tools, and an old electric generator.

The salty sweat made her wounds hurt even more as the day wore on, but Travis never complained. Adriana knew he must be in excruciating pain. Blood was splattered all over the shredded remains of the shirt that hung on his back.

"I'm really sorry about all of this," she said, "you were right; I should have kept my mouth shut. Sometimes I have a difficult time doing that."

"Yeah, I noticed."

She waited a moment and then tried again to apologize.

"Sorry about pushing so hard for everything. I know you were doing what you could for the girls. I should be more patient. This is a bad situation, and Hayes doesn't care about them at all. You're just caught in the middle of it."

Travis stared at her curious.

"How did you know his name?"

Adriana hesitated and cocked her head in surprise.

"What?"

"How did you know the old man's name?" he repeated.

"You... you must have told me," she stammered, "or maybe somebody else said it. I don't know. I heard it somewhere."

Travis stared at her and narrowed his eyes.

"Oh, I'm sure you didn't hear it from me, and I doubt if you heard it from one of the other guys. We're not allowed to use his name around here, especially in front of the girls. The old man is very strict about that. Everyone has to call him boss."

Adriana glanced away, realizing her mistake.

"I guess somebody must have slipped up and said it. Maybe I heard it when I was working at the clinic in Corpus Christi."

A thick silence hung in the air.

"You're lying," said Travis, "you heard it somewhere else. Laura was right; you are still a cop, aren't you? You're down here undercover to bust old man Hayes. That's how you knew his name and probably everything else about this place. You heard it all from the cops. God, how could I be so stupid!"

He jumped up and began pacing back and forth in the small shack. She could see the fury in his eyes. Sweat poured off his face. He picked up one of the big bags of feed and hurled it against the wall.

"All this time, I was trying to believe you. I wanted to believe you. I should have trusted my gut and killed you back in Galveston the first time I saw you. What a stupid, ignorant moron! Damn it! Now you're going to get us both killed!"

Adriana cowered in the corner and didn't say anything.

"Why did I not see this before? No one in their right mind would come here just to save these girls. No one cares about them, and you sure as hell don't care about me! You were lying to me and using me all along."

"That's not true!" she argued. "Maybe I was at first, because that's how I wanted it to be, but everything changed."

He stopped pacing and glared at her.

"What do you mean, everything changed?"

She shrugged.

"Well, I knew you were a cruel, self-centered, lying bastard from the minute I laid eyes on you. That part hasn't changed."

"Thanks for sharing your true feelings."

"My pleasure. But my feelings about the girls have changed. I really do care about them now. At first, I only saw this as a problem to be solved. Hayes was the problem, and I only wanted to take him down. But Hayes isn't the real problem, and taking him down won't cure it. The real problem is that these girls have no life and no future. Yeah, Hayes is taking advantage of that, but getting him out of the picture doesn't give them any kind of alternative. These girls need some way out of this shit hole."

"And you think that you can do that?"

"Yeah, I do! Maybe it's a crazy plan, but I think these girls deserve a chance at happiness. They came into a hard world with nothing but their looks and their wits. We can show them how to use that to get ahead. It won't be easy, but nobody says that life is fair. We know that it isn't. Some get everything, and some get nothing. But these girls do deserve a chance at something."

"And you think turning them all into prostitutes is the answer?"

"It's the world's oldest profession, and you know it. I can't make them all into scientists or engineers, but I can teach them how to be proud of who they are and what they can do. I can teach them how to set goals and work for their dreams. They aren't doomed to be somebody else's slaves for their entire life. They can work hard and put away some money to buy their way out. After a year or two of hard work, maybe they can start over someplace new and reinvent themselves as whatever they want. At least, their future will be in their own hands."

Travis tilted his head and looked at her in disbelief.

"Are you serious? Wow, I'm glad the old man didn't hear you say that! If he had, we'd be having this conversation with the fish at the bottom of the lake."

"Are there really fish in that lake?"

"Probably not, I was only making a point."

"But you understand what I'm saying, don't you? With Hayes, their best hope is to be sold to a kind owner who will use them for a while and then let them go. We both know that isn't likely to happen. Even if it does, and they survive the experience, what happens after that? They fall back into prostitution or drug addiction on the streets? Or maybe they get deported back to Mexico? What kind of future is that?"

"So you're going to be like their guidance counselor or something?"

"No, I want to be more like an older sister who can give them some good advice. Think of it like the girls who work at strip clubs to pay their way through college. It isn't as nice as working at the mall, but it pays a lot better and gets them to their goal. It buys their freedom. We have to look at the big picture and not get hung up on the details."

"Yeah, well, it's the details that are getting us in trouble."

"But you agree with me, right?" Adriana persisted. "What Hayes is doing with these girls is just wrong, and we have a solution that is better for everybody."

Travis glanced around the shack and blew out a big sigh.

"Unfortunately, it doesn't matter what I think, as you can plainly see. Even if I did agree with you, we don't have the power to change anything around here. All the old man cares about is money, plain and simple. Doing things your way will cost him money, and he's never going to agree to it."

"Then we'll just have to get rid of him."

He looked at her and smiled.

"Now you're talking like a real criminal. So are you still a cop or not?"

Adriana shrugged.

"Well, I don't work for the Kemah Beach Patrol anymore."

"Okay, don't say anything else. I probably don't want to know."

"You could always lie about it. You're pretty good at that."

"Don't lecture me about lying. You're in no position to make that argument."

Travis sat back down and cringed at the pain in his back. Adriana moved over and sat next to him. She looked at the deep, red gashes left by Chaco's whip.

"Does your back hurt a lot?" she asked.

"Yes, it does, and that's no lie."

She started to put her arm around Travis and comfort him, but then she decided that wouldn't be a good idea right now.

"Is there anything I can do for you?"

"There are probably a lot of things you can do for me, but now isn't the time. The best thing you can do right now is go back over there to the corner and leave me alone. I need to think for a while."

"I can help you make a plan."

"No, thank you. Your plans don't work out very well for me. I'll come up with something myself. Now that I'm not blinded by lo–I mean, now that I'm thinking more clearly, I can make my own plans."

Adriana nodded and scooted back over into the corner. She let a couple minutes go by and then spoke up again.

"Could you throw some of those bags on the floor and spread them out?"

Travis stared at her.

"What? Why?"

"You know, just spread out a couple of them on the floor to make a sort of bed. The floor is too hard, and I want to lie down on my stomach for a while. We both might as well get comfortable if we're going to be here all day or even all night. We can't sleep on that wooden floor. At least, we can lie down and rest on those bags."

He thought about it for a minute and then shrugged.

"Sure, why not."

She smiled as he wrestled a few of the bags down from the stacks and flattened them together on the floorboards. He leaned back and did a swift sidekick, knocking one of the boards loose on the back wall. Another quick kick, and it went flying back out into the field, allowing a nice breeze to come whistling through the hole.

"Wow! Nice work!" Adriana exclaimed.

Travis nodded.

"We might as well have some air conditioning, too, while we're at it."

"Chaco will be pissed off."

"Good. That gives me extra incentive."

He reared back and kicked out another board a few feet down from the first one. Adriana chuckled.

"Now he'll really be pissed."

"We can only hope," said Travis.

They lay face down on the bags of feed and tried to rest for a while. Their bodies were a few feet apart because of the heat, but Adriana stretched out her hand and tried to touch his fingers. He frowned at her.

"I don't hold hands with cops," he said.

"I'm not a cop anymore," she replied.

"How do I know that?"

"Because now I'm planning to kill somebody."

CHAPTER 21

The day wore on, and time trickled by in tiny increments like drops from a melting icicle. The heat climbed and peaked with the afternoon sun. Hot became hotter, and soon it did not even matter anymore. A few degrees more or less made no difference in the stifling atmosphere inside the shed.

Adriana tried to relax and just focus on surviving the horrible experience. She lay on the feed bags and watched Travis. It was apparent he had been through a lot of other bad times, or had been trained on how to deal with it, perhaps in the military. He seemed to withdraw from reality, almost as if he was meditating or mentally removing himself from the situation.

He lay face down with his eyes closed, motionless and his breathing shallow. Adriana was tempted to shake him sometimes just to be sure that he was still alive. It was eerie to watch, but it looked effective. She decided to mirror his actions and imitate him. Much to her surprise, it seemed to work.

The long day passed in a sort of nightmarish dream state. Minutes became hours, the scorching sun began to ease down toward the distant horizon. They didn't talk or argue anymore. It seemed like a waste of energy to even try. There was nothing more to be said for the moment anyway.

An hour or two before sunset, one of the ranch hands brought them some food and water. The man didn't say anything. He just unlocked the latch, opened the door, put the things inside, and then left again. The sounds of the lock clicking back into place and the man's fading footsteps were enough to shatter any hopes of being released. They both ate their bean burritos in silence, contemplating the night to come.

What concerned Adriana even more was that neither Chaco nor Dusty had come by to gloat or harass them. They must have been very busy to miss such an opportunity. That made her worry about all the girls and what was going on without her and Travis around to protect them. Terrible things could be happening, but they were powerless to intervene or stop it.

"Chaco didn't come back," she remarked.

"Yeah, I know," Travis replied with a scowl.

"What do you think they are up to?"

He frowned and shrugged.

"I don't know, but I'm sure it's nothing good. Chaco hates dealing with the girls. He's got no patience for it, treats them like cattle. Dusty isn't any better."

"Do you think they sold some girls today?"

"I wouldn't be surprised. Hayes wants the money, and they like to get rid of the girls as fast as possible, especially the younger ones that cry a lot. I bet they are up in Galveston right now selling a couple of them."

Adriana punched one of the feed bags.

"Damn it! I hate that man!"

"Which one, Hayes or Chaco?"

"Both of them!"

Travis nodded in agreement.

"Yeah, me too. I've got plans for them, both of them."

"You don't look angry about it though. Why don't you ever get mad and fight back? You let them push you around, and you never say a word."

He grinned and shook his head.

"You don't know me very well, or you wouldn't say that. Their time is coming. But you have to wait for the right time and the right place. I learned that in the military. The success of a mission depends on good planning and great timing. If you rush things, then they don't always turn out the way you want."

Adriana blew out a big sigh of exasperation.

"Well, when is the right time and the right place? I think now is always the right time for just about anything."

Travis chuckled.

"You'll know the right moment when it comes, but it usually isn't now. You have to wait for it. Sooner or later, there is a small window of opportunity when you can have three things happen at the same time. You see a weakness, you do something unexpected, and then you take control of the situation. That's the right time."

"You mean like when you hit Junior on the head with the boat anchor?"

He shrugged.

"Well, yeah, something like that."

"I see."

Adriana smiled and took a last sip of water before settling in for the long evening. The food and water made them feel a little better, so they chatted for a while.

"Would you want to run this operation if the old man was out of the way?" she asked. "I think you would be good at it, and you know all the contacts already. The girls seem to like you despite your many flaws."

"What flaws? I'm more or less perfect. It's other people that screw things up."

"Spoken like a true psychopath. But seriously, would you do it?"

Travis glanced around the shed and thought about it.

"I don't think so," he said, "I don't really want to be the boss of anything. There's too much pressure when you have to trust other people. I'm not good at giving orders or trusting anybody. I just like to look out for myself."

"But what if you had good people to help? I could help you handle the girls, and some of the guys are okay. You could trust Omar and Raul, and maybe Jimmy Ray. They would listen to you."

"I don't know. It's still a lot of pressure. I don't mind being the point person on something to make things happen, but I don't like being in charge and making decisions. That takes a different kind of person who really understands other people. Like you said, I'm not usually worried about what other people are thinking or feeling. I can't anticipate that because I don't really sympathize."

Adriana smiled and caressed his arm.

"I think you sympathize more than you know. You're just used to blocking out all that stuff and pretending it doesn't matter. You act like a lone wolf, but deep down inside you're really a teddy bear."

"I'm not a teddy bear! A grizzly bear maybe, but not a teddy bear."

She giggled and moved a little closer. He gazed into her eyes in the fading light. Adriana leaned over and kissed him. His lips were dry and salty with perspiration, but he didn't pull away. She slipped her tongue inside his mouth, and they shared a passionate moment together.

"You see," she whispered, "you do have feelings. You're a teddy bear."

Travis chuckled and rolled his eyes.

"Hey, don't say that out loud, someone else might hear you and get the wrong impression. I have to maintain my tough macho image."

"Teddy bear! Teddy bear!" she shouted. "Travis is a big teddy bear!"

He laughed and pushed her away.

"Hey, I have a better idea," he said, "why don't you be the new boss? I could be your right-hand man to make sure things run smooth. That way you can concentrate on keeping everybody happy, and I can focus on being the iron fist."

Travis made a fist, and then he growled and pounded on the feed bags a couple of times. Adriana raised her eyebrows and thought about it for a minute.

"That's actually not a bad idea," she said, "I could see that working. I have a lot of good ideas, but I would need a lot of cooperation to make them work. The girls would know that I understand what they are feeling, at least I try, and we really have their best interest at heart. You could make things happen and protect all of us from people like Chaco and Juan the Ripper."

They both got quiet for a moment.

"Yeah... Juan the Ripper," said Travis, "now there is one messed up guy."

Adriana thought about her short scuffle with the creepy guy who attacked Keyla last weekend. Something really bothered her about that. That guy was definitely insane, but he was a lot weaker than she expected after seeing the Ripper's last victim, the dead girl in Houston. And what had he whispered in her ear?

"Do you think it was the Ripper who attacked Keyla," she asked, "or was it just some other psycho prowling the streets?"

"Who knows," Travis replied, "I don't think it was the Ripper though. The guy last week was a nut job with a knife, but he wasn't some big, scary serial killer like the Ripper. I think he was only a pervert copycat."

"Hm… maybe so, but he still scared me."

"Yeah, I could tell by the way you jumped right in there and knocked him on his ass. You didn't look very scared to me."

"That was just adrenaline. I didn't stop and think about it first."

"Well, whatever the reason, you probably saved that girl's life. That took a lot of guts whether you meant to or not."

Adriana felt an unexpected chill go down her spine. The temperature was falling rapidly as the sun went down, and now the sweat on her body made her feel cold.

"I'm going to lie down and try to get some sleep," she said, "would you mind if I cuddled with you for a while?"

"Cuddled? No way! Grizzly bears don't cuddle."

She smiled at Travis anyway and lay down on her side facing the other direction. He huffed and hawed for a few minutes, but at last he settled down behind her. She sensed his presence there and scooted back up against him. A few seconds later, Adriana felt Travis's arm curling in around her waist. She smiled and drifted off to sleep.

It seemed like only a minute later when her eyes snapped open wide.

"Don't move," Travis whispered.

Now she knew what woke her up. A long, cold, heavy rope was slithering across her legs. The rope moved in a slow, continuous motion, easing over her ankles. Trying not to move her head, she peered with caution toward her feet.

"There's a snake in here," he whispered. "I'm going to roll away very slowly and find something to kill it. You stay right there and don't move a muscle."

Travis didn't have to say it twice. Adriana had no intention of moving. Her entire body was paralyzed with fear. She couldn't have moved if she had wanted to.

She watched the snake slide all the way across her and pause a few feet away. The snake lifted its triangular head and flicked its tongue in and out as if it was tasting the air or hunting for something. Adriana heard a slight rustle as Travis rolled away behind her and crept in the other direction. A few seconds later, she heard the metallic clink of some gardening tools banging together.

The shed was dark, and it was difficult to see anything clearly. The snake was a quivering, cord-like shape on the floor. Travis was a big shadow hovering along the wall, edging ever closer.

The snake sensed that something was amiss and coiled itself into a circle. Adriana heard the distinctive hiss and shake of the rattler's tail, and her blood turned to ice. Travis stayed motionless in the darkness.

Without thinking, Adriana shifted her foot back an inch. The snake reacted at once. Its head swiveled toward her, and the tongue flicked in and out as it shook the warning rattle again. She saw the snake draw back his head, getting ready to strike. She screamed as the reptile lunged toward her, but then she heard a loud thump as it struck the blade of the shovel instead.

Travis held the shovel between her and the snake as he leaped toward its neck. The rattler twisted around to face his attacker, but Travis was even faster. He flipped the shovel over and slammed the blade down, slicing the snake in two.

The body of the serpent continued to wriggle and squirm, but the head lay flat on the floor gasping for its dying breath. Travis was taking no chances. He lifted the shovel and pounded it on the rattler's head several more times to be sure it was dead. When he was satisfied, Travis picked up the snake's lifeless body and tossed it to the back of the shed.

"Damn it!" he yelled.

Adriana was still quivering in shock.

"That... that was a rattlesnake," she stammered.

"Good observation skills," Travis said with a sarcastic tone, "what clued you in, those diamond-shaped markings on the back?"

"But how did it get in here? Has it been in here the whole time?"

Travis frowned and snarled in anger.

"I don't think so. I thought I heard some footsteps a little while ago. I think that someone brought us a little gift during the night."

"Well, I don't think that I'll be sleeping in here anymore."

"Me neither. I've had enough."

He walked up to the door and kicked it open, splintering the wood frame around the latch and sending it flying into the darkness.

"Let's get out of here, I'm done with this bullshit. It's time to kick some ass and make things happen."

CHAPTER 22

It was not yet dawn when they crept out of the shed and into the adjoining pasture field. There were no guards posted, so Travis and Adriana walked away from the big ranch house and back toward the lake. They moved across the flat, dry dirt and didn't stop until they had almost reached the dormitory building.

"Where are we going?" Adriana whispered.

"I'm not sure," Travis replied, "it won't be long before they realize we're gone and start looking for us."

"Shouldn't we leave here? Can we take one of the trucks and just go?"

Travis thought about it for a minute.

"That's tempting, but it doesn't really solve anything, does it? They'll probably come looking for us at first light."

"But they won't find us," Adriana argued, "we could be long gone by then. The real problem is that all the girls will still be here, and we won't be able to help them get away. Everything would go back to the way it was before."

"I could live with that," he said, "what really bothers me is Chaco and that damn whip. I want to take that thing and shove it down his throat."

"We could come back later for that, maybe with some weapons and some help. Let's wait until we have a plan."

"I don't want to wait. I've got a score to settle."

Adriana blew out a big sigh and rolled her eyes.

"What is it with you and this macho bullshit?"

"Just shut up and follow me."

He led her back along the narrow road to the dormitory building. They paused at the corner and peaked around. There was no one in sight. Travis grabbed her hand, and they crept to the door and eased it open. He wedged a small block of wood in the doorframe to keep it from closing all the way.

"I thought the doors were all locked," she whispered.

"Everything is designed to keep people in, not to keep them out," said Travis. "You can open all the doors from the outside. We just have to be careful not to lock ourselves in someplace."

Adriana nodded, and they continued on through the building. The girls were still sleeping in their bunks, but two of the beds were empty. She tapped on Travis's shoulder and pointed to the empty cots.

"Look, Amanda and Claudia are missing. Do you think they sold them?"

"Maybe. Either that or they are trying to escape."

She frowned, concerned now about the two missing girls. They walked back through the room and into the shower area.

"I want to get cleaned up a little and then find a place to rest for a while," said Travis, "let's take a quick shower first and then go to the storm shelter."

They turned on the faucet and started peeling off their clothes. The water was chilly, but it felt good after spending yesterday in the oppressive heat of the shed. Adriana closed her eyes and let the cool water flow over her head and down her aching body. The gash on her back from Chaco's whip began to sting as the wound cleansed itself. She couldn't imagine the pain that Travis must have been feeling with all the raw flesh on his back and shoulders.

She heard the soft patter of bare feet on the tile floor and peered toward the sound. The four Laredo girls were standing in the doorway and watching them take a shower. Yasmine put one finger on her lips for a second, and then all four of them moved over closer.

"We were worried about you two," said Vera, "we didn't know what happened to you yesterday, and the other guys wouldn't tell us anything. They just laughed when we asked them. Everyone thought you were dead."

"We nearly were," said Adriana, "Chaco locked us in a shed, and then somebody put a rattlesnake in there with us."

"How did you get out?" asked Wanda.

Adriana smiled and nodded toward Travis.

"My knight in shining armor rescued me," she answered.

"I don't know about the shining armor," Ursula remarked, "but I do admire his long sword. Maybe we should thank him for you."

"Go right ahead," said Adriana, "I'm sure he would appreciate it."

Ursula and Wanda took off their clothes and kneeled down in front of Travis. He stood there naked, letting the water splash across his shoulders and stream down his back. Ursula reached out and grabbed his penis, massaging it in her hands. Wanda put her hands down below and began to caress him between the legs.

Travis glanced down, and then he started moaning with pleasure. Ursula inched closer and slid his penis into her mouth. Wanda worked her hands around and continued to massage him. After a minute or so, they switched places, and Ursula massaged his genitals while Wanda sucked on him.

The others watched in fascination for a moment, but they began to get excited as well. Yasmine and Vera took off their clothes and pushed themselves up against Adriana. Vera kissed her hard on the mouth while Yasmine dropped to her knees. Yasmine licked Adriana's wet pussy, letting her tongue roam free around and inside all of the crevices. Vera continued to kiss her, using her tongue as well. She placed her hands on Adriana's breasts, massaging and squeezing them both.

Adriana closed her eyes and felt the heat building inside of her. She imagined that it was Travis kissing her that way, hard and with passion. She felt Yasmine slide three of her fingers up inside of her, thrusting them quickly in and out. The pleasure was surging and spreading all over her body.

She heard Travis groan louder and glanced over at him. Ursula and Wanda were both on their knees in front of him, their mouths open wide. Adriana saw him grimace, and then the muscles of his body all clenched simultaneous as the powerful orgasm came. Streams of milky semen flew from the end of his rigid penis onto the waiting tongues of the two girls. Ursula held him in her fingers and squeezed it dry.

Seeing that triggered something primal deep within Adriana, and she felt the eruption of her own climax only seconds later. Marvelous sensations rippled through her body, making her shiver all over. She leaned her head back and cried out with ecstasy as streams of hot hormonal juices flowed down her legs. Yasmine chuckled, and then she grabbed Adriana's ass with both hands and licked her clean.

Adriana looked at Travis and saw him grinning.

"What? You thought men were the only ones that could have sex for fun?" she said. "Women can do it, too."

Travis held up both hands and shook his head.

"Oh, that's fine with me. It gets me excited to see it."

She let her gaze wander a little further down his body.

"Yeah, I think that's pretty obvious."

Ursula and Wanda were both still on their knees in front of him. It looked as if they were preparing to start working toward a second coming.

"Okay, ladies, I've think you've shown Travis enough appreciation for now," she said. "We need to get out of here and find a place to rest for a while. What happened to Amanda and Claudia? I didn't see them out there."

"Chaco took them away yesterday," said Yasmine, "I think he was taking them to Galveston. That old cowboy guy went with him."

"Aw shit," Adriana exclaimed, "he's going to sell them! We've got to stop this, Travis. We've got to do something."

"It's too late for that now," he mumbled.

"It may be too late those two, but what about the rest of the girls? We have to put a stop to this."

Travis thought about that for a minute. He seemed to have trouble concentrating with Ursula still licking his penis.

"Stop it, Ursula. Let him think. We've got to do something."

She gave Travis one more good lick, and then she sighed and backed away. He splashed some water on his face and frowned at Adriana.

"Okay, let's go to the storm cellar and wait there. If Chaco went to Galveston, then they will be back any minute. We need to rest and come up with a plan."

"Take us with you," Vera pleaded, "please! Don't leave us here!"

Adriana shook her head.

"We can't right now, but we won't leave the ranch without you, I promise. You all wait here and try to get the other girls ready in case something happens. Travis and I will figure out something, but you girls need to be ready to help when the time comes. Keep your eyes open and stay together."

The Laredo girls nodded. They all got dressed again and then moved into the dormitory. The other girls were stirring now and curious to know what was going on. They tried to follow as Travis and Adriana headed for the door. The Laredo girls held them back and huddled with the others to explain the situation.

Travis took Adriana's hand and led her out across the field to the storm shelter. They made their way down the concrete steps and ducked inside the room as daylight was breaking on the horizon. Travis found an oil lamp and lit the flame.

"Let's try to get some sleep," he suggested, "we need to be fresh when we go back outside and face the music. I feel exhausted."

"Not me," said Adriana, "I'm wide awake now. I guess the shower woke me up. There's no way I could go to sleep right now."

"Well, you need to try. At least lay down for a while."

Adriana smiled a wicked smile and began to peel off her clothes. She lay face down on the big table with her arms and legs spread wide apart and her butt in the air.

"Okay," she said, "how about this? I'll just lay here and rest. Would you mind blindfolding me to block out the light? And hand me one of those vibrators, please."

Travis stared at her and shook his head.

"You are unbelievable. When you come over to the dark side, you come all the way, don't you? You're a really bad girl now."

"Oh, you have no idea how bad I can be. I'm just now figuring that out myself. I think you need to punish me a little because I've got all kinds of wicked thoughts running through my head. You need to tie me up and force me to endure the consequences of all those bad things I want to do."

He took some rope and started tying her hands and feet loosely in a spread-eagle position. Then he blindfolded her, and Adriana grinned.

"Now what are you going to do to me? Are you going to punish me?"

"No, I'm going to put a sock in your mouth so I can take a nap."

"What? No! You can't do that! That's not fair!"

Travis chuckled.

"Hey, I'm the one in control here, and I say we need to take a nap."

"Aw, come on! Take advantage of me! I'm waiting…"

She squirmed around on the table and groaned. He hesitated for a moment, and then at last, he gave in.

"Okay, but only for a few minutes. Then we take a nap. Deal?"

"Sure. You probably can't last more than two minutes with me anyway."

"Oh, we'll see about that."

He laughed and crawled up on the table, and then they played for a while. Travis grabbed a paddle and started smacking her on the butt. Adriana pretended to protest, but she wriggled her ass higher begging for more. He took off his shirt and pulled it over her head like a hood.

"Now you're in for it," he said, "you've had this coming for a long time, so just shut up and enjoy it."

Travis squeezed lubricating oil into his hands and between her legs, spreading it in. He found a vibrator and turned it on, inserting it into her vagina and sliding it in and out until she was dripping with wetness. Then he moved it up higher and began to work it in and out of her anus, gradually deeper each time. She moaned with delight.

"I want you," Adriana whispered, "fuck my ass."

He slid the vibrator back down to her pussy and slipped it inside. Then Travis took off his jeans and crawled up on the table behind her. His cock was rock hard with excitement seeing her like this. He put the tip of his penis against her ass and pushed it up inside. Adriana opened herself wide to receive it, and he drove it in to the hilt. She gasped with the sudden pain and pleasure of the new sensation.

Adriana moaned and yielded as Travis pounded her ass faster and faster. The slim vibrator was still deep inside of her, too, causing her entire body to quiver with pleasure. Their passion burned and spread like wildfire. In a matter of seconds, they both exploded with orgasmic ecstasy. They collapsed on the table panting for breath.

She was wrong. He lasted almost eight minutes.

CHAPTER 23

Adriana woke up several hours later sore, sweating, and hungry. Travis had untied her, but there was no comfortable place in the storm shelter for them to sleep. Her back was still burning from the sting of Chaco's whip, and the temperature inside the closed room was escalating as the heat outside rose.

She opened her eyes and saw Travis sitting with his back against the door.

"Good morning," she said, "or is it afternoon now?"

"I think it's afternoon based on the heat and the cramps in my stomach."

"So what do you want to do now? I'm sure they're searching for us."

Travis nodded.

"Yep, no doubt Chaco is furious and looking to stick us back in the shed," he responded, "we are going to have to face him again sooner or later, but I'm not going back in that shed."

"Me neither," Adriana agreed, "you want to try sneaking out of here, or do you want to talk to Mr. Hayes again? I'm with you either way."

He thought about it for a minute.

"Let's try talking to the other guys first. Chaco might back off if he sees that he's not in control. There's no glory in being the big dog if nobody listens to you."

Adriana rearranged her clothes and blew out a big sigh.

"Okay," she said, "I'm ready when you are."

Travis pushed the door open, and they stepped outside. The sun was high in the sky and shining like a fiery torch. She felt the heat radiating off the dry ground as they climbed the stairs and walked out into the pasture.

They didn't have long to wait. As they were crossing the big field, Chaco and the other guys came around the corner of the dormitory building and spotted them. The men all stared at Travis as they ambled up the long dirt road. Travis and Adriana didn't slow down, and soon they were within twenty yards of each other.

"Stop right there!" Chaco commanded. "Where the hell have you been, Miller? We've been looking all over for you. You're supposed to be in the shed."

Travis shrugged and smiled.

"Well, we were lonely and wanted somebody to talk to," he replied. "I'm a real friendly person, and I missed your smiling face. Besides, it was getting a bit crowded in there with all the snakes."

The other men glanced at Chaco but didn't say anything. Chaco turned around to face Travis and Adriana, and the other guys spread out in a loose semicircle behind him. Omar and Raul stood on one side, Dusty and Jimmy Ray on the other. Chaco grabbed his bullwhip and let the end fall heavily on the ground.

"It's a shame that rattler didn't finish the job," said Chaco, "it would have saved me a lot of trouble. Now I'll just have to do this myself."

"Don't bite off more than you can chew," Travis warned him, "I'm done taking orders from ignorant assholes like you. Why don't you put your toys down and face me like a real man, or do you even have the balls to do it?"

Chaco growled in anger.

"You talk tough, Miller, but you're just pussy-whipped and showing off for the new girl. That shit may impress her, but it don't mean squat to me. It's time somebody put you in your place and wiped that stupid grin off your face."

Travis laughed and Chaco scowled even more.

"And you think that you're the man to do that, *cabron*? Just because you can push those little Mexican girls around, you think you're a big man? Let's see you back that up then. Bring it on you big, ugly son-of-a-bitch."

Chaco raised his arm high to crack the whip, but Omar stepped forward and grabbed him by the wrist. The two men glared at each other.

"No whip this time," said Omar. "If you want to punish this man, do it with your fists, *mano-a-mano*. This is going to be a fair fight, or it's not going to happen with me standing here."

Chaco looked around at the other guys. They all nodded in agreement and took a couple of steps back.

"Cowards," Chaco shouted, "you're all a bunch of traitors and cowards! Just wait until I finish with him. I'm going to kick your ass next, every one of you!"

Omar grinned and jerked the bullwhip out of his hand.

"You can start with me," he said, "just as soon as you finish with Travis. I'll be waiting right here, and I'll be looking forward to it."

Dusty put his hand on the grip of his pistol. The other guys all stared at him, and he let his arm dangle back down by his side.

Chaco grunted and moved forward. Travis didn't budge. Adriana had seen fight scenes in the movies that seemed to last for hours, but she knew that real life wasn't like that at all. In real life, things happened fast.

She watched as Travis took a deep breath and prepared himself. He relaxed his shoulders and waited for Chaco to make his move.

Chaco paused for a second, then he rushed at Travis like a raging bull. Travis ducked and shifted to his left, bringing his right fist up hard into Chaco's gut. The big man stopped and wheezed as the air went out of his lungs. With a smooth, arcing motion, Travis brought his left fist up and nailed Chaco with a quick left cross to his temple. Chaco staggered sideways.

"We can stop any time you're ready," Travis offered, "you don't have to prove anything to me. Just shut up and walk away while you still can."

Chaco grunted and glared at him.

"I'm going to kill you with my bare hands!" he yelled.

The big man turned and lunged at Travis with unexpected speed. Both men went down on the ground grappling with each other. The other guys all shuffled closer, but no one made a move to interfere.

Travis worked his left hand free and slapped Chaco hard right on top of his ear. Then he stiffened his fingers and jabbed them like a knife into the big man's throat right below his chin. Chaco began to cough and clutched at his neck. He rolled away to catch his breath again. Travis lost no time in scrambling back to his feet.

"Quit while you can, asshole," said Travis, "you're starting to make me angry. I don't want to kill you, but I will if I have to."

Chaco rolled over and stood up again. He tried to say something, but his raspy voice failed him. Balling up his hands in frustration, he roared and ran at Travis once more. Travis was ready, and he reacted with a well-timed spinning back kick. The heel of his boot connected with the side of the big man's head. Chaco was stunned and fell to his knees.

"Stay down," said Travis, "you're not going to win this fight."

The big man huffed and puffed for a moment. Then he reached down and slid a long hunting knife out of his boot. He snarled and forced his body upright again. Chaco glared at Travis and stumbled toward him.

"I'm going to kill you!" he screamed.

The long blade sliced back and forth through the air, and then he jabbed the tip directly at Travis's stomach. Travis shifted to one side and let the knife pass by. He grabbed Chaco's wrist and rotated his arm. Then he brought his knee up hard right into his elbow and shattered the joint. Chaco bellowed in agony as the knife tumbled to the ground. Travis scooped up the knife and stuck it deep into Chaco's thigh.

"I told you to stay down!" Travis shouted, as he pushed the big man over. "Don't test me again! Next time I will put your ass in the ground permanently!"

Chaco wallowed around in the dirt and screamed in pain. The other guys looked at Travis in astonishment and wondered if they were next. Dusty's hand began creeping toward the pistol again.

"Don't do it," Omar warned him, "it's over now, just let it go."

Travis glanced at Adriana and then at the other guys.

"Asshole had it coming," he said, "at least he can still walk away. Anyone else want to dance with me?"

He scanned the group, but found no takers. Adriana moved over and stood close beside him. Travis put his arm around her.

"No more of this bullshit!" said Travis, "from now on, we treat each other like real human beings and not like animals. Anybody have a problem with that?"

The other four guys all looked at each other and then back toward Travis. Dusty pointed at Chaco.

"What about him?"

"I reckon he needs a doctor," Travis replied, "are you volunteering to take him to the hospital? If not, that's fine with me. We can just leave him out here and let him crawl back to the ranch house whenever he feels up to it."

"I'll take him," said Dusty. He moved over to help Chaco.

"What about Hayes," asked Omar, "what are you going to tell him?"

Travis glanced at Adriana and chuckled.

"I'm going to tell him the truth, like always. Chaco was riding in the back of the pickup truck and fell out. It was an accident. Did anybody else see anything different?"

The other guys all smiled.

"No, that's pretty much what I saw," said Jimmy Ray.

"Me too," Raul agreed, "and he was holding that knife for some reason. I didn't even know he had one."

Omar laughed.

"Well, it looks like you're calling the shots, tough guy," he said, "so what now? Should we all go up to the ranch house and discuss this with the boss?"

Travis considered that for a moment, and then he shook his head.

"No, I think that can wait until tomorrow. Right now, I'm tired, and I'm hungry. Why don't we all go back to the dorm and have some dinner with the girls? Then maybe we can take a shower and relax for a while. That okay with everyone?"

"I don't know about that shower part," said Adriana.

He laughed and started walking.

"Am I missing something?" asked Omar.

"You remember those girls from Laredo," said Travis, "they can be very nice in the shower, wash all of your troubles right down the drain."

"Hmmm, I like the sound of that, and it is Saturday night. I try to shower at least once a week whether I need it or not."

"You guys are so nasty," said Adriana.

"That's just the way you like us," said Travis.

She glanced up ahead and saw the girls peeking around the corner of the building. They were all anxious to know what was going on and what that meant for their future. Adriana wondered the same thing.

CHAPTER 24

Big Bill was not a happy camper. Adriana could tell that by the way he pointed the gun at them. It was really no surprise since they were threatening to tear down the empire he had worked for years to create. She leaned back in the chair and crossed her arms.

"I can understand your resistance to change, Mr. Hayes, but we can't continue to treat those girls like livestock. They're not horses or cows. They are real people with real feelings. If we treat them right, then everyone will be happy and successful. Why is that so difficult for you to believe?"

Hayes slammed the gun down on his big oak desk.

"Because, missy, I have about forty years of experience doing things a different way. My way works, and I've made a lot of money to prove it. I don't need you young, starry-eyed punks telling me how to run my business. I only need you to follow orders and get things done. Did your time in the shed not teach you anything?

Do you want to spend a couple more days in there thinking things through?"

"Look, boss, I know you're upset about the way things have been going lately," Travis interjected, "but we're going to turn this operation around. Whether we like it or not, the world is changing, and what worked in the past may not work in the future. But we can take advantage of that and do even better than before. We're only asking for a little time to get everything set up and running."

"You've had time!" the old man shouted.

Travis shook his head.

"Really, we haven't, boss," he replied, "it's only been a couple of weeks. And I know you're anxious to see some results, but it's going to take a little longer."

"Damn it, Miller, you're asking a lot," said Hayes, "Junior would have already had things going full speed. You haven't accomplished anything so far."

Adriana glanced over at Travis and saw him roll his eyes.

"And now Chaco is out of commission," Hayes added, "I can't believe he fell out of that damn pickup yesterday and hurt himself so bad. He's going to be in the hospital for a while. He may not ever be back to work."

"Is that what the other guys told you?" asked Travis.

Hayes nodded and puffed on his cigar for a minute.

"We're going to miss that surly bastard around here," the old man said, "at least he made us a little money the other night, but not nearly as much as I was hoping."

"Selling those girls is not the way to make money," said Adriana, "when we sell them, then they are gone forever. We've lost them. What we need to do is upgrade them and make them even more attractive. I know how to make these girls beautiful. When they are happy and healthy, these girls will be irresistible. And we can teach them the skills they need to be successful. Travis and I have a plan that will do that, but we need your support to make it happen."

The old man grunted and frowned.

"You're not asking me for support, you're asking me for more money."

"But not that much," Travis argued, "the first thing we want to do is just change the atmosphere around here. Right now, it feels like a prison, and these girls are always miserable enduring one day at a time. This is mid-July, and that building where they live doesn't have air conditioning. It's usually over a hundred degrees inside of there. There is no television, no music, and nothing but crappy food to eat."

"This isn't Disney World, and they're not on vacation. That building is just a holding pen until I can move them on, so why should I make them comfortable?"

"Because we want them to be happy and healthy," Adriana responded, "we're not planning to move them on. After we invest the time and money to make them attractive, we want them to stay with us for a long time. Think about it, Mr. Hayes. When you look at a woman, and she smiles at you, don't you find her more attractive?"

Hayes laughed and slapped his hand on the desk.

"Do you know how long it's been since a woman smiled at me? What a stupid question! And the last woman I had wound up running off with some other guy, so why do I care? I hope they all die and rot in hell!"

Adriana could see that they weren't making much progress. She glanced over at Travis and he shrugged, he was out of ideas.

"Please, Mr. Hayes, give us a chance to change your mind," she persisted. "I don't know what happened in the past, so I can't explain that. But you're still a young and handsome man, and soon you will be even more wealthy. I'm sure there must be dozens of women who would line up for a date with you."

The old man's face turned a little pink, and Adriana could have sworn he was almost blushing at the thought. Maybe she had finally hit a soft spot. He puffed on his cigar for a moment and let the smoke drift lazily up toward the ceiling.

"You really think so?" he asked, "I don't believe any woman would even look at an old dinosaur like me when they could chase after young boys like Miller there."

"You're wrong, Mr. Hayes," Adriana argued. "Women like maturity and stability. They want a man they can respect who can take care of them."

Hayes snorted, "You mean they want a man for his money."

Adriana shook her head.

"No, that's not what I mean at all. Think about what these girls have seen, what a lot of women have seen. They see men that are selfish and greedy and ruthless like those guys in the drug cartels. They see men that are cruel and have no regard for life or family. Guys like Travis are a dime a dozen. Girls know that they can't depend on someone like that to carry them into the future. They don't want some useless, ignorant drifter like him to be the father of their children."

"Thanks a lot," said Travis, he leaned back and crossed his arms.

"Hey, I'm only being honest here," Adriana responded, "the world is a tough place. Women learn quickly that you can't trust anyone. Everyone lies and cheats and uses other people. Women are desperately searching for a man that can protect them, someone reliable and dependable who is worthy of their love. If they can find a man like that, age doesn't matter. Older is actually better because those guys have knowledge and experience. Men like Mr. Hayes are a lot more attractive than younger airheads."

Travis stared at her in shock, not believing his ears. Hayes was smiling.

"I like what you're saying," said the old man, "it makes a lot of sense to me, but how do I know that's true? One minute you're talking about these girls like prostitutes, and the next minute you're talking about wives and children. Which is it?"

"What I'm talking about are the basic rules of attraction and survival, Mr. Hayes. Marriage is really prostitution in a different form. The only difference is that you commit yourself to one customer for the rest of your life. You focus on making him happy, and he does the same for you. What makes it work is when you add mutual respect."

The old man burst out laughing so loud that his voice echoed down the hallway. Even Travis chuckled at the thought.

"So marriage is really long-term prostitution," Travis remarked, "now that's an interesting way to look at it. You certainly have a strange view of the world."

"Only the sexual part of the relationship," Adriana explained, "the other parts are something different, like being a parent, managing the household–all of that other stuff requires different skills. For women, emotional attraction is separate from physical sex. There are a lot of women who marry older men just for their maturity and stability. They are looking for men who are successful in life, not for the money, but because they think of older men as more desirable emotional partners. Men who are confident and secure are going to value a solid relationship with a good woman. A man like that is someone they can trust and have faith in. For a woman, quality in a relationship is all about emotional strength, not passion or physical strength. Sure, the young studs are fun for a while, but for the long run, a girl would rather have the coach than the players."

The room was quiet for a minute as they all pondered this.

"I think you're wrong," Travis argued, "I think a lot of women marry for money. Look at all those groupies that follow athletes and rock stars. They aren't doing it because those guys are mature and stable. They are the biggest players in the world."

"Yeah, but those aren't mature women either," said Adriana, "those are crazy, mixed-up girls who don't have a clue about life. Our girls won't be like that. Our girls know how stupid that is, and what life is really all about."

"Are we talking about the same girls," said Hayes, "that bunch of teenagers in the dorm building? They don't know anything!"

"You might be surprised at what they know and what they've seen," said Adriana. "They have a different perspective on things because of where they come from and what life has been like so far for them. They are wise beyond their years."

The old man stared at her for a moment.

"Maybe I'm missing something here," he said, "what is your point?"

"My point is that most men really do not understand women at all, and you are in a unique position to take advantage of that."

"Explain that to me, but keep it short and simple this time."

Adriana sighed and leaned forward in her chair. She saw Travis lean forward at the same time, watching her.

"Okay," she said, "when you think of a confident, successful, sexually attractive man, what name comes to mind?"

Hayes chuckled and puffed on his cigar.

"Honestly, I never think about men as being attractive. You lost me."

"If you could change places with any man in the world, who would it be? What name goes with success and sexual attraction like nobody else?"

Adriana put her fingers on top of her head and wiggled them.

"Playboy," Travis shouted, "Hugh Hefner and the Playboy bunnies!"

"Exactly," said Adriana, "every man has a fantasy to be like Hefner with a house full of young, beautiful, sexy girls to play with. You, Mr. Hayes, already have exactly the same thing. We can make those girls beautiful and sexy. You will be surrounded by them. Every man in the world will come to you for advice and to get hooked-up with your girls. You are sitting on a gold mine here. We just need to develop it."

The old man grinned and rocked back in his big leather chair. Adriana could tell that Hayes liked the idea. She could see him digesting it, turning it over and over in his mind, fantasizing about girls and sex and money for years to come.

"But this isn't the Playboy Mansion," he said at last, "and it will never be."

"Why not?" asked Adriana. "If you don't want to rent a place in the city, that's fine. We can fix up this place. We can add a giant swimming pool. We can build some really nice rooms for the girls to live in, and we can get sexy lingerie and bikinis for them to walk around in all the time. You can have your own private club right here and charge other men a fee to be members. They will gladly drive for hours to get away from their boring lives and spend time here instead. And they will pay a thousand dollars a night to spend time with one of your girls. You can just sit back and enjoy life while the money comes rolling in."

Hayes smiled and slipped the gun into his desk drawer.

"I got to admit, I like this idea a lot better than trying to run a brothel up in the city. But what about immigration? Won't we have a problem with that? We'll be all in one place and sitting ducks for them to raid us all the time."

"You can hire them," Travis suggested.

"Hire the border patrol guys?"

"No, the girls," Travis clarified, "open a small business here, a bar or restaurant or something, and hire all the girls with a work visa. We can make them look legal. And whatever else they do on the side won't be mentioned."

"I don't know anything about running a bar or a restaurant," said Hayes, "won't we lose money on that?"

"It doesn't matter," said Adriana, "you'll be making so much money on the side business that you can afford to hire a manager to run that for you. But my guess is that your customers will pay any price you ask for food or drinks when they're here, just like they do at a strip club in the city. I bet you'll make a big profit on that stuff, too."

"You've got me convinced," said Travis.

The old man hesitated a minute, then he nodded.

"Okay, let's do this thing. How do we get started?"

Adriana smiled and leaned back in her chair again.

"I think the first step is to improve our employee relations," she said, "I think you ought to spend some time getting to know the girls. They need to see you as their friend, their *patron*, not as the mean guy who keeps them prisoner. We have to break down that image so you can earn their trust. Everything else will be easy after that."

Hayes sighed and puffed on his cigar, excited now about the future.

"And how do we do that?" he asked.

"Let's have a party," Adriana suggested.

CHAPTER 25

They heard the loud roar of the diesel pickup truck as Big Bill pulled up outside of the dormitory. The girls were all gathered inside still finishing their lunch. All of a sudden, the room got quiet, and all conversation stopped. The girls glanced around at each other for a moment, and then all eyes turned toward Adriana.

"What's going on," asked Sofia, "somebody is coming for us?"

Adriana stood up and smiled at the group.

"It's not what you think. Actually, I think you're all going to like this. Travis and I talked to Mr. Hayes for a long time yesterday about the way things are, and I think we convinced him to make some changes. At least, he has a more open mind now. I don't know what kind of changes he is going to approve. We will have to wait and see, but hopefully it will make things better for everyone."

The girls stared at her for a second, and then they all began whispering to each other. Adriana saw a lot of doubt in their eyes and anxious expressions on their faces. After what they had been through so far, it was understandable. The murmurs got louder and lunch was forgotten.

The door swung open wide and Travis strolled into the room followed by Omar and Big Bill Hayes. Travis took his usual position in the center of the room and raised both hands to get everyone's attention. The other men stood on either side of him. He smiled at Adriana, then he nodded to the other girls.

"*Hola* ladies! It's nice to see you all looking fresh and lovely after that delicious meal, but I hope you're not completely full yet. The boss has a great surprise in store for us today, and I know you're going to like it."

The girls glanced at each other wondering where the delicious food was that they had missed. They stared at the slop on their plates and then looked at Travis. Adriana stepped forward and pointed to the old man.

"For those of you who haven't met him yet, this is the boss," she said, "He owns this ranch and all the property that he graciously shares with us. This is the great man who generously provides all of our food and clothes and supplies."

Hayes touched the brim of his cowboy hat with his finger and gave a slight nod, but there was no hint of a smile. The girls glared at him in silence.

"The boss wants to get to know you girls," Adriana added, "he is always so busy running the ranch that he doesn't have much free time. But he has agreed to take a couple of hours off today and throw a little party for you. This is your chance to meet him and let him know how much you appreciate what he is doing for us."

"You mean what he is doing to us," Sofia mumbled.

Everyone heard the comment, but they pretended to ignore it.

"Why don't you all finish cleaning up the dining room and then come outside?" Travis suggested. "We brought some tequila and beer and lots of ice. We can sit around down by the lake and relax for a while. We even have some music, and we bought some bikinis if anyone wants to go for a swim."

Adriana watched the girls' reaction. Some of them appeared to be excited by the news, but most of them still looked skeptical. Bianca and a couple of the others seemed almost angry about it.

"Sure, we can all have a margarita and drink a toast to Amanda and Claudia," she said, her voice filled with bitterness, "if they are still alive."

Travis grabbed Hayes by the arm and pulled him toward the door while Omar focused on herding the other girls together. Adriana moved over to separate Bianca and Sofia from the crowd and talk to them in private.

"Please, girls, don't do this," she urged, "don't say bad things like that in front of Mr. Hayes. We do not want to make him upset with us. He is finally opening up his mind and his heart to treat us in a different way."

Sofia rolled her eyes.

"Bullshit," she said, "that is a cruel man, and he will never change. He brought us all here with lies and promises that he does not honor. We are treated like cows, not like people. He buys and sells us as if we are nothing."

"You have seen what he does," Bianca added. "You are already treated differently because of your lover, but our lives do not matter to him at all."

"That is what we are trying to change," Adriana insisted. "I know that you have all suffered here, and that is a big disappointment. But remember where you came from. Things were no better for you in Mexico. At least we are closer to our dreams now. We have to keep fighting for them."

Bianca snarled with frustration.

"I will fight him all right," said Sofia, "I will claw his lecherous eyes out. Then I will cut off his penis and feed it to him!"

"No! No," said Adriana, "I didn't mean to fight in that way! I mean we should be friendly and win him over with our smiles. Please, at least try to be nice for a little while. He may surprise you. This is our chance to let him see us as friends instead of enemies. Please swallow your anger and think about the future."

"I am thinking about the future," Bianca argued, "I am wondering how long it will be until he sells me to one of his friends."

Sofia nodded.

"Please," Adriana responded, "make an effort to be a better friend so that he will not want to see us go. That is our only chance."

The other two girls sulked for a moment, and then they all went outside to join the crowd down by the lake. Travis and Omar had set up some lawn chairs and were trying to get some music going. Hayes was milling around and staring at all of the girls. Adriana walked over and offered to help.

"What can I do?" she asked.

"How about serving the drinks?" Travis replied, "I'll get the stuff from the truck and bring it over. You can get everything set up on one of those tables. Maybe if we can get some alcohol flowing, then everybody will loosen up a bit."

"Good idea."

The guys carried a couple of large coolers over to one of the wooden tables and dumped bags of ice inside. Adriana stuck the beer in the ice to give it a quick chill.

Then she found some mixer and started pouring up some strong margaritas in the plastic cups. The girls swarmed the tables like hungry ants and gulped down the drinks faster than she could refill them.

"Look what I found!" Travis shouted.

He pulled some huge bags from the back of the pickup and tossed them to Omar. They wrestled them over to the tables and opened them up.

"Swimsuits!" he shouted, "Free for anybody who wants one!"

The girls got even more excited and crowded around. A couple of the girls started digging in the bags while the others pushed and shoved to get closer. They decided to speed up the whole process by dumping the entire contents of the bags onto the tables. Colorful nylon and spandex spilled all over the place, followed by a frenzy of stirring and snatching activity.

Travis grabbed Hayes by the arm, and the two men ducked back into the dining room. A few minutes later, they both emerged wearing baggy swimming trunks. Adriana looked at them and laughed. Travis had a lean, muscular body, but his tan lines distorted the athletic image. Hayes was out of shape. He looked like a small polar bear in a pair of Bermuda shorts.

The men strolled toward the edge of the lake. Without their cowboy boots, both of them walked in a halting, tentative manner like their feet were sore and blistered. The effect was almost comical, and some girls began to point and laugh. Adriana cringed, knowing that would not go over well. She shouted encouragement.

"It will be a lot better when we get a real swimming pool, right Travis?"

Travis grimaced and nodded as he took another painful step.

"Sure, that will be great," he agreed. "Then we can get some sandals or something and walk across the smooth concrete instead of this rough ground. Damn, I had no idea there were this many rocks out here!"

"This is bloody hell," the old man shouted, "I hate this!"

"Just a few more steps," said Adriana, "there is a big patch of grass and sand next to the water. That won't be so hard on your feet."

"We should have parked the truck closer," Hayes remarked.

"I'll move it later," Travis offered.

Adriana kept pushing the drinks, and a few of the girls were starting to show the effects of the alcohol. Most of them had stripped off their clothes and put on one of the bikinis. Some were wearing only the bottom part. Jimmy Ray and Raul had also stopped by to enjoy the show.

Omar cranked the music up louder and started dancing with one of the girls. Most of the others bobbed their heads and swayed their hips to the beat. A few girls waded into the lake holding their plastic cups up high.

Hayes glared at the water for a while, then he overcame his fear. The old man slogged out into the murky shallows as if he was pushing through a deep snow drift. Adriana watched his progress and grinned, and then she noticed that he wasn't holding a big plastic cup. She picked one up and mixed a cold margarita with ice.

"Here, take this," she said to Vera, "take it to Mr. Hayes."

Vera nodded and hurried toward the lake. Sofia was lurking near the edge of the water and intercepted her there. She snatched the cup out of Vera's hand and shoved her away. Sofia smiled and waded into the water, creeping toward the old man. Adriana watched her, fearing the worst.

Sofia moved closer to Hayes without attracting his attention. Hayes was focused on the other girls, paying special attention to the ones without a bikini top. Some of them were laughing and splashing each other. Sofia crept around behind the old man. She paused for a moment, and Adriana saw her mischievous grin. She hesitated for only a moment, and then Sofia lifted up the cup and poured the margarita on top of the old man's head. The ice-cold liquid ran down his back, and Hayes squealed like a pig.

"That should cool you off, *perverso cabron*!" Sofia yelled.

She was still laughing when he spun around and punched her hard in the jaw. The girl went down with a loud grunt, but Hayes wasn't finished. He jerked her back up with one hand and punched her over and over in the face. Blood spewed out of Sofia's nose and streamed down out of her mouth. Then her eyes rolled back in her head as she lost consciousness and dangled limp from the old man's clenched fist.

"Stop! Stop it," Adriana shouted, "it was only a joke! She didn't mean it!"

Travis was already on the move, dashing out into the water to grab Hayes and hold him back. The old man let her go, and Sofia collapsed with a splash. The other girls rushed over to pick her head up and keep her from drowning. Tiny ripples of red water danced in every direction.

"Let her go, boss," Travis yelled as he grabbed the old man's arm, "she was only playing around. She didn't know it was going to make you mad."

"Stupid bitch," Hayes shouted, "they're all a bunch of stupid little whores!"

"She didn't mean anything, Mr. Hayes!" Adriana shouted back.

"This was all your idea!" he replied, pointing at her, "you and Miller. I should have known it would turn out this way. You're both full of shit, and I'm tired of your advice. I'm done with you! I'm done with all of you!"

Everyone froze and watched as the old man stormed out of the water and walked to his truck. He swung open the door and climbed into the driver's seat. Then he started the engine and roared off toward the big ranch house.

CHAPTER 26

Scared and anxious, they all waited through the rest of the day for something bad to happen, but it never did. The girls took Sofia back to her bunk and tried to make her feel a little better, but there wasn't much anyone could do. Both of her eyes had swollen shut, her nose was broken, and a couple of teeth dangled on one side of her mouth. It was a vicious, savage attack that no one had expected.

Adriana used the rest of their medical supplies trying to mend the damage. Travis stayed with the girls while Omar and the other guys cleaned up the party debris and put everything away. All the women huddled inside the dormitory and whispered amongst themselves. The men regrouped later in the afternoon out by the lake, and Adriana went outside to join them.

"What the hell was that all about?" asked Jimmy Ray. "I didn't really see what happened. One minute we were all drinking and having a good time, and then the next minute the boss is beating the shit out of that girl."

"He just snapped," said Omar, "Sofia poured a drink on his head, and that really set him off for some reason."

"He is a cruel and heartless man," Adriana remarked. "We tried to open his eyes and make him see the girls in a different manner, but it didn't work. I thought maybe there was still a spark of humanity deep inside of him, but I guess I was wrong."

"There's nothing human inside of him," said Travis. "The old man never really cared much about anyone but himself. Now that Junior is dead, even that little bit of emotion is gone."

"Oh, there is emotion," said Jimmy Ray, "but not the good kind."

"We've seen this kind of thing before," said Omar, "haven't we, Travis?"

Travis nodded.

"Yeah, he's acting like the drug lords and the cartel guys. Those men act like they hate the whole world. Their soul is black and cold. Any sign of compassion is smothered because they see it as a weakness. They don't care about anybody, not even the women or the children. Those people use everyone and just take whatever they want. They kill for pleasure to show the world how tough and ruthless they can be. That kind of man is not even human. They are only demons that look like men."

The guys all milled around and thought about that for a minute. Raul went inside and came back out with a six-pack of beer that he had stashed someplace. Everyone took a can and popped the top.

"So what are we going to do about this?" Jimmy Ray asked. "I'm not really sure what to do now."

"The real question is: what is the old man going to do?" Travis replied. "Like it or not, we all still work for him. That hasn't changed."

"Maybe it should change," said Adriana, "it's obvious that Hayes is a psychopath. He is clearly not rational anymore. You can't trust a man like that."

"Yeah, but he still owns everything." Travis argued. "This is his property and his business. We can't just take it away. I don't have the money to buy the whole ranch. Hell, I don't even have enough money to buy one of the trucks."

The other guys all nodded in agreement and kicked some dirt around.

"We don't have to buy him out," said Adriana, "but we can't let him continue to run the business and control our lives. There's no telling what he might do."

"We don't have to do what he says," Jimmy Ray pointed out.

"Yeah, but then he might decide not to pay us," said Raul, "he still controls all the money. We don't know where he keeps it, and we sure don't carry any checkbooks or credit cards. How do we buy food or gas without Hayes?"

"Good point," said Travis.

"We should find out where he keeps it," Adriana suggested, "I bet he has a lot of cash hidden somewhere in the ranch house. Or maybe he has a safe. Do any of you guys ever take him to the bank? Do you know if he has a bank account or a safety deposit box somewhere close by?"

The men looked at each other, and they all shook their heads.

"I don't think so," Travis concluded. "Hayes is real old-fashioned, and he doesn't trust anybody, not even the banks. As far as I can remember, he has always run the ranch and the business with cash. He always pays us in cash."

"That would make it a lot easier to hide things," said Adriana. "I bet he doesn't want any paper trail, so he never has to report anything to the government. He probably files just enough information to stay clear with the tax people."

"If the feds ever wanted to take him down, that would be a good way to do it," Travis remarked. "It would be a great excuse for raiding this place. They would have a tough time proving anything, but it would probably keep the old man tied up in court for the rest of his life."

Adriana smiled at the thought. She glanced around.

"Where is Dusty? I haven't seen him since Hayes left."

Omar pointed to a dust cloud coming from the ranch house.

"I bet that's him heading this way in the pickup."

They all turned and watched as the swirls of dust moved closer and closer along the dirt road. A truck was coming slowly toward them. Dusty was at the wheel, and a cluster of men were hanging on the back.

The pickup drove around the corner of the dormitory building and parked right in front of the door. Four armed men jumped out of the back. Dusty swung the driver's door open and stepped out. He glared at Travis and grinned.

"Well, ain't this a cozy little group," he said. "I see you guys are all taking a break from your little party. The boss was wondering how things were holding up after he left. Looks like things kinda broke up since."

Travis and Omar stepped up to face Dusty. Adriana hung back next to the tables with Raul and Jimmy Ray. The four guys from the pickup truck formed themselves into a line behind their new leader. Travis smiled.

"You been up at the big house kissing ass all day, Dusty? I know you're real good at that. You suck his dick, too?"

Dusty's face got beet red in a heartbeat.

"Shut up, Miller! I'm tired of your shit! You think that you're so tough, you and Omar... hard ass soldier boys. But you don't know nothing! Your time is coming, you can bet your sorry ass on that."

"Why are you here, Dusty," asked Omar, "and who are those guys?"

"They're your replacements," he answered, "they follow orders, and they'll do whatever I say. The boss told them that I'm in charge now. They aren't going to listen to you or Travis or anybody else but me."

"I don't think you can handle all that responsibility," Travis responded, "that might require too much thinking, and you're not very good at that."

Dusty pulled a pistol from the holster on his belt. He glanced over his shoulder and shouted orders to the men behind him.

"Okay, boys, we got a job to do. Take these varmints inside and keep an eye on them for a minute. One of you, grab that gear out of the truck. Let's move."

He waved the pistol toward Adriana and Travis.

"You all get inside, now! And don't try anything!"

Adriana walked into the building, and the other guys followed. One of Dusty's men held a gun on them and motioned them into a corner of the dining room. The other new guys followed Dusty into the girls' barracks carrying some rope and handcuffs. Adriana heard the girls screaming and yelling at them.

"Tie them all up," Dusty commanded, "use the ropes and tie them to their bed, any position you like! I don't care. If any of them resist, smack them around a little until they do what you want. Do it!"

She could not see the girls from where they were, but Adriana could imagine the struggle happening in the bunk room. Shouts and screams echoed through the building as Dusty's men went about their work. She saw the tension and frustration in the faces of Travis and the other guys huddled there with her.

It seemed to take a long time, but Dusty and his men walked back into the dining room. Dusty had a smug expression, but the other men looked worn out by the struggle with the girls.

"How will they go to the bathroom?" Adriana asked.

Dusty hesitated for a minute, then he went to the corner of the dining room and picked up a stack of plastic cups.

"Set one of these next to their beds," he ordered his men, "we wouldn't want to have any accidents during the night."

Travis had both of his hands balled tight into fists. Adriana braced herself for some kind of sudden move. She could see the other guys watching him, too. But Dusty stood too far away, and he kept the pistol leveled at Travis.

"Don't even think about it, Miller," he warned, "I've been dreaming of the day when I put a bullet in your brain. I would love to have an excuse right now."

The air crackled with tension as the room filled with a pregnant silence. Travis clenched his jaws, but then he relaxed his hands.

"You put that gun down, or I'll make you eat it," said Travis, "but I know you won't do that because you're nothing but a chicken-livered piece of shit who can't think for himself. I feel sorry for people like you."

Dusty's face turned deep red as he simmered with anger. His finger tightened on the trigger, but then he backed off.

"Put the handcuffs on them," he ordered, "hook them up to the tables or whatever you can find in here. Make sure they're not going anywhere."

Adriana and the other guys were dragged around the room and cuffed to the heavy dining room tables.

"Hey, what about my plastic cup?" asked Omar.

Travis laughed. Dusty nodded to his men, and one of them went around the room putting a plastic cup next to each of them.

"Are you happy now?" Dusty smirked.

"Why don't you come over here and hold it for me," Omar suggested.

Dusty chewed on his lip for a moment and then stomped toward the front door. He pointed at his men.

"I want two of you on guard duty at all times," he ordered, "work in two teams on four-hour shifts. Keep this door locked and make sure they don't get out. Nobody goes through that door until I get back. Got it?"

The four new guys followed him out the front door, and they slammed it shut. Adriana heard them do something outside to block the door and then fading footsteps as they all walked away. She sat down on the floor and closed her eyes, expecting another long and miserable night ahead.

A few minutes later, Adriana heard the soft patter of bare feet and glanced up to see Wanda and Yasmine staring at her.

"What are you girls doing walking around? I thought they tied you up."

Yasmine held up a small pocket knife and grinned.

"Girls from my *barrio* carry a knife."

"Where?" asked Travis.

"You don't want to know," Yasmine replied.

"But that doesn't help us," said Adriana. "We're in handcuffs."

It was Wanda's turn to grin and hold something up.

"Women in my profession carry handcuff keys," she said. "You never know when a customer might forget what no really means."

"I love women in your profession," said Jimmy Ray.

"Then I will unlock you first," said Wanda.

The girls went around the room and unlocked everyone's handcuffs. Adriana and the boys went into the bunk room and found the other girls all sitting on their beds and whispering to each other.

"What now?" she asked Travis.

"Now we wait for our chance to get out of here. We have to be ready whenever it comes, so I guess we should get some rest."

"Do you want some more beer?" asked Raul. "I know where we stashed all of the things from the party. It's in the cabinets with the kitchen stuff."

"Even the tequila?" asked Yasmine.

Raul smiled and nodded.

"Then let's continue the party," said Adriana, "but in a calm way. We don't want the guys outside to get too curious."

"Maybe we could all take a shower," said Travis, "I'm feeling a little dirty."

Adriana sighed and rolled her eyes.

CHAPTER 27

They heard the trucks arriving just after dawn, more than one this time. The girls stopped talking and listened to the sounds of oversized tires skidding in the dirt and steel doors slamming. There was a lot of commotion outside, men jumping down from the truck bed and running around shouting to each other. Adriana looked at Travis and the other guys. They were all tensed and ready for a confrontation.

"Get all the girls in their bunks," said Travis. "I don't know what is coming, but maybe we can keep them out of it. Hurry!"

Adriana scurried around the dormitory room making sure they all got sorted out again. They didn't attempt to put the ropes back or pretend to be tied up. It would have been a useless exercise anyway.

The men moved back into the dining room area and regrouped just inside the front door. Adriana stood in the back of the room close to the dorm entrance. They all waited anxiously and listened to the noise outside. She heard the unmistakable voice of Big Bill Hayes yelling commands, and shivers went down her spine.

All of a sudden, the front door swung open and Hayes stomped into the dining room with Dusty right on his heels. This time, there were eight new guys including the four from yesterday. Travis stepped forward to meet them.

"Good morning, boss, did you come to have breakfast with us?"

The old man hesitated, thrown off balance by Travis's good-natured sarcasm, but he soon recovered his scowl.

"I don't think so, Miller," he replied, "I'm bringing in a new team to replace you ungrateful bastards. They're here to do things my way. We don't need you anymore."

Travis grinned.

"Are we getting a nice severance package? I could sure use a vacation."

"You're lucky I don't sever your goddamn head," Hayes shouted, "I've treated you like family for years, and look at how you repay me! You bring in a bunch of new whores and try to ruin my business. Well, I've had enough of your shit! I'm going to show you who's boss, and then I'm going to kick your sorry ass out of here."

He pulled a revolver out and pointed it in the general direction of Travis's gut. Travis and the other guys moved back a step.

"Dusty," the old man barked, "get your boys in here and round everybody up. I want you to take them all up to the corral, right now!"

The newer guys were also carrying guns, and they waved them around. They rushed into the building and began herding everyone outside. Travis and the guys were huddled in one place while Adriana and the girls were pushed together in a small cluster a few feet away. Some girls were reluctant to obey orders from the new men, so Dusty slapped them around a little to make them more compliant.

Adriana watched it all and fumed with anger. She glanced at Travis and saw him keeping score as well. His eyes were like flint, and she could tell he was calculating the odds and waiting for a chance to make his move. Omar and Jimmy Ray were lingering close to Travis and looked like they were itching for a brawl as well.

"What about that breakfast, boss?" Travis yelled. "Can we all grab a quick bite before we go? It might be a long day."

Hayes glared at him and started to say something. Then he changed his mind and got into the pickup. The motor cranked up, and the truck roared away.

Travis turned to the other guys.

"Sorry, no bacon and eggs today, boys. It looks like we may lose a few pounds before this is all over."

"No problem," said Omar, "I wasn't hungry anyway."

"Me neither," Jimmy Ray echoed, "I need to lose some weight."

Raul chuckled and patted his stomach, nodding in agreement.

"Quit your yakking, dickheads," said Dusty. "Okay, everyone start walking. I want you all into the corral, let's go!"

The new men took positions behind them, and Dusty led the way toward the old corral. Travis and his guys followed Dusty. Adriana lagged a few feet back and led the girls in a ragged group. They all began walking up the long dirt road toward the ranch house.

The old barn sat over on the left side of the ranch house with a big corral adjacent to it. The corral had been used in the past as a holding pen for horses and cattle. It was a large, oblong enclosure covering hard-packed ground with no grass or trees. The border was marked by a thick split-rail fence made of rough wood.

The girls sulked and dragged their feet, easing closer to the edges of the road as they went. The new guys shouted and shoved, trying to keep them all moving. Adriana smiled and did nothing to hurry them along. Travis and his guys strolled casually ahead of her with no sense of urgency.

Dusty turned around every minute or so to yell and grumble, but it had no effect on their speed or motivation. The group flowed steadily toward the old corral with the velocity of an arctic glacier.

It took the better part of an hour for them to reach the barn. Dusty unlatched the gate of the big corral and swung it open. He and his men pushed everyone inside. Hayes ambled out of the ranch house and walked over to the fence.

"Strip them all down," the old man commanded, "I want to see nothing but bare skin! Toss all of their clothes outside the pen. Get some rope and tie Miller and his boys to the fence with their arms wide apart. I want them all to enjoy the hot Texas sun today. This is going to be a glorious day!"

Hayes laughed and strolled back toward the ranch house. Dusty and his men went to work. A few minutes later, they had Travis and his guys strapped to the fence. The girls all crowded into the middle of the corral, naked and afraid. Adriana sat with them and waited to see what came next. They huddled on the ground close together leaving only enough room for a little breeze to cool them if any came along.

Dusty and his men finished up their work and then moved outside of the corral. They didn't seem to know what else to do, so they left two guards posted and went away. Even those two got bored after a while, and they left in search of a cooler spot.

The rest of the day was like a living hell. The temperature soared over a hundred degrees, baking the dry earth beneath it. The sun shone bright and hot in a clear, blue sky. Adriana hung her head and closed her eyes, just trying to endure each minute. The sweat poured from her body and in an instant evaporated in the sweltering heat.

Hours passed. No one came to check on them. The girls began to whisper among themselves, and Adriana knew what they were thinking. She could see it in their eyes. Travis and his guys appeared to have missed their chance. Everyone was growing more and more desperate by the minute.

Twilight came at last, and the two guards returned. Dusty arrived a few minutes later with the other men. They opened the gate and prodded the girls to their feet. Some of the weaker ones leaned on the other girls for help. When everybody was ready, Dusty motioned them toward the gate.

Adriana glanced back over her shoulder as they filed out of the corral.

"What about Travis and the other guys?" she croaked.

"The boss said to leave them here," Dusty replied.

"You can't do that! They need water! They'll die if you leave them out here all night. Please, these are your friends!"

Dusty shook his head.

"They're not my friends. They used to work here, that's all. It's up to the boss now. I'm only following orders."

"Please! Don't leave them here like that! At least untie them!"

"I can't do that," said Dusty. "Boss said to leave them. Now move!"

He waved his gun around some more. Adriana was hesitant, but she followed the other girls out of the corral. They bunched together outside the gate, and Dusty's men pushed them back toward the lake. The group moved out into the dirt road and began the long trek to the dormitory building.

The girls were all weak and dehydrated. The road seemed to be a mile longer now than it was this morning. Adriana walked behind the others, helping the smaller ones who struggled. They shuffled and staggered at a snail's pace just trying to put one foot in front of the other. Progress was slow. Several of the girls had to stop and rest for a moment or vomit on the side of the road from heat exhaustion and nausea.

Two of Dusty's men stayed behind to guard the guys in the corral, and two others peeled off and went to the ranch house. Dusty walked with the group about halfway, and then he also left and headed toward the house. The remaining four new men herded the group back toward the distant dormitory.

It was an arduous journey, but Adriana felt better than she had all day. At least now they were moving, and the blazing sun had dipped below the horizon. A cool breeze kicked up, and the night air was invigorating. She noticed that a couple of the other girls were perking up as well. As they neared the building, she saw them starting to whisper back and forth to each other.

Yasmine glanced over her shoulder and dropped back to walk next to Adriana.

"We've got to do something," she whispered, "some of these girls can't take it anymore. They're going to make a run for it."

"Not yet," Adriana responded, "we need to recover from this first. If we all take off running now, they will catch us or kill us. The weaker ones won't make it. Tell all the other girls to be patient for a little while longer. Wait until we get back to the dormitory. We can get some water and figure out what we're going to do."

"Have you got a plan?"

"I'll come up with something."

Yasmine nodded and began to move around the group, whispering to the others. Several of them stared at Adriana, and she felt the pressure of their unspoken fears. She would have to step up now and earn their trust again. The responsibility fell squarely on her shoulders to lead them as best she could. Adriana just hoped that somehow she could find the courage and ability to deserve their trust.

As they neared the end of the road and the end of their journey, Adriana saw the dark ripples of the lake and felt relief. Their clothes were stacked there in a pile outside the front door. Dusty's men fanned out into a ragged semicircle.

"Get your clothes and then get inside!" one of the men shouted.

The girls were quick to comply, snatching up their garments and carrying them into the building. The guards stood close by leering and making lewd comments as they all passed through the door. Several of the girls glared at them but didn't respond.

Adriana was the last to pick up her clothes. She made a show of getting dressed slow and provocative, smoothing down the wrinkles. Her flimsy panties were bunched in her hand as she sauntered toward the building.

"Good night, boys," she said in a sultry voice, "we're all going to take a shower now. Maybe you can come in and check on us one more time after we all get clean. We want to go to sleep feeling safe and secure tonight."

Adriana paused in the open doorway and blew them all a kiss as she dropped her panties across the threshold. She went inside, and the door slammed closed. But with her underwear wedged underneath, the latch did not click shut.

She waited for a minute and listened. The guards all laughed and made crude comments to each other, but none of them came over to check the door. She heard the sound of footsteps moving away, then the faint murmur of conversation fading into the distance. Adriana smiled. It was time to make a plan.

CHAPTER 28

Adriana walked through the dining room area and back into the bunk room. Some girls were still taking a shower, but most were resting on their cots. They all perked up and stopped talking when she entered the room. Adriana went over and sat down on the bed next to Yasmine. The others gathered around them.

"So what is the plan?" asked Yasmine. "We're all fed up with this. We have to get out of here, and we have to go tonight. The old man has clearly lost his fucking mind. We can't stay here anymore."

The rest of the girls all nodded in agreement.

"I hear you," Adriana said, trying to be as calm as possible, "but we need to be smart about this. We have to be very careful. We may only get one chance."

"One chance is all we need," said Wanda, "the new guys don't know anything. We can get past them and run for the fence."

"There is more than one fence," said Adriana, "they have guns and four-wheelers and horses. They may even have dogs. We don't really know what we're up against."

"I don't care," said Bianca, "we've got to try it anyway. We should go right now while it's dark. At least some of us might make it."

"That's not good enough for me," Adriana argued, "I don't want to leave anyone behind. Look around. Some of these girls are too weak to run. Look at Sofia and Laura and some younger ones. They won't get far. They will get killed or captured and brought back here to suffer even more. Can the rest of you live with that?"

"I can," Bianca exclaimed, "I don't care what happens to the weaker ones! I say it's every woman for herself."

"And what about the men," asked Adriana, "are you going to leave them there in the corral tied to the rails? The old man will kill them all for sure. We have to find some way to cut them loose. They can help us escape. We need them to go with us."

"I don't need any man to help me," Bianca responded, "they already had their chance, and they did nothing. I say we just go and leave them here."

Adriana looked around at the other girls.

"What about the rest of you? How many of you want to leave Travis and the other guys tied up? Raise your hand if you want to abandon them."

No one raised their hand.

"What do you suggest then?" Yasmine asked. "You know more about this place than any of us. Do we even have a chance?"

The girls stared at Adriana, waiting for an answer. She smiled.

"Of course we do. We use what we have to take advantage of their weakness, just like we would on the streets. Men are always men, no matter what the situation. Except for animals like Chaco, and maybe Dusty, they would rather look at us than shoot us. We can use that. We can catch their eye and distract them. And while they are watching our tits or our ass, we can take their weapons away. We can kill them if we have to. That is our best chance to make this work."

The group fell silent, and the girls all glanced at each other. One by one, each of them nodded in agreement. Even Bianca nodded as well.

"Good," said Adriana. She looked at Yasmine, "gather up any knives or weapons that we can find and give them to the strongest girls. Then, we should all lie down for a couple of hours and get some rest. We're going to need it."

Yasmine and Bianca got busy while the other girls finished up their showers and laid down to rest. But everyone was too nervous to sleep. After two hours of tossing and turning, they all started whispering again.

"Okay," said Adriana, "I guess it's time to get things started. Is everyone ready?"

"As ready as we'll ever be," Yasmine replied.

They all nodded in agreement.

"Good. Let's take this one step at a time. Who has the best tits?"

The girls looked at each other's chest for a minute.

"I think it's Helen," Vera suggested, "or maybe Teresa."

"Okay," said Adriana, "Helen and Teresa both come with me. We'll go up to the front door, and you girls take off your shirts to get the guards' attention. We'll try to draw them both inside. I assume only two of them are out there, but we don't know for sure until we open the door. Who has a really cute ass?"

All the girls glanced over their shoulders and tried to estimate the relative appeal of their backside. Four of them raised their hands.

"Okay," Adriana continued, "I want you girls to take off all your clothes and get into the shower room. Start the water running. Get wet and soapy, then turn your back to the doorway. Laugh and giggle a lot when the guards come in. You're the bait. We want to lure them into the shower room. Drop the soap or whatever you have to do. Yasmine and Wanda, you two get on each side of the shower entrance out of sight. Grab a knife and be ready when the guards get close. The rest of you just be ready to jump in when the time comes. Everyone clear on the plan?"

"Give me a knife," said Bianca, "I want to be part of this."

"Me too," Sofia mumbled through swollen lips.

The other girls stared at them in awe as they both picked up a blade.

"Okay, let's move," Adriana ordered.

Wary, she got up off the cot and walked through the dining room to the front door of the building. Helen and Teresa followed on her heels. Her panties were still wedged in the crevice below the door, so Adriana pushed it open a few inches. As she expected, two of Dusty's men were standing about twenty feet away. Neither of them were paying much attention. One of the men was smoking a cigarette and staring across the lake.

Adriana stepped out and held the door open.

"Hey boys, you want to come inside and play with us for a while?"

The men were surprised, but soon recovered. They reached for their guns, but then they stopped when Helen and Teresa peeled off their shirts. Both of them grinned and walked toward the door.

"Well hello, ladies," one of them said, "you're looking mighty fine tonight. Did you get all clean and rested up?"

"Easy there, Vince. We're not supposed to talk to them," the other man warned.

Adriana smiled.

"Now do we look dangerous to you? Look how friendly we are. Why don't you both come in for a while and spend some time with us? We're all very lonely. We really appreciate the company of a good man. Come on in."

She let the front door ease halfway closed again as she motioned for the girls to go inside. Helen and Teresa rubbed their hands across their chest and then stepped back into the dining room. Adriana lingered at the doorway, holding it open a tiny crack.

Dusty's men hustled over to the door and rushed inside just in time to see Teresa and Helen walking across the room. They both glanced back at the men with a flirtatious grin, and then they strutted out of sight into the bunk room.

"Hurry boys, you can still catch them," Adriana urged, "and I think I hear some of the other girls taking a shower. You might want to check on them, too."

The two men dashed through the dining room and were running by the time they got to the bunk room. Adriana hurried along behind to keep an eye on them. She paused and watched them creeping down through the row of beds. Helen and Teresa continued to play their parts, winking and smiling as they strolled back toward the showers. Dusty's men followed them like puppy dogs chasing a ball.

The girls in the shower began to giggle and kick a bar of soap around on the floor. They took turns bending over and trying to pick it up. The men were attracted to the fresh eye candy and ambled over to take a closer look. The naked girls in the shower smiled at them and crooked their fingers, beckoning the men to come inside. They both took one cautious step through the doorway, and then all hell broke loose.

Adriana watched from across the room as Yasmine and Bianca leaped on the two men from each side of the door. Blades flashed in the glistening water, and blood poured onto the cement floor in bright red streams. Five seconds of screaming and slashing was all it took. The two men lay dead on the slick shower floor. The other girls quickly turned off the water.

Vera took the guns from the dead men and handed them to Adriana.

"What now?" she asked.

"Now we go hunting," Adriana answered, "we're going to kill them all."

They left the bodies right where they fell, and everyone put on their clothes. Now they had two guns as well as their knives. Adriana carried one of them and gave the other gun to Sofia. She wasn't sure if Sofia knew how to use a gun, but she was certain of her willingness to do it.

The girls were quick and quiet as they exited the building, watching for signs of the other guards. They split into two groups and then began creeping up the long dirt road toward the ranch house. About halfway to the house, Adriana spotted two more of the men coming their way. They didn't seem to be in any hurry, so maybe they were coming to relieve the two dead guys and didn't suspect that anything was wrong.

Adriana motioned her group a little further off the road and signaled for those on the other side to do the same. The two guards were busy chatting with each other as they walked. They seemed surprised when they looked up and found themselves in between the two clusters of women.

"Hey! You're not supposed to be out here!" one of them shouted.

The two men separated, and each ran over to the side of the road to gather up the girls. Several of the girls were quick thinkers and pulled up their shirts. The men were distracted from their task. Blades flashed in the moonlight, and both of the men went down in seconds.

"Nice work!" said Adriana. "Let's go!"

Both groups continued on toward the ranch house, but at a faster pace now. They were excited and encouraged by their success. They moved on down the road and were nearing the house when Adriana motioned for them all to stop. She could see Travis and his guys still tied up at the corral with two guards standing nearby.

"Vera, go tell Sofia and the other group to wait here while we cut the guys loose. We should only be a few minutes. Tell them if something goes wrong, they should move into the ranch house and do their best to get control of it. They will be safer in there than out here in the field."

"Okay!"

Vera dashed across the road and crouched next to Sofia in the darkness. Adriana nodded to Yasmine and the others in her group. They crept forward without a sound. The two guards at the corral were both sitting against a fence post dozing. Wanda separated from the group and moved around the outside of the corral, cutting the ropes that tied the guys to the fence. She was working on the last one when the guards heard the noise and opened their eyes. They reached for their guns.

"Don't move," Adriana commanded, pointing a pistol at them, "stand up slowly and turn around. Keep your hands away from your belt."

The two men hesitated but got to their feet. They turned around to see Travis and the other guys staggering across the corral toward them.

Adriana glanced at Yasmine.

"Get some of that rope and tie them up."

"Not good enough," Yasmine responded. She pounced like a jungle cat, slashing their throats and shoving them both to the ground. The girls watched them bleed out in the dirt like slaughtered animals.

Travis and the boys stumbled out of the corral and rushed over to help, but their help wasn't needed. He looked at Adriana and smiled, pain still showing in the parched, gritty wrinkles around his eyes.

"Hey, beautiful, did you miss me?"

She stared at him and couldn't help but laugh. His haggard appearance reminded her of a walking scarecrow except without the plaid shirt.

"Not really," she replied, "but we were running out of things to do, so we came by to see what you guys were up to. A few of the girls were a little worried about Omar. I thought we might go inside and talk to the old man for a while. You want to come?"

"I thought you would never ask."

They turned toward the ranch house, and that's when they heard the gunshots.

CHAPTER 29

Travis stopped and looked at Adriana.

"Are the rest of the girls near the ranch house?"

"They were supposed to wait for us, but you know how Sofia is. It sounds like she decided to move forward without us."

"Is she armed?"

"Yes."

"Shit! We've got to get over there and see what's going on."

Yasmine grabbed the guns from the dead guards and handed them to Travis. He gave one to Omar and kept the other for himself. He glanced at Adriana.

"You girls wait here while we check it out."

"Hell with that," she replied, "we're all coming with you."

Travis and Omar raced toward the ranch house with Jimmy Ray and Raul right on their heels. Adriana and the girls followed a short distance behind them. They ran around the corner and saw some other girls crouching on the ground outside.

"Where are they?" Travis shouted.

The girls all pointed at one of the side doors. One of Dusty's men was lying dead only a few feet away.

"Sofia shot the guards and went inside," said Vera, "a couple of the others went with her, but we waited out here."

"Is anybody hurt?" asked Adriana, scanning the group.

They all shook their heads. They heard another gunshot.

"I'm going in," said Travis, "you stay here and take care of them."

"Bullshit," Adriana responded, "I go where you go."

Travis blew out a big sigh of anger and frustration.

"Okay, Jimmy Ray and Raul, you guys stay with the girls. Omar, you're with me. We don't know what's behind that door, so stay low and move fast. If we aren't back in fifteen minutes, you guys find a truck and get the girls out of here. Ready?"

He glanced around at all the nervous faces and then bolted for the door. Adriana and Omar were right behind him. Travis yanked the door open and rolled inside. Omar covered him for a moment and then ducked into the hallway. Adriana got down on the floor and crawled in after them.

She saw the outline of a man propped against the wall for a brief second before Travis put a bullet in his head. It was another of Dusty's men. Omar ran on past him and into the next room. Travis caught up, and they both paused to assess the situation. There was no sign of anyone else. Adriana moved up closer to Travis.

"Dusty? Hayes? Where are you?" he yelled.

"I'm in here," a faint voice answered.

"Where is here?" shouted Omar.

"I'm barricaded in the kitchen. Don't try to come in here, or I'll shoot."

"Come on, Dusty," said Travis, "you know us. We're old friends. Throw out your gun and come on out here. We're not going to hurt you."

"Don't let that crazy girl shoot me either," he replied.

"She's not here anymore," said Travis, "it's only me and Omar. We need you to help us find the old man before she does. Come on out."

"You promise that you won't kill me?"

"I promise."

There was a lot of banging noise like furniture moving, and then the door on the far side of the room creaked open. Dusty tossed out his gun and stepped through the doorway with his hands up.

"Don't shoot," he reminded them.

Travis glared at him and cocked his head.

"You know, Dusty, I sometimes have been known to lie a little."

He raised his gun and shot Dusty twice in the chest. Adriana looked at Travis in shock for a moment, then she dashed over and picked up Dusty's gun.

"Desperate times," Travis said with a shrug.

Omar was already moving down the other hallway. Travis and Adriana walked a few steps back. The end of the hallway was bathed in darkness, and all the doors were closed. They paused for a moment. Adriana heard the distant sound of a girl crying, then a man screamed. The three of them ran in that direction. They found the old man's bedroom door shut and locked.

"Sofia? Sofia is that you?" Adriana shouted. "Are you all right?"

For a few seconds, no one responded. Then Sofia spoke up.

"I'm okay now," she said, "I was shot, but now I'm okay."

Adriana looked at the guys and motioned for them to be patient.

"What was all that screaming about? Is Mr. Hayes all right?"

Sofia laughed a maniacal laugh.

"Mr. Hayes is fine. I have him tied to the bed. He's not going anywhere."

"Was that him screaming or you?"

"I think that was him," Sofia replied, "I cut off one of his ears."

Adriana's eyes grew wide, and she glanced at the guys. They were getting anxious to make a move. She shook her head at them.

"Sofia, honey, we need to get you to a doctor. Is it okay if we open the door and come in there with you? I need to bandage up your wounds."

"Don't come in here," she warned, "I still have my gun! I just need to spend some more quality time with my lover. I'm going to rearrange his face a little, and then I'm going to make him into a woman so that he understands how I feel about things. It won't take me very long."

They heard the old man start screaming again. Travis glanced at Adriana.

"Sofia has lost her mind," he whispered, "we've got to stop her. She will sit on that bed and torture him until they both bleed to death."

Adriana thought about it and nodded in agreement.

"You're right, but take it slow. If she panics, she might kill all of us."

Travis grunted in frustration. He pointed at Omar.

"Do a quick walk-through and make sure no one else is in the house. Then go back outside and tell the others what is going on. Take them all into a big room some place and secure the house for the night."

Omar nodded and scurried off. Adriana moved closer to the door.

"Sofia? Can I come in there with you? I'm worried about you, sweetheart."

The girl laughed again, and Adriana felt cold chills go up her spine.

"You won't have to worry much longer. My lover and me are going away soon to someplace special. No one will ever have to worry about us again."

They heard the old man scream again, and this time he didn't stop. His unearthly wails echoed off the walls and soared into the night sky like a demon from the depths of hell. Travis shoved Adriana aside and kicked in the bedroom door. They both rushed into the room, and then they froze in horror.

The old man was tied to a wooden four-poster bed in a spread-eagle position. He was covered in blood. Even in the dim light, Adriana could see streaks of red sprayed on the walls, puddled on the sheets, and dripping off the mattress. Whatever clothing he had been wearing was ripped to shreds.

"Sofia, sweetie, please put the knife down now," she said, "I think Mr. Hayes has learned his lesson. We need to think about getting you to a doctor."

The girl stared at Adriana with glassy, bloodshot eyes. She was sitting in between the old man's legs with a knife in one hand. Her other hand was holding a large chunk of bloody flesh that had once been attached to the man's body. Sofia leaned forward and tried to stuff it into his mouth.

"Come on, honey," Adriana said, "I think you've done enough. Hayes is already dead, so you can't punish him anymore. Please drop the knife and let me take a look at your wounds."

She eased a few steps closer to the bed, and Travis moved around behind her. Sofia closed her eyes and cried, her chest heaving with each breath. Adriana noticed two dark stains on the front and back of her shirt that were growing.

"Hand me the knife, Sofia."

Adriana stretched out her hand and moved to the side of the bed. Sofia turned to look at her. She reached out with both arms like a baby wanting a hug.

Travis shouldered Adriana out of the way and grabbed Sofia as she fell. He took her in his arms, and she clung to him like a child. The bloody knife clattered to the floor as she wrapped both of her arms around his neck. The back of Sofia's shirt was wet and sticky around two large, gaping holes. He pulled Sofia off the bed and picked her up in his arms.

"Tell the other girls that I'm taking her to the hospital," Travis whispered.

"But she'll never make it," Adriana argued, "she's lost too much blood. Let me patch her up first."

"Don't waste your time. I'll take her someplace while you get the others settled down here for the night. I should be back before daybreak."

"Someone needs to stay with her at the hospital."

"I'm not taking her to the hospital."

"But you said–"

"I said tell the other girls that I'm taking her to the hospital, but she isn't going to the hospital, and she isn't coming back. Nobody needs to know the truth. Don't tell them what we saw. Close the door to this room and don't let anyone in here. You and I are the only ones who will know what really happened. I'll be back soon and help you clean up. Sofia is gone. Hayes is gone. It will be better for everyone, trust me."

An awkward moment of heavy silence hung in the air between them. Adriana was still not ready to accept it. She shook her head in denial.

"Look at the old man's body," said Travis, "she shredded his face. She must have stabbed him about a hundred times. This girl is insane. Sofia is a danger to us all. I can't even feel her heartbeat anymore. Let me put her out of her misery."

The emotional pain was tearing her apart, but Adriana knew that Travis was right. Letting Sofia die would be the merciful thing to do. Even if she lived, she may never be sane or rational again. And they had no idea what she might say. A doctor might decide to put her in a mental asylum, or send an army of people to the ranch to investigate her story. Sofia might go to prison or be deported back to Mexico, and neither one of those options would be any better for her.

Adriana leaned forward and kissed her on the forehead. Then she nodded to Travis, and he carried her away.

Pulling the door closed, she walked back through the house. The other girls were gathered in the big front rooms and were trying to make themselves comfortable for the night. Several of them were still quivering with nervous excitement and glancing around like they expected something more to happen any minute. A few of them were staring at the door that Travis had just passed through carrying Sofia outside.

Someone had removed the bodies of Dusty and his men. Omar was trying to get the girls settled down and reassuring them as best he could. Adriana walked in the room and stood next to him. Everyone stared at her.

"Okay, ladies, I think it's finally over," she said. "Mr. Hayes is dead, and I think the rest of his men are probably dead, too."

She glanced at Omar for confirmation, and he nodded.

"What happens now," asked Yasmine, "are we still going to leave? Do we have enough trucks to take everybody?"

Adriana hesitated and took a deep breath.

"I think that will be up to you."

"Me?" said Yasmine.

"I mean all of you," she clarified, "you are all free now, but we have no place to go. We have no money. We have no one coming to help us. We're on our own. You want to go back to Mexico? You want to go into the city and take your chances on the streets? What do you want to do?"

The girls glanced at each other and thought about it for a moment.

"Where is Travis?" Bianca asked. "He will know what to do."

"Travis went to take Sofia to the hospital," Adriana lied, "he will be back soon. Until then, I think we should all try to relax and think about this some more. Omar and the other guys will take good care of us and protect us, but they are exhausted now. We should find some food and drinks for everyone and then rest for a while. We will make better decisions in the morning. Agreed?"

They all nodded and began to mill about the room.

"Good job," Omar whispered. "We all need to get some rest."

Adriana nodded.

"We can talk about this when Travis gets back."

Omar chuckled.

"You mean if he comes back."

CHAPTER 30

The sun was climbing into the bright, blue sky and still there was no sign yet of Travis. Adriana was beginning to get worried. The guys had been whispering back and forth to each other all night. She didn't know if that meant they were trying to get themselves organized, or if they were all planning to leave.

The girls had been whispering, too. Most of them seemed content to wait for whatever came next. They were accustomed to doing that anyway. But a few of them were showing signs of growing desperation and restlessness. They knew things weren't really over yet, and they were anxious to get on with it.

A couple of the older girls managed to scrounge up some coffee and breakfast for everyone. Adriana did a quick check and was surprised to find that no one had fled during the night. She took that as a good sign. Maybe it was fear or maybe it was hope, but at least most of the group had decided to see things through together.

Omar sidled over and stood next to her.

"What are you going to tell them now?" he asked.

Adriana sighed and shrugged.

"I don't know," she said, "I'm not really good at being a leader. Maybe you can just take over and be in charge for a while. Do you have any ideas?"

He put his palms up and backed away.

"No way! I'm not going to be responsible for what happens to all of these people. I can look out for myself, but these girls don't stand a chance if they try to leave here. They will probably all be dead or deported within a week. I don't want something like that on my conscience."

"Then what do you suggest?"

"I say let Travis do it. He likes being the center of attention."

"But what if he doesn't come back? Then what?"

"Then it's on your shoulders. You're the only one they'll listen to anyway."

Adriana sighed and stared at the floor. She knew he was right. Grabbing a plate of tortillas, she moved around the dining room of the ranch house chatting with all the girls. Most of them seemed tired and anxious, but in good spirits.

She paused in the middle of the room and put down the plate.

"Good morning, ladies, can I have your attention please? Thanks to you all for the support last night. We are now free of the chains that were holding us here. Mr. Hayes is dead, and there is no one forcing you to stay here anymore. So what do you want to do?"

"Where is Travis?" one of the girls asked.

She glanced at Omar for a second.

"He should be back any minute now," Adriana answered, "but Travis is not the boss. He does not own you. You are all free to do whatever you want."

Yasmine laughed.

"Really? Like what? Can you give me some money so that I can go to Dallas or Houston and start a new life there? I have no documents to stay in this country legally. I have no home here, but I do not want to go back to Mexico."

"I was born in the United States," Adriana replied, "and I am a U.S. citizen. I can find work somewhere. Any of you that want a home are welcome to stay with me for as long as you like."

Everyone was silent for a moment.

"That's a very generous offer," said Bianca, "but that is too much to ask. Twenty people cannot live on the back of one. We must find our own way."

"What will happen to this place?" asked Vera. "Surely that old man had money around here somewhere. We should look for it."

"That's a good idea," Adriana agreed, "let's do that. Everyone finish your food, and then we will search for the money."

Just as they started cleaning up, she heard the sound of a big pickup truck rolling down the gravel driveway. Travis pulled up right in front of the ranch house and turned off the engine. Everyone hurried outside and bunched up on the covered porch to see what was going on.

Travis lingered in the cab for a moment, rubbing his face with both hands. At last, he swung open the door and climbed out. He started walking around the back of the truck and then stopped when he saw the huge crowd staring at him. His tired face lit up with a smile.

"Hi everyone! This is a sight I never expected to see, all of these beautiful women waiting to welcome me home. Did anybody save me some breakfast? I'm starving!"

Adriana ran down the steps and gave him a big hug and a kiss.

"I missed you! I'm glad you came back."

"Was there ever any doubt?"

Omar shook his head and chuckled.

"I think some of us may have been wondering," he said, "we were deciding what to do next. You have any thoughts about that?"

"Why ask me? I'm not the boss."

"You are now," said Adriana, "the old man is dead, along with all of his minions. You know more about this place and his operation than anyone. We were all hoping that you might kind of take charge for a while. But don't worry, I'm sure we'll let you know if we don't agree with you."

Yasmine smiled and pointed her knife at Travis.

"Thanks so much for your vote of confidence," he said, "but you know I'm not really the leader type."

"Yes, you are," Adriana argued, "you like being in charge and doing whatever you want to do. Now is your chance, just don't blow it or there may be consequences."

"That's what I'm afraid of. You guys are pretty hard with the consequences."

"You can handle it. So what should we do next?"

Travis sighed and thought about it for a minute.

"Okay, here's what I'm thinking. The old man must have some money stashed here someplace. He didn't trust banks, or anyone else for that matter. A lot of his deals were in cash because they were on the shady side of legal or the other side of the border. First thing we need to do is find the safe or the strong box where he kept his cash."

"Good," said Adriana, "we're in agreement already! That's exactly what we're planning to do right now. What else?"

"I think Omar and me should collect all the bodies and get rid of them. We can haul them off into a field someplace and burn them. That includes anything that might be considered evidence, like the mattress, clothes, or whatever. Just in case someone comes poking around, we can lie about it for now and pretend everything is business as usual. We can pretend the old man is sick and not talking to anybody."

"For how long?" she asked.

"We'll figure that out later. Right now, we're only buying some time."

"What about Raul and me," asked Jimmy Ray, "you want us to help you?"

"No, I want you guys to get with a couple of the girls and figure out how we can make this place livable. We can't all stay in the ranch house, but the dormitory building is horrible, especially in this heat. Maybe we can put in a couple of small air conditioners in the windows or something. I know we need to upgrade the beds and the showers. Make a list of everything and about how much it would cost. Pick a couple of the girls who have been here the longest. Once we find some money, we can start making changes."

"So you intend for us to stay here," asked Bianca, "we're not leaving?"

He glanced at Adriana then shrugged.

"I don't know the answer to that one yet. I'm not going to force anybody to stay here against their will. I think Adriana has some good ideas about that, but I don't know what the rest of you think. Maybe you should all think about it for a day or two and then we can discuss it again. Some of you might want to stay, some of you might not."

"Are you going to sell anybody?" asked Helen.

Travis shook his head.

"I'm not going to sell any of you. I'm going to sell the boat, though. I made a few phone calls last night when I was gone, and I think I found a buyer. I will know in a day or two. That should get us some quick cash anyway."

"Is that why you took so long?" one of the other girls asked.

"Uh, yeah, that's the reason," he replied. "I took Sofia to the hospital, and then I made some calls while I was waiting."

"Is she going to be okay?" asked Bianca.

"No, I'm sorry, but she didn't make it. The gunshot wounds were fatal, and the doctors couldn't save her."

The girls looked at each other, nobody seemed surprised at the news.

"Okay, let's all get to work then," Adriana prodded, "three or four of you go with Jimmy Ray and Raul to look at the dormitory building and see what we can do with it."

"Don't forget about the bunkhouse," Omar suggested.

"The what?"

"The guys have a bunkhouse in back of the barn," Travis explained, "I forgot about that. It's where we slept and stored our clothes and stuff. It has a separate shower and everything. It's not as nice as the ranch house, but it's better than the dorm."

"How many people does it hold?" asked Adriana.

"About ten or so the way it is now."

"Super! We should take a look at that. It might be cheaper to expand that and the ranch house instead of fixing up the dormitory building. I'm sure most of the girls would rather stay closer to the house. The dorm building holds a lot of unhappy memories."

"All right then," said Travis, "let me get a quick cup of coffee and rest for about twenty minutes, then we'll get started."

"Come with me," said Adriana, "let me fix you some breakfast, too. You've been up all night, and you look exhausted."

They started toward the kitchen and the rest of the crowd dispersed. Adriana got some leftovers and put them on the table. Travis pulled out a chair and sat down as she handed him a cup of coffee.

He wolfed down the food like a hungry coyote. Adriana watched him and smiled.

"You did great," she said, "I know you don't think of yourself as a leader, but you have a way of inspiring people, giving them hope and confidence."

Travis shook his head.

"I don't know about that. You ladies did great last night without me. I let myself get hogtied in the corral until one of the girls cut me loose. I'm not proud of that. I should have made a move sooner. That was a bad mistake."

"Everybody makes mistakes. Nobody is perfect."

"Yeah, but sometimes mistakes get people killed."

"Don't worry, babe. I've got your back, and you've got mine. We'll look out for each other from now on."

Adriana leaned over to give him a kiss just as Omar ran into the room.

"You've got to come see this," he exclaimed, "you won't believe it!"

They hurried after him down the hallway to the old man's bedroom. Omar took a knife and started ripping up the bloody mattress. Travis and Adriana stood beside the bed and watched him in confusion.

"What the hell are you doing?" asked Travis.

"Look," Omar shouted, "look inside the mattress! I picked up his body and saw these deep gashes on the bed where Sofia had cut it up. It was too dark to see last night, but look at it now."

Travis and Adriana moved to the edge of the bed and leaned over to take a closer peek. The bloody mattress was torn and shredded all over where Sofia had gone crazy in her killing frenzy. But there was something stuffed down inside some gaps.

"Sofia didn't do all of this," Omar said excitedly, "the mattress had already been cut open and sewed back together in several places."

"Why," Travis asked, "was the old man too cheap to buy a new mattress?"

Omar reached inside one of the holes and pulled out a long, leather belt with lots of small pockets. He smiled like he had just won the lottery.

"Money belts! The old man was keeping his cash in money belts stuffed inside of his mattress. Can you believe that?"

Adriana reached over and took the belt from Omar's hand. She unfastened one of the little pockets and peered inside. The boys watched as she pulled out the cash and counted it. Her eyes got wide with surprise.

"There is a lot of money here," she said. "I don't know if all the pockets have this much, but we need to check."

"Do you see any more of those belts?" Travis asked Omar.

He nodded with enthusiasm.

"I see at least four more."
Travis looked at Adriana and smiled.
"It looks like we're in business."

254

CHAPTER 31

They heard the big trucks rumbling up the driveway right around lunchtime. Jimmy Ray and Raul had just come back from the store with a load of food and supplies. The girls were gathered in the kitchen at the ranch house going through everything. This was the happiest that Adriana had ever seen them.

A few girls grabbed some food and started talking with excitement about a plan for dinner. Travis was the first to notice the sounds of the strangers approaching. He glanced at Omar and the two of them ran out of the room. They came back a few seconds later, carrying guns.

Adriana caught his eye and tried to get the girls quiet.

"What's going on?" she asked.

"We've got company. Don't know who it is yet. Might be something, might not. Keep everyone out of sight until we know more."

"Quiet everyone," Adriana shouted, "stay here, I'll be right back!"

She followed Travis and Omar onto the front porch of the ranch house. Adriana caught a quick glimpse of movement in of the corner of one eye. She guessed Raul and Jimmy Ray were lurking out of sight somewhere nearby.

A big, black SUV was making its way toward the house with a large farm truck trailing behind it. The SUV looked like a luxury model, maybe a Cadillac Escalade. The truck behind it was a big diesel flatbed with three armed men standing in the back. Both trucks slowed as they neared the house. The SUV eased to a stop about fifty feet from the porch. A stocky Mexican man swung the drivers' door open and climbed out of the front seat. He took a moment to adjust his dark sunglasses.

"*Hola la casa*!" he yelled in Spanish.

Travis stuck a pistol in the waistband of his jeans and sauntered down the steps. He paused about halfway to the SUV. Omar stood halfway between him and the house with a shotgun in his hands. Adriana waited by the door and watched.

"Howdy," Travis replied, in a manner that was not friendly at all, "who are you, and what do you want?"

The stocky man smiled and walked around the car. He opened the back door, and a smaller Mexican man got out. The smaller man lit up a long cigar and took a couple of puffs. He gazed all around, and then he began walking slow toward Travis. The two men stared at each other for a few seconds.

"Who are you, and what do you want?" Travis repeated.

"They call me El Guapo," the Mexican man said, "perhaps you've heard of me, particularly in Laredo. I control the business there."

"In case you hadn't noticed, this ain't Laredo, and I don't really care what you do down there. I only want to know why you're here."

The man took a few more puffs of his cigar and glanced around again.

"Where is the old man?" he said at last. "I heard that he was having some trouble lately. I thought that I would come by and see what I could do to, uhm... help."

"What do you mean exactly," asked Travis, "you mean to help the old man, or do you mean to help create a more trouble?"

The Mexican man smiled and shrugged.

"I am open to either possibility, as long as there is some benefit to me. I really do not care what happens here as long as you and I understand each other."

Travis nodded.

"Then I think we can agree on that. The old man has decided to retire. He wants out. His son is dead, so there is no one to take over the business. My partners and I have worked here for years, so we want to give it a shot. We're going to make some changes, but nothing that affects you. As far as we're all concerned, Laredo will always be your territory, and we respect that. If we need to do any business down that way, we want to deal only with you and your people."

El Guapo smiled again and puffed on his cigar.

"So where is the old man now? Did he take his money and go to Florida?"

Travis glanced at Omar, and they both chuckled.

"Let's just say he moved a little further south. He's not here anymore, and you won't be seeing him again, except maybe on November first."

The man thought about it for a moment, and then he understood the joke. Travis was referring to *Dia de los Muertos*, the Day of the Dead. The Mexican nodded.

"Then I will not be able to collect the debt that he owes me."

"What debt? Hayes doesn't owe you anything. He always kept everything neat and tidy. Cash on the barrelhead. He never borrowed money from you or anyone else. You're full of shit."

El Guapo stopped smiling and threw his cigar on the ground. The Mexican guys standing in the truck all pointed their guns at Travis.

"Okay, maybe I missed something," Travis said, backing up a step, "maybe he had some deal with you that I didn't know about."

He turned around and shouted to Adriana.

"Do you know if Hayes owed Mr. Guapo here any money?"

She scowled and made a serious face like she was concentrating.

"Hang on a minute, let me go inside and check the books."

The men all watched each other and waited while Adriana ducked back through the front door. Sweaty fingers slid up and down trigger guards and everyone held their breath. She came back out a minute later with Yasmine and Bianca.

"Yes, I believe he did," Adriana yelled, trying to be nonchalant about it.

The girls walked out to where Travis was standing, and Adriana handed El Guapo a money belt. He glanced at her and then at the other girls.

"This is the ten thousand dollars that he owes me?"

Adriana shrugged.

"That is only five thousand, but we can give you five more next month. We need the money right now for some business expenses. With the management changes, we are going to make some other changes in the operations. We need the money for that sort of thing right now."

"What kind of changes?" the Mexican asked.

"We want to start an escort service," Adriana responded, "we have a lot of pretty girls with great skills. I think it will do much better than whatever Hayes did before. But you know what? You're a successful businessman, and we would love to hear your ideas about it. Would you like to come inside for a drink? Come on in, bring all the other guys, too. You can meet the girls, and we can talk about it for a while."

She took El Guapo by the arm and began pulling him toward the front door. The other men weren't sure what to do. Everyone froze and watched.

"*Jefe*?" shouted one of the men in the truck.

El Guapo glanced back over his shoulder, then motioned for the other guys to follow him. Travis and Omar stepped aside as the Mexicans climbed down from the truck and hurried after their boss. Yasmine and Bianca smiled at them and winked.

Vera was waiting at the door and held it open as Adriana led El Guapo into the ranch house. The other girls giggled and crowded around him as he came into the room. Travis and Omar stood behind the Mexican guys just inside the door. Wanda eased up next to Travis with a knife in one hand.

"El Guapo, these are my girls," Adriana said with pride, "they would be happy to get you something to eat or drink. I know you've been traveling this morning, and you're probably a little tired. Have a seat on the sofa here and chat with them. Would you like a cold beer or do you prefer something stronger?"

She leaned in close and smiled as El Guapo sat down, accentuating her cleavage as much as possible. Helen and Teresa moved over next to the other men and smiled at them. For a moment, everything was quiet.

"Bring me some tequila, if you have it," El Guapo demanded, "and some beer for my men. Then I want you to sit beside me and tell me about what you have in mind."

Adriana nodded toward the kitchen, and some girls scurried away. Travis and Omar held their positions, but the Mexican guys allowed Helen and Teresa to guide them over to the chairs on the other side of the room. Yasmine and Bianca continued to smile and wink as they sat on the floor next to the sofa. They both leaned back on their hands and stared up at El Guapo with innocent eyes. Adriana almost laughed because they were being so obvious.

"We have a plan for the business," she said to El Guapo, "we want to change it to an escort service. Some of our girls have fantastic skills, and we don't want to lose them. We think that we can make more money by training them and finding customers that will come back again and again. Our girls want to be the best. We want to create something that is guaranteed to succeed. We want to create sexual addiction."

El Guapo stared at her in surprise.

"Sexual addiction? Is there such a thing?"

"Of course," Adriana replied, "if you spent the night with one of my girls, I can guarantee that you will never forget it. You would come back for more, and you would spend whatever it takes to get that satisfaction over and over again. Just look at them. How could a man say no to that?"

Adriana glanced at the girls, and a couple of them peeled off their shirts. All the Mexican guys nodded and started mumbling in Spanish. El Guapo grinned. Ursula handed him a bottle of tequila and a glass. Gloria passed out bottles of beer to the other Mexican guys. Everyone paused for a drink and relaxed.

"Why don't you let Bianca and Yasmine give you a quick tour of the place and tell you about our plans?" Adriana suggested. "I'm sure you will be very interested and have some good ideas. You may even decide that you want to become partners with us and invest money in our business. We would certainly welcome a smart and powerful man like yourself, and you could come to visit us as often as you like."

El Guapo poured himself another large shot of tequila and tossed it back. His eyes roamed around the room for a minute, then stopped on Yasmine and Bianca.

"I will go with these two girls and hear what they have to say."

The two girls jumped up and smiled at him. Yasmine took the bottle of tequila and the glass. Bianca grabbed him by the hand and began leading him back toward the bedroom. The others sat silent and watched them walk out.

Adriana looked at the other Mexican guys.

"Anyone else want a tour or some tequila?"

The men glanced back and forth at each other, not sure what to do. After a moment, one of them stared at Helen's chest and spoke up.

"Tequila for me," he said. His companions all nodded.

Helen smiled and led them into the kitchen to find another bottle. Travis moved to the sofa and sat down next to Adriana.

"What are you doing?" he whispered. "Are we going to kill them or invite them over for a slumber party?"

"Patience, I'm using the weapons that we have. We can win this battle without even firing a shot. Let me do things my way."

Travis growled in frustration, but he didn't argue.

Twenty minutes later, El Guapo came strutting back into the room with Yasmine and Bianca at his side. He was smiling ear to ear, and the bottle of tequila was empty. He glanced around for the other guys.

"*Vamanos*," he shouted, "we are done here!"

Adriana got up from the sofa and walked El Guapo to the front door. She pushed open the door, and they waited on the front porch as the other Mexican guys scrambled outside and climbed back into their truck. She gave him a hug and a quick kiss on both cheeks. El Guapo raised her hand to his lips and kissed the back of her fingers.

"My dear, it has been a pleasure. I look forward to seeing you again."

"You are welcome anytime," she responded, "a gentleman is always welcome in our home."

They smiled at each other while Travis rolled his eyes. The stocky man held the door open on the SUV. El Guapo walked out and got inside. Both of the vehicles cranked up their engines and drove away.

"He forgot the money belt," Omar observed.

"No, he didn't," said Adriana, "he left it on purpose. That gives him an excuse to come back. We have a new partner, and we have the protection of the cartel. Nothing can touch us now."

CHAPTER 32

By Friday evening, things were beginning to settle down. Life was almost normal again, but the new normal was a very different world. The group had become more like an extended family now. Everyone was trying hard to get along with each other, but there were still a lot of unanswered questions.

A couple of the girls were miserable and wanted to leave, so Adriana gave them each a thousand dollars and sent them on their way. Raul volunteered to drive them to the bus station in Corpus Christi. The others decided to stay and see what might happen with new hopes and dreams for the future.

She was sitting next to Travis on the front porch of the ranch house. They were sharing a bottle of wine and talking about their own dreams. The girls had cooked up a terrific dinner, and both of them were feeling full and content.

"So when do you want to go look at some property?" she asked.

"What property?" he said. "What are you talking about?"

"Remember our original plan was to rent a place in the city for an escort service. That way we would be closer to the customers and could provide more security for the girls. We need to get things rolling so that we can generate some income."

"Are you sure that's the way you want to do it? I kind of like the idea of building something here and adding a swimming pool. It wouldn't be nearly as risky as trying to operate in the city."

"We could do both once we have the money, but I think we should try to keep the business separate from our home. What if someone wanted to get married or have kids? We need someplace private for our home life."

Travis arched his eyebrows in surprise.

"Get married and have kids? Who have you been talking to?"

Adriana shrugged and smiled.

"Nobody. It was just a thought."

He chuckled and stared at her. She looked him in the eye and stretched up to wrap both of her arms around his neck. He leaned down lower and kissed her on the lips. They pressed their bodies together and enjoyed the moment. Adriana could feel the passion and desire burning inside of her, and she knew Travis felt the same.

"You want to go to bed now? It's starting to get dark."

"It's way too early to go to sleep."

"Who said anything about sleep?"

Travis smiled, then he kissed her again. Adriana closed her eyes as he pulled her closer and hugged her tight. Then she heard a soft bang as the door slammed behind them. She opened her eyes to see Omar standing there.

"You ready?" he asked Travis.

"Ah... yeah, I guess so," he replied.

"What," she said, "what's going on?"

"We're going to Houston tonight. I forgot to tell you."

Adriana crossed her arms and took a step back.

"Tonight? You're leaving tonight? What for?"

"I found a buyer, and he wants to do the deal early tomorrow. We need to leave tonight in order to be there early and get everything ready."

"You're selling one of the girls?"

"No, I'm selling the boat, but I have to deliver it to the buyer in Houston. Omar is going to drive up and bring me back. We should be back by lunchtime tomorrow."

"Ugh! Why didn't you tell me?"

"Sorry, I just forgot."

Travis nodded to Omar, and they both walked away. Adriana sat down in one of the big chairs on the porch and sulked. She thought about things for a while and after some time, her anger went away as well. The evening air was warm and comforting. She leaned her head back and closed her eyes, feeling the wine relaxing her body.

Adriana heard a sound, and her eyes snapped open. She felt a painful twinge in her neck. Had she fallen asleep in the chair? It was dark now outside. Bright pinpoints of starlight flickered in the nighttime sky.

Then she heard it again, soft footsteps creeping around the corner. Adriana stared intently in that direction. She could see the vague outline of someone there next to the window. The light from the window was behind them, bathing their face in an inky blur.

"Who... who is it?" she stammered. "Who's there?"

The shadowy form crept closer but didn't respond. It moved with ease making little sound. She watched as it came up the porch steps and stopped no more than ten feet away. Adriana grabbed the arms of the chair with both hands, trying to think of some way to defend herself or escape. She heard the soft hiss of a match and saw a brief flicker of flames. The unmistakable odor of cigarette smoke drifted by.

"Johnny?" she whispered.

"Hello Adriana," he answered.

"Johnny, is that really you? I thought you were dead!"

"The news of my death has been greatly exaggerated. As you can plainly see, I'm still very much alive and well."

He held the burning match up in front of his face and smiled. Adriana could see the deep scars that lined his brow, the sallow complexion, and the dark circles around his sunken eyes. He looked more like a walking corpse than a living man.

"Johnny, you don't look very good. Are you sick? Can I take you to a doctor?"

He chuckled and shook his head sadly.

"Thanks for your concern, but there is no cure for what I have. I know there is something wrong with me. I've been that way for a long time. I just couldn't hide it anymore. There is nothing anyone can do for me now."

"We can get you some help, Johnny. You need to be in the hospital."

"They can't help me. I have AIDS. I'm dying now, and there is nothing they can do to stop it. Each morning that I wake up is a surprise to me."

"Why are you here? Why don't you go someplace and try to get treatment?"

"I came here to rescue you, Adriana. We're partners, and that's what partners do for each other. I let them take you away before, but now I've come to take you back."

Johnny coughed and bent over, spitting out his cigarette. He then straightened up again. Reaching down, he pulled a long hunting knife from the sheath on his belt. He held it up in front of his eyes, watching the shiny metal blade gleam in the moonlight.

"Come on, Adriana. It's time to go now."

"Where are the others, Johnny? Where are the police?"

"They're not coming. It's just you and me against the world now."

He started to laugh and staggered in her direction. All at once, the front door swung open wide, and Laura stepped out holding a gun. Johnny turned his head toward her, and Laura fired two shots into his face. His dead body hit the ground with a loud thud. Laura stood there and stared at him, her face a frozen mask of fury.

"Why did you shoot him?" Adriana asked.

"That's the man who killed Keyla," she replied, "that's Juan the Ripper."

Laura started to cry, and her hands started to shake. Adriana moved quickly and took the gun away from her. Then she wrapped her arms around Laura and held her tight.

The other girls heard the gunshots and rushed outside to see what was going on. Someone turned on the porch lights. Two of the other girls were also holding guns.

"It's okay, baby, it's going to be okay," she whispered to Laura, "no one is going to hurt you now. No one is going to hurt any of you ever again."

The other girls looked at Laura and Adriana, then they stared down at Johnny's lifeless body. The two girls with guns both fired a bullet into his head just to be sure. Adriana kissed Laura on the cheek, and then she handed her off to the others.

"Someone find Raul or Jimmy Ray, and ask them to take care of the body," she ordered, "the rest of you get back inside in case he isn't the only one prowling around out here tonight."

The other girls glanced at each other and then started shuffling back inside. She took one final look at Johnny and wiped the tears away.

CHAPTER 33

No one got much sleep Friday night, but everyone was anxious to get up and start a new day on Saturday. Nightmares were best forgotten in the bright light of the morning sun. The girls all got up and went about their business, letting Adriana sleep in a little. She heard them getting organized and dividing up their work for the day. It was still amazing to her how resilient they were, and how quick they bounced back from even the most traumatic experience.

Adriana was still lying in the bed when she heard the bedroom door creaking as it swung open. She saw Travis peek in and smile at her. He sauntered over and sat down next to her on the bed.

"You're back," she said. "Did you sell the boat?"

Travis held up a fistful of crisp bills and grinned.

"I did. Now we have a wad of cash to live on for a while. There's enough here to pay for our building repairs and get some new clothes for everybody."

"Great! I knew we could count on you to take care of us."

He laughed.

"That's not what I'm hearing, I guess I missed all the action last night."

Adriana sat up in the bed and leaned back against the wall.

"We had an unexpected visitor. We took care of it. It was no big deal."

"Wait until you hear the other version of the story."

"What do you mean?" she asked.

"According to the girls, they were attacked by Juan the Ripper last night, and you took him down all by yourself."

"What?"

"You should hear them," said Travis, "first, you protected them from old man Hayes, then you protected them from the cartel, and now you've killed Juan the Ripper. You're their hero, Adriana. You're like Wonder Woman or something. All the girls love you like you're their mother."

"Now wait a minute. I'm not that old. Maybe their older sister."

"I don't know why you want to have kids," he chuckled, "you've already got at least twenty of them!"

Travis leaned over and took her in his arms. Adriana kissed him. The stress she had been feeling for days welled up inside of her. A rivulet of tiny tears began streaming down her face and gathered on their lips.

"What's all this?" he said in surprise. "Wonder Woman doesn't cry."

Adriana buried her face against his chest and held on tight.

"Hold me for a minute, Travis," she gasped, "please, just hold me."

He wrapped his arms around Adriana and enveloped her in his love. She could feel the strong beat of his heart and the firm grasp of his muscular arms. There was no denying the love and desire that he felt for her. She could feel it in the way he touched her and held her close. He didn't have to say it. She knew it was real.

She wanted the moment to last forever, but she realized it had to end. Adriana leaned back and swiped the salty tears from her face. Travis looked into her eyes.

"Are you okay?"

Adriana nodded.

"I'm fine. I'm just a little emotional today for some reason."

Travis tilted his head and grinned.

"Okay then. Now change your clothes and put on your game face. We're going out here to have lunch with the kids. We don't want them to see any weakness, do we?"

"Of course not. Toss me my jeans and a shirt."

Travis grabbed some clothes and handed them to her. He watched her change and smiled at the glimpses of her naked body. She put both of her hands under her long, dark hair and tossed it back to hang freely behind her.

Then she stared at him.

"Hey Travis? When you sold the boat, and you had all that money in your hand, why didn't you just take it and leave? Why did you come back for me?"

He looked at the wall for a moment and shrugged.

"I don't know exactly. I never even thought about it."

"A month ago, you would not have even hesitated. You would just go."

Travis grinned and moved up closer to her. He put his arms around her.

"I guess I'm a different man now. Something changed, and I like it. You make me feel loved and wanted, like I'm a hero or something. I like that feeling.

It makes me want to be a better man. It makes me want to be with you forever."

Adriana smiled and nodded.

"Yeah, I know what you mean. When I first met you, I could not imagine a life with a man like you. But now, I can't imagine what life would be like without you, and I don't want to find out."

"Me neither."

He kissed her again, soft and tender this time.

The bedroom door burst open and several of the girls rushed in.

"Enough of that nonsense," Yasmine shouted, "we have work to do, and you two are in here wasting time! We have a contractor out front who wants to talk about the new additions to the house."

"And another guy who wants to talk about where we want the swimming pool," added Bianca, "that's important stuff!"

Adriana looked at Travis and smiled.

"It's not too late to run away," she whispered, "but please, take me with you."

Travis laughed and glanced around the room at all the smiling faces.

"Not a chance! How could I ever leave a family like this?"

She hugged him tight.

"We're all yours."

END

About Your Author

I was born and raised in the southern United States, but I have traveled to many other places in the world. I find the different people and cultures fascinating. My education and work experience began with accounting and finance. But as with everything else, it has gradually evolved more and more to computers and information technology. Our lives today are centered on talking with each other through the flows of bits and bytes.

More than twenty years ago, I started writing stories to capture all of the interesting thoughts and impressions lurking in my imagination. These stories became an important part of my life and I decided to share this by creating fictitious people and places in my mind. These people could say and do anything that I had ever seen or thought about. They are all very real to me with their own unique personalities, motivations, and quirks. They live in my head every day, and through the magic of books, I can share all of it with you.

Today, I am the luckiest man on the planet. I am married to a beautiful lady from Colombia and I'm the proud father of some wonderful children. I love animals, mysteries, and salsa music. Life is a very precious thing. Take time to ride a Harley, smoke a pipe, eat a taco, cuddle with a cat, or drink a cup of tea. Enjoy every moment of it with me.

Amazon Author Page:
https://www.amazon.com/author/loroberts

Website: www.loroberts.com
Facebook: LeeRoberts
Twitter: Lee Roberts@LeeORoberts67

Other HellBound Books Titles
Available at: www.hellboundbookspublishing.com

Twerk

An addictively dark, psychological thriller laced with steamy romance, mystery, action and suspense; Twerk exposes the working lives of Las Vegas strippers behind the glamor - the challenges, the rewards, and the deadly risks. Desire, a spark, a decision made too fast (in haste), and a Las Vegas stripper is plunged into the depraved world of a psychopath. But is she the only target of his twisted desires?

A regular Sunday night in a Las Vegas strip club is rocked when a local oddball dies mysteriously, during a private dance.

Amber falls immediately in lust with the hot paramedic who arrives, and follows him outside, anticipating sizzling romance. But, her casual encounter quickly descends into a terrifying, twisted nightmare from which she is unable to escape.

Spells in Waiting

For as long as she can remember, Lauren Merriweather has fought to separate herself from her mother - by focusing on school and developing her healing powers. Like her mother, she's a natural-born witch, but unlike her mother, Lauren is not a killer driven by hatred.

But, when a fight with her rampaging mother drives Lauren to seek relief in alcohol and mindless flirting, her world is twisted violently out of her control.

Lauren's attraction to David is as immediate as it is undeniable - to the extent that she forgets about the spells that have, until now, kept her from getting close to a man. David Fredricks is the government operative investigating her mother for murder, and he and his partner have identified that Lauren is their best lead.

As far as David is concerned, Lauren and her mother are both witches, and that makes them little better than monsters. Lauren's allure doesn't change the fact that her mother is a vicious serial killer, and he's prepared to do whatever it takes to stop her.

An interrogation goes too far, and Lauren finds herself bound to David in a way that neither of them could ever have imagined - and her very survival depends on her trusting the same people who stole her identity.

Flanagan

"Straw Dogs meets Fifty Shades - heart pounding, gut-wrenching, sexy as all hell and with a twist you'll never see coming!"

Meet the Sewells, your typical, all-American couple; happily married for ten years, respected high school teachers, still crazy about one another and with a secret, shared dark side.

During their annual Spring Break vacation to recharge their batteries and reconnect as a couple, they are waylaid by a perverse gang of misfits in the one horse, North Texas town of Flanagan.

Taken hostage as the focus of the gang's twisted games, the Sewells are brutalized into performing increasingly vicious physical, sexual and emotional acts upon one another, until events take an unexpected turn - triggered by an unintentional death.

As their circumstance descends into the worse nightmare imaginable, the Sewells find themselves involved in an altogether different situation...

The Waning

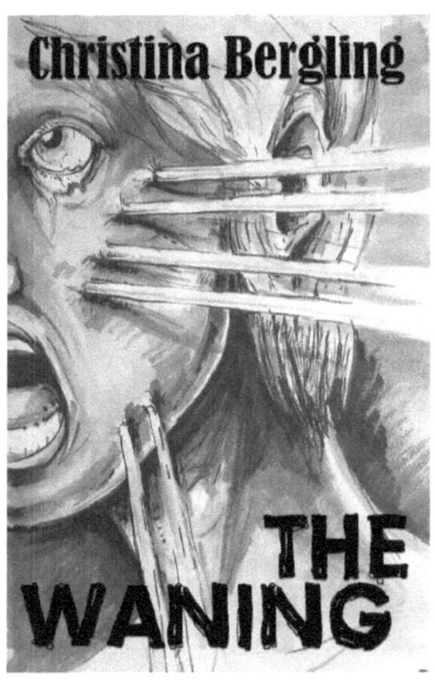

Beatrix woke up in a small metal cage, Lost in the darkness, a persistent dripping sound her only company.

She was celebrating a promotion that was the culmination of her entire ruthless, driven career; a promotion that would cement her status enough for her to take her relationship with her girlfriend out of the lesbian closet; Beatrix had finally made it.

And then she was here, disoriented and petrified in a blackness she could not define. Yet the reality of her Master may be even more terrifying than the crushing darkness and enveloping isolation. He appears as an ominous shadow in the doorway of her cell, never speaking. Instead, he teaches Beatrix the language of pain and torture, of submission and obedience, of domination and possession

With each passing day, the fight and hope in Beatrix begins to shrivel and wane. With each savage beating, her survivalist instincts rise up to overwhelm the person she was. With each dehumanizing condition, she begins to forget who she was and the life from which she was ripped.

Can Beatrix ward off the psychological breakdown of her Master? Can she resist the temptation to survive and thrive through submission? Either Beatrix will succeed at surviving and escaping the torments of her Master or her Master will succeed at breaking her completely and reforming her into his design for a human possession…

The Pleasure Hunt

After meeting the mysterious *Dark Dance* on the casual encounters website, The Pleasure Hunters Club, *Sexy Cupid* finds himself enchanted by a enigmatic seductress – *Dark Dance*.

After experiencing bizarre, nightmarish visions during their first physical liaison, *Cupid* awakes on a bench somewhere in Louisville, unable to get the mystifying creature off his mind. As he begins to search both online and through the seedy streets of the city for her, he uncovers harrowing truths about the object of his obsession, truths which fill him with both indomitable dread and inexplicable love for her.

By the time *Cupid* begins to understand the terror he faces, the shackles on his soul are already too tight as the ancient monster has her talons dug well into his flesh.

Every time he is swept away to her world of Theia - the Moon Realm - she extracts and devours yet another piece of his very essence, and despite the merciless torment of his encounters with his obsession - and the warnings of, a menacing stranger - he presses on to find her, dragging himself deeper into her darkened realm.

Cupid soon finds that he may have but one opportunity to escape the demonic *Dark Dance*, but the bewitchment she has cast upon his heart may deter him from making a stand; with his soul about to slip down the gullet of the beast, *Cupid* has to make a decision before he is forever wrapped in the wicked thaumaturge's wings of eternal damnation.

Depraved Desires 2

 A dark and wonderfully stimulating collection of the disturbingly erotic from the very best authors in the business - all lovingly selected by the internationally renowned authoress Bonny Capps.

Seventeen mouthwateringly delectable tales from: Duana Monroe, Jacob Mielke, Matt Payne, Ken Goldman, M.J. Sutton, D. Norfolk, Mawr Gorshin, J. Stanley, Tim J. Finn, Shane Porteous, J.L. Boekestein, Becky & Lee Narron, Marela Aryan Ballot, Becky Narron & J.L. Boekestein and Jennifer Lynne

Schlock! Horror!

An anthology of short stories based upon/inspired by and in loving homage to all of those great gorefest movies and books of the 1980's (not necessarily base in that era, although some do ride that wave of nostalgia!), the golden age when horror well and truly came kicking, screaming and spraying blood, gore & body parts out from the shadows...

This exemplary 80's themed/inspired tales of terror has been adjudicated and compiled by one Mr Bret McCormick, himself a writer, producer and director of many a schlock classic, including *Bio-Tech Warrior*, *Time Tracers*, *The Abomination*, *Ozone: The Attack of the Redneck Mutants* and the inimitable *Repligator*.

Featuring stories from: Todd Sullivan, Timothy C Hobbs, Mark Thomas, Andrew Post, James B. Pepe, Thomas Vaughn, Edward Karpp, Jaap Boekestein, Lisa Alfano, L. C. Holt, John Adam Gosham, Brandon Cracraft, M. Earl Smith, Sarah Cannavo, James Gardner, Bret McCormick, and James H. Longmore.

**A HellBound Books LLC
Publication**

http://www.hellboundbookspublishing.com

Printed in the United States of America

9 781948 318495